I0689213

DIE
FOR ME

DIE FOR ME

BOOK 3: THE TATE CHRONICLES

K. A. LAST

www.kalastbooks.com.au

Copyright © 2016 K. A. Last. All rights reserved.
First published in Australia 2016 by K. A. Last.

The right of K. A. Last to be identified as the author of this work has been asserted by her under the *Copyright Amendment (Moral Rights) Act 2000.* This is a work of fiction. Names, characters, businesses, places, events and incidents are either the products of the author's imagination or used in a fictitious manner. Any resemblance to actual persons living or dead, or actual events, is purely coincidental. This work is copyright. Apart from any use as permitted under the *Copyright Act 1968,* no part of this publication may be reproduced, stored in a retrieval system, recorded or transmitted in any form or by any means, electronic, mechanical, photocopying, recording or otherwise, without the prior written permission of the publisher.

K. A. Last
kalast@kalastbooks.com.au
www.kalastbooks.com.au

ISBN: 9780994217578

Formatting and cover design by KILA Designs | www.kiladesigns.com.au

For Mum and Dad, because your love is infinite.

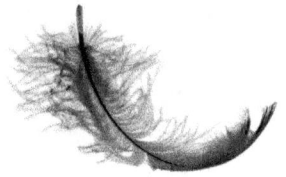

And when Love speaks, the voice of all the gods
Make heaven drowsy with the harmony.
William Shakespeare – *Love's Labour's Lost,
Act IV, Scene III*

GRACE

Leaves and sticks crunched beneath my feet as I ran. Branches whipped my face, and I drove deeper into the forest, refusing to give up the chase. The moonlight caught the vampire's pale skin as he flashed between the trees.

He was fast!

I misted to try and get closer to him, but I couldn't get close enough. The vamp dummied to the left then switched quickly to the right, leaping into the air and grabbing the closest tree trunk like a cat with its claws out. He glanced over his shoulder before shimmying into the canopy above.

I stopped at the base of the tree and put my hands on my hips, craning my neck.

"Good escape plan." I watched him move through the branches.

"Come and get me. Then you'll see how good it is." The vamp jumped from an outstretched limb and landed in another tree, sending leaves tumbling to the ground.

Great. A smartarse vamp. Just what I need.

I was sick of it—sick of chasing them, sick of fighting them. Sick of everything my existence had become. It had been more than three months since I'd gone to the city to find Josh. I'd found Seth as well, and Ryan had ended up dead. I'd done the wallowing thing, and tried the happy thing, but now I was at the stage where everything was all too much. In my line of work, I had to take the good with the bad, but when the bad outweighed the good—why did I bother?

Because it's what we do, Archer popped into my head. *We keep going, no matter what.*

I glanced around the forest but couldn't see him. *Where are you?*

In stealth mode, he thought.

I resisted the urge to roll my eyes, looking again and spotting him behind a tree about ten metres away.

Yeah, really stealthy, Arch, I thought. *Bet I can beat you to him.*

My brother moved from the base of the tree, taking a few steps back then running up the trunk until he caught a branch a little way above his head. He swung himself up with ease, but before he'd made it any farther, I misted and landed on the next branch above him.

"Hey, that's cheating!" he said.

"No, it's resourceful."

I searched the trees from my higher view point and spotted the vamp making a getaway through the canopy, jumping from tree to tree. He wasn't far enough away that I couldn't catch him, but when I went to mist again, I heard something else coming through the forest.

The undergrowth rustled with the sound of running feet, and I estimated maybe two pairs of boots pounding the ground. Two vamps burst through the trees in a blur, followed by a cloud of black mist. Seth materialised below us long enough to shout at Archer.

"Get your butt back in the game!"

Then he was gone again.

"Go," I said. "I've got this one."

Archer dropped to the ground and took off into the trees after Seth, no questions asked. That was what I loved about him. He got in there and did the job. No questioning the meaning of everything, like I'd been doing lately. Archer said we should keep going like we always had, because that was how you dealt with the loss and the grief. If we didn't stop, then we didn't have to think about it. But I was over people dying, and having to be the strong one through all of it. After so long fighting, maybe I'd reached my breaking point.

I sighed and scanned the forest again for my runaway vamp. I caught him clinging to a tree trunk near the path that wound through the forest. It took less than a second to mist to where he was. I landed on the path as he was about to drop to the ground.

"Hi there." I pulled a stake from my belt and curled my fingers around it. "Fancy seeing you here."

The vamp grunted and headed back up the tree. I conjured a fire ball in my free palm, rolling it between my fingers for a moment before letting it loose. It sailed over his head and landed in the top of the tallowwood. The leaves crackled and burned, raining little pieces of ash onto his head like black confetti.

I pulled my arm back to throw another fire ball, but I'd barely conjured it before Seth appeared at my side and grabbed my wrist.

"What the hell are you doing?" he said. "You'll burn down the forest."

I let a breath out slowly, then gave him the meanest look I could manage. "I'm fighting the only way I know how." And I didn't just mean physically.

"Think ... before you make stupid decisions."

"What's up your butt?" I pressed my lips together and yanked my arm away from Seth.

When we'd first come back from the city, everything had been fine. He'd done a great job of keeping me smiling. But in the past month or so, everything between us had started to fall apart; Seth had become overprotective and annoying. I couldn't help thinking it had something to do with Josh. It always did. But I hadn't chosen him, I'd chosen Seth, and for some reason he couldn't be happy about it. He was angry about something but he wouldn't share it with me, and I was angry at him for being angry.

"Don't do anything stupid," Seth said.

"Yeah, because we both know that never happens."

I focused on the vamp up the tree. The fire had gone out, but he was trying to make himself invisible by keeping still. It wasn't working.

I misted and landed on a branch next to him. He whipped his head around and glared at me, right before I punched him in the face. The impact jarred through my knuckles, making them ache. It was weird, because it had never hurt like that before. He growled and lunged at me. *Finally! He's going to fight back.* They were no fun when they didn't fight back.

The vamp grabbed me around the throat and shoved me against the tree trunk. My foot slipped, and I fell onto the thick branch beneath me, crying out as my body connected with the wood. A sharp pain pinched my side. I wasn't sure if the cracking sound was the branch or my ribs breaking. The vamp fell on top of me, and I cried out again, clenching my teeth against the pain. His legs and arms flailed as he tried to scratch my face, but at least he'd let go of my throat.

"Need any help up there?" Seth asked.

"No. I got this." I wrapped my arms around the vamp's neck and squeezed.

We rolled off the branch, and I ended up on top, my body slamming into him as he hit another branch below. This one snapped and we kept falling, bits of tree scratching my face and arms. I pushed him away and misted, landing on the ground a few seconds before the vamp fell into a heap in front of Seth. I raced forward and staked him in the chest before he could get up. The dust flopped to the forest floor and mingled with the leaves and debris.

When I straightened up, I winced and put a hand over the wound in my side. My palm came away bloody, and I wiped it onto the leg of my jeans, hoping Seth wouldn't notice.

"You okay?" he asked.

"Fine." I clenched my teeth and forced a smile. I didn't

want him to know how much it hurt. "Are we done for the night, or do you think there's more?"

Archer barrelled through the trees and onto the path, stopping to catch his breath. "Definitely more … maybe two or three." He panted, resting against a tallowwood.

A possum scurried along a branch overhead, and a twig snapped in the darkness. Something moved behind us, and then a flash passed through the trees straight ahead.

"Looks like they've split up," Seth said. "Let's go." He moved towards Archer who pinched the bridge of his nose with his thumb and forefinger.

"Don't you ever just … let it go?" Archer said.

"What happened to, 'we keep going'?" I asked.

"That's only when I haven't covered myself in the dust of five vamps. And I'm really, really tired."

Seth clapped him on the shoulder. "Toughen up, Tate. You coming, Grace?"

Pain burned my side in fiery licks, and I tried to stand normally, hoping Archer and Seth wouldn't notice.

"I'll take that one." I thumbed towards the shed, looking for a reason to head towards the clearing. "I'll meet you back at home."

Seth stared at me for a long moment, and he tried to penetrate the edges of my thoughts with his mind. But I had my wall in place like I always did. It wasn't because I didn't trust him; I wanted to be able to share things with him on my own terms.

Sure you're okay? he asked in my head.

I'll heal, I thought. *Go and kill some vamps.*

He eventually turned away and Archer followed, both of them jogging along the path and disappearing into the darkness.

When they were out of sight, I relaxed against a tree and took a look at my side. A coin-sized hole marked my top. Blood had seeped into the fabric, pasting it to my skin in a dark, sticky mess. When I peeled the fabric away, a piece of tree branch stuck out of the wound by about a centimetre. I hoped the other end of it wasn't in me any farther than that. The last thing I needed was the stick pretending it was an iceberg.

Blood slicked my fingers as I tried to grip the end of the piece of wood. My jaw ached from clenching my teeth, and I realised after trying for a few minutes to pull it out, I needed something to grab onto the stick with. Poking it made it hurt more. I had to get home.

My vision clouded and I rested my head against the tree. My stomach clenched, and a sick feeling washed through me. I hadn't felt woozy like that since I'd made the decision to tell Josh what I really was, and the sensation was not one I favoured. My hair clung to the rough bark when I pulled my head away from the trunk, and I blinked a few times to focus. Someone stood in front of me, smiling. The man's face split into three blurry masses, and then he bared his teeth.

Great. He wants to eat me.

I was about to pass out on the forest floor, but before he could lunge and sink his teeth in, I misted back to the clearing. I needed to work fast if I wanted to clean myself up before Archer and Seth got home. The first-aid kit was in the cottage, so with my last bit of strength I pulled myself up the steps and through the front door.

Fifteen minutes, a pair of tweezers, several gauze

K. A. LAST

pads, some iodine, and two Panadol later, I'd patched myself up as best I could. My wound should have healed by now, but it hadn't, and there had never been a time when my bumps and scrapes hadn't healed themselves. I wasn't sure what scared me more—how much it hurt, or not knowing what the hell was happening to me.

2

GRACE
Two weeks later, Tuesday afternoon

A knock sounded on my bedroom door and I rolled my top down to cover my side.

"Come in." I flopped onto my bed and winced at the dull ache from my injury a couple of weeks before. Why was it still bothering me? I was an angel. It should have healed fast, but it hadn't, and I was confused as to why.

The door swung open and Seth leaned against the frame. "How was your last exam?"

I smiled. "Archer cheated the entire time."

He laughed. "No one will ever know."

"I'm glad school's over. We never have to go back."

"Abby might think differently … the formal …"

I groaned. "I told you, I'm not going."

Seth stared at me and didn't reply. He'd never force me to do something I didn't want to do. Abby was a different

9

story, and I wasn't looking forward to making her listen the next time I told her I wasn't going. So far, every time I'd said no she'd ignored me and changed the subject.

I pressed my lips together and crossed my legs on the bed. Seth had something he wanted to say; I could tell by the way he looked at me. I could also tell it was something I probably didn't want to talk about.

He came over and sat on the edge of the bed, gently grabbing my ankles so he could unfold my legs and wrap them either side of him. Leaning in, he kissed me softly, letting his lips linger for a second.

"You okay?" Seth tucked my hair behind my ear and ran his thumb over my cheek. "The formal could be a good distraction."

"I'm ..." I nodded and rested my cheek on his shoulder, hiding my face. I'd been telling everyone I was fine. He wrapped his arms around me and I tucked my face into the crook of his neck. Seth fell onto the bed, pulling me with him. I cried out then winced, thankful Seth couldn't see my face and that he probably took my little yelp of pain as surprise.

Seth pulled me on top of him and I straddled his waist, leaning down to kiss him again. He rested his hands on my hips and I tensed, not wanting him to touch the tender wound on my side, or see the patch covering it. It was a miracle I'd made it this long without him finding out about my non-healing abilities. I should have told him about it when it had happened, but it scared me. I didn't want him and Archer worrying about me. And besides, I'd always looked after myself. I wasn't the kind of girl who needed help, or who asked for it.

Seth squeezed my hips and ended our kiss. "When are you going to tell me what's bothering you?"

I sat back and ran my fingers through my hair. "Nothing's bothering me."

He regarded me with dark eyes. "I know you, Grace. Don't say it's nothing."

"Yeah. Well, I know you, too." I flung one leg over him and jumped off the bed. "You've been hiding something from me since we came back from Wide Island."

The mention of our time in the city threw a heavy shroud of silence over us. Seth took a deep breath and ran a hand down his face, staring at me from where he lay on the bed. I crossed my arms and waited out the silence.

"I liked it better when you were over here," he finally said.

I moved back to the bed and sat on the edge, hugging myself, careful not to put too much pressure on my right side.

"I miss him." I stared at the scuffed toes of my boots.

Seth touched my back and trailed his fingers down my spine. "Do you mean Ryan, or—"

"Of course I'm talking about Ryan."

After everything that had happened, Josh's name was not a word I could freely say around Seth. He sat up and nestled in behind me, pressing his chest to my back and wrapping his strong arms around me. I slipped my arms around my stomach, under his, to relieve the weight of his embrace.

"I wouldn't be upset if you ... wanted to talk about someone else."

11

I snorted, turning to look at him. "Yeah, you would."

"Grace ..." Seth sighed and pressed his lips to my neck. "The past is in the past. And no matter what you do, I will always love you. Always."

I rested my cheek against his and closed my eyes. "I know." And I also knew what he wanted me to say back to him. I did love him. I'd shown him that many times. I'd fallen apart over him, and that was the main reason I hadn't told him yet. I was scared if I did that it would all disappear. That somehow he'd leave me again. The last time I'd told someone I loved them, I had to be the one to leave. The word love and I didn't have a good history. I tried every day to show Seth as much as possible how strongly my heart beat for him, but I couldn't say those three words. I was waiting for the right time.

Seth hitched my leg and spun me around to face him. *And you don't think now is the right time?*

You snuck into my head! I thought.

He stared at me, his mouth set into a firm line. He wasn't angry, but he was hardly smiling either. *You haven't let me do that in a long time.*

I reached up and ran my thumb over his lips in an attempt to relax them. *Maybe I do want you to hear me say it.* "But in here," I said aloud, placing my palm over his heart.

His lips parted and my gaze dropped from his eyes to his mouth. Heat rose into my chest, consuming me with a powerful desire laced with panic. What if something happened to me, and I never got to tell him how much I loved him? What if my inability to heal myself meant that losing him was also a possibility? The panic over the thought consumed me, and I grabbed Seth's face with both hands, pulling his lips to mine, crushing them with desperation. I couldn't get enough of him, and something inside me snapped. I tasted the salt of my tears as they ran over our lips and into our mouths.

Seth broke our connection, his lips moving to speak.

"I love you," I said, before he could form words. "I love you so much it hurts."

He leaned forward and rested his forehead on mine, stroking my cheek with the tips of his fingers. I clung to him like he was my life source and without him I'd die.

"Why are you crying?" he whispered into my hair.

Because I'm scared, I thought. *I've already lost you twice. I promise you won't lose me again.*

We sat on the bed in each other's arms, and I spent a few minutes wandering what else was wrong. When he'd first come into the room he'd wanted to talk about something, and it seemed we'd gotten side-tracked.

"I know there's something else you want to say," I said.

Seth loosened his embrace and I stood, hoping I could keep my feet after riding the emotional roller coaster.

"You need to come downstairs. Archer wants to have a meeting." Seth looked up at me and half-smiled.

"Since when did he become the boss?"

"Since you decided to give up the fight." Archer stood in the doorway, his hands stuffed into his jeans pockets. "You were taking too long." He glared at Seth.

Seth stared him down, raising an eyebrow. "Tactful."

"It's my middle name. Come on. I'd rather not talk in a room with you two and a bed."

Seth slipped his hand into mine and we followed

Archer down the metal stairs to the bottom floor of the shed. I already knew what this was going to be about. Archer wanted me to fight again, and like every time he'd tried to put his foot down for the past two weeks, I'd do the same and say no. I had a wound that wouldn't heal, and I didn't want another one before I could work out what was wrong with me. Still, I gave him points for persistence.

Archer stopped in front of the kitchen table and turned to face us, leaning back against the edge and crossing his legs at the ankles. I sat on the arm of the couch and tucked my foot behind my knee. Seth flopped onto the couch and put his hand on my back. I wasn't a hundred percent sure where he stood with the situation. Whenever Archer called one of these meetings, Seth said he wouldn't force me to do something I didn't want to do.

"Before you say it, Arch, the answer is still no."

He scowled. "Come on, Gracie. Fighting. It's what we do."

"Did," I said. "I've told you, I don't want to do it anymore. I'm fallen now. There's no rule that says I have to keep the mission."

"What about doing the right thing?" Archer waited for an answer, but I wasn't playing the game. "What about protecting me?"

"I can't heal you anymore," I said. "And you have Seth, who's willing to fight in my place."

Archer's gaze flicked to Seth then back to me. He licked his lips and shook his head. "I can't believe you've given up."

I closed my eyes and counted to five. The speech was

getting old, and I wanted to tell them why I'd decided to stop fighting, but it didn't seem like a good idea. They'd treat me differently if they knew I could get hurt. I was the same Grace, and I refused to become the main guest at their pity party. They were doing fine without me.

"I think what Arch means," Seth said, "is the situation is getting worse."

"Really? Because I thought he was trying to make me feel guilty," I said.

"I can try harder." Archer glared at me and pushed off the table. He clenched his fists and the sudden display of anger caught me off guard.

"What are you going to do, beat it into me?" I asked. "I've made my decision. I don't want to fight anymore."

"Things are getting out of hand, Gracie." Archer took a step forward. "You need to suck it up, get over whatever it is that happened, and get your arse back out there."

"What I need," I said, as calmly as I could, "is for everyone I love to stop dying around me."

"Well, one day I'm going to end up dead," Archer said, "because you don't have my back anymore."

"Calm down," Seth said. "I told you she wouldn't have changed her mind."

I couldn't believe what I was hearing. Archer had never used this tactic before. It was usually the *please tell us what's wrong* card. Maybe he thought it was time to try something else.

I stood from my perch on the arm of the couch and walked towards the shed door. "I'm done listening to you, because you don't seem to be hearing me."

When I reached the door, I grasped the knob and

turned, but I only got it halfway open before Archer was at my side shoving it closed. Seth was at my other side in an instant, but I ignored him. I wasn't entirely happy with the fact he wasn't arguing for me. He seemed to be sitting on the fence a bit too much, which made me think he agreed with Archer more than I wanted him to.

Slowly, I turned to face my brother. "Angry doesn't suit you, Arch." I opened the door again, and this time he didn't stop me from walking out into the warm afternoon sun.

"Why won't you tell us what's going on, Gracie?" Archer yelled after me.

Because it's none of your business, I thought. And I was too scared to tell them.

Neither of them replied.

ARCHER

Grace's hair swayed around her shoulders as she walked across the clearing. I was so angry with her I didn't know where to put the energy, and for some stupid reason, all I could think about was how much her hair had grown in the past few months. Was I only noticing it now? Had I been so caught up with fighting that I'd missed whatever else she'd been going through?

I scoffed at myself. It was only hair.

Seth came out of the shed and stood beside me. He waited until Grace had disappeared into the forest before speaking. "She needs time."

"To do what?" I asked. "Mope around and make everyone else miserable? Refuse to help us do what we're meant to do?" I clenched a fist, wanting to punch something. "What she needs is to get back in the game. We need her back. In case you haven't noticed, the vamps are getting worse.

Word is out there's no active hunter in Hopetown Valley."

"You're a hunter."

"It's not the same."

"We can't force her," Seth said.

"Whose side are you on?"

Seth gritted his teeth and ran a hand down his face. "I'm not on anyone's side, Arch. And if I were it would be hers. Let her make her own decisions. We can continue the fight until she's ready."

I walked to the middle of the clearing and tilted my head to the sky, opening my mouth and letting out a scream that echoed off the shed wall and bounced into the forest. It should have made me feel better, but at that point the only thing that would was Grace telling me she hadn't completely abandoned me.

"And what if she's making the wrong decision?" I asked. "I can't do this by myself."

"You've got me," Seth said.

I snorted and headed towards the car port and the old truck that sat in the end space. "You coming?" I called over my shoulder. "We've still got some daylight." And I needed to take my mind off Grace or I'd explode.

Since we'd come back from the city, Seth and I had tried getting along better, something that wasn't going too well right then. The old truck seemed to have become a facilitator in our conversations. We'd been working on getting the Bedford running again. Actually, Seth had been working on it. I mostly watched. But even after all the chit-chat and male bonding sessions, I still didn't like the guy.

I slid my fingers under the hood and jiggled the rusty

catch. The hinges groaned as I lifted it and propped it open. Seth grabbed the tool roll from the front seat and got to work tinkering. He'd already pulled half the engine apart and put it back together again, and she still wouldn't kick over.

Seth worked in silence, and I watched him unscrew nuts and do them up again. I didn't have much of an idea when it came to cars. Pa had taught me how to fight, not change spark plugs.

I twirled a spanner in my hand and leaned against the side of the truck. "How long are we going to let this go on for?"

"As long as she needs." Seth grabbed a rag and wiped the grease from his hands.

"That's not the answer I wanted."

"I know which answer you want, Archer, but I'm not going to give it to you." Seth went to the driver's side door and got in the truck. The engine whirred when he turned the key, but it still wouldn't kick over.

I looked at him through the open passenger-side window. "Who died and made you boss?"

"Charlotte and Ryan died." Seth got out and slammed the door. "And no one made me boss. She needs more time."

"Don't say her name again or I'll ... I want my hunting partner back. Her substitute sucks. And why are you so against her hunting?" I asked.

Seth looked at me across the hood. His eyebrows set in a stern frown. "I'm not against her hunting."

"Do you think I'm stupid? You think because I can't read your mind, I can't read you? You're the last person who stops her from doing what she loves. What she's supposed to do. You're the last person who'd stop her doing anything."

"I'm not stopping her." Seth clenched his fists then pushed off the hood of the truck. "I'm not going to force her to do anything."

I stared at his back as he walked across the clearing towards the shed. So much for male bonding, and taking my mind off Grace. I bit back my anger and followed him. He had to see that Grace getting back out there and dusting some vamps was the best thing for her. It was the best thing for all of us. I couldn't do it without her. *We* couldn't do it without her. She could always get the population under control, but without her it was like we were fighting for nothing.

I pushed through the shed door and went to the sink to get a glass of water. Seth sat on the couch with his elbows resting on his thighs and his face in his hands. He didn't often show emotion other than anger. Or at least the permanent scowl on his face made him look angry all the time, so I was instantly worried.

"Why don't you want her to hunt?" I asked. "Because that's it, isn't it? You don't think she needs time. You flat out don't want her hunting. I've never known you to let her hold back on anything. You've always let her go and never stood in her way, even when you were trying to get her to talk to you all those years. You always knew when to back off. And you always let her make her own mistakes."

Seth raised his head and fixed me with a dark stare. "You're right. I don't want her to hunt."

"But that's not your choice to make."

"It's not yours either." He glared at me. "And she could get hurt."

"What the hell does that mean? This is Grace we're talking about."

Seth's jaw clenched and he stood up, running a hand through his cropped blond hair. "I don't want her getting hurt."

I stared at him, my fingers aching from clenching my glass of water. He wasn't telling me something, and the second I'd had the thought, his frown deepened. "What are you holding back? Come on, Seth. Stop messing with me."

"You have to trust me."

Usually I was good with the snide comebacks, but this time I raised my eyebrows instead and wondered when the glass in my hand would shatter.

"I think I need some air." I set the glass on the table and headed for the door.

"You know I love her," Seth said.

I stopped with my hand on the doorknob and turned to face him. "So you keep saying. But she needs to see what's going on. Someone has to pull her out of this bubble she's put herself in, because the Grace I know would never turn her back on this place."

"We can handle the fight without her," Seth said.

"Yeah, until someone else gets killed." I yanked the door open. "Who knows how many people in the area have already died? I don't want that to be Grace's wakeup call. I don't want any more blood on my hands."

I slammed the door and stalked across the clearing to the path. If I knew Grace like I thought I did, she would've gone to the family cemetery, and I wasn't done talking to her. Yes, Charlotte and Ryan were dead, and what we did sucked sometimes, but running away from our problems wasn't going to fix them.

If Grace had taught me anything, it was that.

4

SETH

I picked up the glass Archer had left on the table. A crack ran from the rim and stopped halfway down. I wanted to hurl the glass at the wall, and watch it shatter into tiny pieces, but I set it back down instead.

I couldn't tell Archer I suspected Grace had an injury that hadn't healed properly. He'd start asking questions. And I couldn't tell Grace she'd been marked, because that was a conversation I wasn't ready to have. I'd left it too long, and if she did find out, she'd be angrier with the fact I hadn't told her than she would be with the dying issue itself.

Grace could die and it was my fault, stemming from the aftermath of an agreement I'd made with Michael more than ten years ago. I'd hoped I'd be able to find a way to fix it, but that didn't seem to be the case. The rules kept changing. And if Archer knew his sister wasn't immortal anymore, he would hate me more than he already did.

The terms of my agreement with Michael were something no one was ever meant to know. Ever. Grace had been made to hunt. It was her purpose, and I'd had a hand in taking that away from her all because I'd wanted her back. Maybe she needed protection from me more than anything else.

My guess was Archer would head for the Tate Family Cemetery. Grace went there when she wanted to think and talk to Ryan. I wanted to stop Archer from seeing her. He was angry. Trying to talk to someone when you were angry didn't always go down so well. I knew from experience.

I closed my eyes and honed in on Archer. He hadn't made it far. I misted and landed on the path a few metres in front of him. He looked up, his hands stuffed in his pockets, and scowled.

"If you're in such a hurry to get to Grace, why aren't you running?" I asked.

"I'm thinking."

"Does it hurt?" I gave him a half-smile.

"Get lost, Brone." He shouldered past me.

I laughed. "You must be really angry, calling me by my last name."

"There are no words foul enough in the English language to describe how I feel about you."

I fell into step beside Archer and we walked in silence for a bit.

Archer glanced at me from the corner of his eye. "You can mist. Why not go and warn her I'm coming to give her what for?"

I took a deep breath. "I can't find the cemetery on my own with the magical charm mojo thingy your family has going on. And besides, I like walking." I waited for him to respond but he didn't, so I continued, "When I was in Heaven, I loved walking everywhere. So many of the angels would orb where they wanted or needed to be, but I liked to walk. Grace thought I was crazy—"

"You are," Archer said.

"Aren't we all?" I crossed my arms. "She was always in a hurry to get places. She'd laugh at me because I took so much longer to get anywhere. But the time wasn't the point. I always got where I needed to be, but I also enjoyed the journey."

Archer slowed and we stopped on the path, facing each other. "You have some philosophical moral to this story, don't you?"

"It's not always about where we end up, Archer. Grace probably needs to start hunting again. But she's spent her whole life fighting and running. Can't we let her walk for a while?"

"I think I like you better when you're mean," Archer said. "I'm still going to talk to her." He took a few steps, but I didn't move. "You coming or what?"

I thought about it, but then decided I'd let them have it out. Fighting together was something they'd done for a long time. Archer's anger over the whole situation was a family issue. Maybe she'd open up to him, even though she hadn't to me.

"I'll meet you after dark for patrol," I said. "Go easy on her. She's more fragile than you think."

Archer stopped briefly to give me one of his, *I hate you* looks, but I turned and headed back towards the shed before he could say anything. I stuffed my hands into my pockets and kicked the dirt as I walked, watching the late afternoon light filter through the trees. The forest was a little too quiet, but I'd had enough practice at knowing when someone was watching me not to react.

The leaves crunched under my feet as I kept moving, waiting for Michael to announce his presence. I wasn't about to let him get me riled up. I'd had enough riling for one day.

I'd made it most of the way back to the shed, and he still hadn't said anything.

"You know, it's rude to spy on people." I stopped in a small clearing.

Light lit up the shadows and millions of tiny spheres floated in the air in front of me. They spun until they got bigger and formed the shape of a person.

"I don't spy—I watch," Michael said, crossing his arms.

"Same thing." I glared at him and walked on, brushing past his shoulder and picking a line through the tallow-woods. "What do you want?"

Michael fell into step beside me and I did my best to make it hard for him, moving close to trees and through gaps not wide enough for the two of us.

"We need to talk."

"So talk," I said.

"She's still here."

I wanted to say "So what?" But I said nothing and kept moving. Maybe if I ignored Michael, he'd go away. He'd never stipulated any specifics when I'd seen him last. All he'd told me was that Heaven wanted Grace back, and in order to get there she had to die for the one she loved the most. I'd spent a lot of time thinking about who that would be, and I'd come back with three possible options. Although there was always a loophole when it came to the way the Council thought, so with any of my picks I could be totally off the mark.

Grace was capable of intense love for more than one person. All angels were. It was the way we were originally conditioned, to love unconditionally and intensely. But it didn't matter. I didn't want her dying for anyone, even if it meant I had to take a one-way trip to the In-Between.

"Seth!" Michael grabbed my arm and pulled me to a stop. "Ignoring this won't make it go away."

I stepped forward and shoved him as hard as I could. Michael stumbled backwards, clenching his fists, but he didn't fall. He never did when I tried to fight him. He was an archangel, and far more powerful than I'd ever be. He shoved me back but I managed to hold my ground.

"Why have you put this on me?" I said. "Do you enjoy making my life a misery?"

Michael regarded me for a moment, lifting his chin and staring down his nose at me. "I told you when you were first cast down. It's far from over."

"And here I was thinking you'd been talking about me, and what I did, but no. You had to bring Grace into it, too."

"She's been a part of this from the beginning, whether you like it or not," Michael said. "And you've only got yourself to blame for that."

"This should all be over. She's told me how she feels."

27

"It doesn't matter anymore!" Spit flew from Michael's mouth as he yelled. He took a deep breath, puffing his chest out and standing taller. "I want what's best for Grace. She has to come home."

"And you'll go to any length to get her there." I shook my head and closed my eyes for a moment. Arguing with Michael was like dragging hot needles across my eyeballs. "And what's best for Grace," I said, gritting my teeth, "is what *she* wants. Not what you, or I, or anyone else tells her she needs. Are we done?" I clenched my fists, itching to punch him. When he didn't answer I turned and headed towards the shed.

Michael followed me in silence, and I wanted nothing more than to turn around and give him what he expected. But fighting him never got me anywhere, although sometimes it did make me feel better.

We reached the clearing where dull shadows danced across the grass, moving gently with the breeze. I stalked across the open space with Michael at my heels. His silhouette slowed as we passed the trampoline, but I refused to turn around and face him.

"You have to get her to fight again," Michael said. "She has to die."

I stopped, staring at a patch of ground where the grass didn't grow. The last thing I wanted was to turn and face Michael. I was sick of him, sick of his rules and demands. Sick of the way he'd tried to manipulate me.

"I will not force her to do anything," I said.

"Who said anything about forcing her? All you have to do is convince her to fight."

This time I couldn't stop myself from facing him.

Michael made me so angry. My fist was clenched, ready to strike, but I held back.

"And what if I refuse?" I squared my shoulders and lifted my chin.

Michael stood with his feet apart, one arm across his chest and the other up; his finger tapped his mouth, and his lips held a small smile.

"You know what's at stake, Seth."

"I don't care about oblivion," I said. "All I care about is Grace, and I know she won't want to go back."

Michael laughed. "Have you actually asked her what she wants?"

"If Heaven wants her so badly, why don't *you* ask her?" The words were out of my mouth before I could stop them, and I instantly regretted it. I didn't want Michael anywhere near Grace.

He laughed. "You have to be the one to tell her."

"Why?" I asked, shifting on my feet, my nails digging into my palms until they drew blood.

"Because I like watching you suffer."

The tattoo on my inner left forearm burned, and blue celestial fire glowed in Michael's eyes. The tattoo had been a constant reminder of what I'd done when I fell, and even though I had Grace now, the past haunted me. Michael and I had a connection I couldn't break, and I hated that he had so much power over me. I shook my head and looked away, unable to stare at the fire in Michael's eyes any longer.

"What you're doing is wrong. You're tricking her into returning to Heaven. I know Grace, and if given the choice, she'd say no." I pinched the bridge of my nose with my fingers, wishing I could argue my way out of the mess we were in. "I never thought the Council would resort to blackmail."

"You have to do this, Seth," Michael said. "You have five days." He orbed, and his light filled the shadows for a moment before dissolving into nothing.

Five days.

It wasn't enough time.

When it came to being with Grace, forever was not enough.

5

GRACE

The sun dipped below the trees and the forest settled into dusk. I pushed through the undergrowth until I reached a low stone wall. At first there was nothing but grass and fallen leaves in the small clearing on the other side of the fence, then a moment later headstones and the mausoleum shimmered into view. Our family cemetery had been protected by a charm right from the day I buried my first grandfather. No one could find it unless they had Tate blood running through their veins.

Off to the right stood the mausoleum, and on the left, in line with the wall were two rows of headstones. Some of the earlier ones were overgrown, but the most recent were tidy, with flowers at their bases. Pa had died almost two years ago, but I visited him regularly.

The other fresh grave was Ryan's. Next to that was a cross marking a memorial for Charlotte. Archer hadn't wanted it, but I'd insisted. He never talked about her, and I wanted him to remember her, even if he thought he didn't.

I sat on the wall and put my legs over to the other side, then walked to the end of the row and sat on the grass in front of Ryan's grave. My fingers worried at the laces on my boots, and I took a deep breath.

"What should I do?" I asked, staring at the inscription on the stone. *Gone but never forgotten.*

The irony of the statement we'd chosen for Ryan wasn't lost on me.

"I want to tell them," I said. "But I don't want them to worry about me."

Leaves rustled, and I glanced over my shoulder to see Archer jumping the wall.

"I always worry about you, Gracie." He came and sat beside me, staring vacantly at his hands as he pulled pieces of grass between his fingers.

"I was wondering how long you'd take to get here," I said.

Archer pulled his knees to his chest and rested his chin on them. "I'm sorry I got so angry." He tilted his head and stared at me.

"Yeah, you did get pretty mad."

"Why won't you tell me what's going on?"

I sighed. "I don't want to talk about what you want me to talk about."

Archer grabbed my hand that played with my laces. He slipped his fingers through mine and squeezed. "I'm worried."

"Which is one of the reasons I don't want to tell you what's bothering me."

"There's more than one reason?" Archer raised his

eyebrows. "This has to stop. You have to stop hiding from me."

"Arch, I'm not hiding."

"Then what are you doing?"

"I'm ... I don't know." I pulled my hand from his and got to my feet, brushing the grass from the back of my jeans. "I'm tired of everyone around me dying."

"What about me? Do you care if I die?"

Was he an idiot? Of course I cared. "What do you think?"

"I can't keep fighting without you, Gracie." Archer didn't move. He stared at Ryan's headstone. "Without you by my side ... it's like I'm missing my right arm or something."

"Then don't fight. We don't have to fight anymore."

I didn't see why he was so adamant to keep fighting. If he stopped, then a new team would be sent, and all our problems would be over. I was tired of it. Tired of everything that came with the responsibility of being a hunter. I was hardly a Protection Angel anymore. I couldn't keep Archer safe. I couldn't even keep myself safe, so what was the point?

"I can't believe you said that." Archer got to his feet and faced me. "This is our mission. It's what we do. You can't give up because it got hard."

"I'm fallen, Arch! It's not my mission anymore."

"If you believe that, then ... What happened to fighting for what you believed in? What happened to goodness, and defeating the evil that tries to drag us down every day?"

"Are you done?" I crossed my arms and turned away.

Archer grabbed my arm and spun me around. "No. I'm not done. And neither are you." He glared at me, his eyes dark and full of anger. "If we were done, then we'd have been replaced by now. They haven't replaced us."

"But you've been keeping things under control." I frowned at him.

"That's the thing," Archer said. "At first we were. It was like it's always been … enough to dust one maybe two every night. On the odd night we'd do three, but now … we're looking at bigger gangs moving through the area. You need to start hunting again."

"I don't want to."

Archer ran a hand through his hair. "You need to be there. We're a team. We work better, and faster, and more efficiently than any other hunting team I know."

"Well, that's a great comparison," I said. "We only know one other hunting team."

"I don't want to force you, Gracie, but we need more muscle. Otherwise people are going to die."

I glanced at Ryan's headstone. "Everyone's already forgotten him, like he never existed. We're the only ones left who remember."

"Abby remembers, too," Archer said.

I shook my head. "It isn't enough."

"Yeah." Archer said. "Nothing ever is."

Ryan's death had triggered the start of the end for me, even before I'd discovered I couldn't heal myself. But how could I make Archer understand I was done? We were standing in a secret cemetery full of our dead ancestors who were also my brothers, fathers, and my grandfathers. The whole concept of the mission suddenly seemed like the most messed up thing in the world. I hated the Council for putting me through it in the first place. I hated having to say goodbye to every single one of my brothers because of it. I didn't want to lose anyone else I loved.

"Listen to me, Arch. Look around us. We're surrounded by dead people. Our parents … and grandparents … My brothers. Ryan." I watched as Archer's gaze floated over all the graves. "In no more than seven years, I'm supposed to die and be born again, only this time it won't happen, because I fell and broke the cycle. You will never have a child who will grow up to be me. We're the last Tate generation because of what I've done."

"It doesn't mean you should give up."

I swatted my cheeks, wiping away the tears that slowly rolled down them. "What if the Council hasn't replaced us because they're punishing me?"

"That's ridiculous." Archer scoffed and put his hands on his hips.

"Is it?" I shook my head and stared at the ground, the grass and dirt blurring beneath my tears.

"Why would you think they're punishing you, Gracie? I mean … apart from the obvious."

I raised my head and stared into Archer's eyes. His anger had fallen away, replaced with worry and fear. He bit his lip and waited. *Maybe I should tell him what's wrong.* He was my brother. If there was one person I could trust, it was him.

I took a deep breath and lifted my top to expose my right side. "If they don't want to punish me, then why is this happening?"

Archer's eyes widened at the sight of the patch. A small amount of blood had seeped through, marring the white surface. He reached out and touched my hip, and

I flinched. The wound site ached, and I pulled my top down again to cover it.

"You haven't healed?" he said, letting his arm drop to his side. "But you always heal."

"I haven't been wounded in a fight since Wide Island … until a couple of weeks ago."

"Has Seth seen it?"

I shook my head. "I don't let him … look at me … with the light on. And we haven't …" I twisted my fingers together. "Do I have to have this conversation with you?"

"No, I'm good." Archer raised his hands in defence.

"This is why …" I said.

Archer covered his mouth with one hand, his fingers digging into his cheeks. "You stopped …" He rubbed his chin.

I nodded. "Now do you understand?" I asked. "I can't heal myself like I used to be able to. It's scabbed over a little, but it aches, and I don't know why."

"What does this mean?"

"What if I get to the point where I can't heal at all, Arch?" I said. "What if … I get injured so badly—"

"I would never let that happen. We've made it this far."

But how could he promise that? I couldn't guarantee his safety any more than he could mine. We were both like time bombs waiting to explode.

"The mission will eventually kill us both," I said.

"You don't know that … You don't know if you'll die."

"Arch, if I can be wounded, I can die."

"Have you told Seth any of this?"

I pressed my lips together and shook my head. What was I supposed to say to him? He'd accuse me of not trusting him, when all I really wanted was for him to love me and not feel as if he had to protect me. I'd never wanted to be a burden on anyone. I was supposed to be the protector.

Archer came over and put his hand out. I grabbed it and he pulled me to him, wrapping me up in a warm hug.

"We'll get through this," he said, pressing his cheek to my hair. "We're in this together. We always have been."

He took my hand and led me to the stone wall. The cemetery shimmered away to nothing once we stepped over the threshold—our family protected from the outside world. We walked through the forest together in silence, and I listened to the sounds of the breeze between the trees, and the animals scurrying through the undergrowth, coming out for the night ahead.

"Will you hunt tonight?" I asked as we neared the end of the path that led into the clearing at the shed.

"I hunt every night." Archer stopped and faced me, stuffing his hands into his pockets. "Will you?"

I toed the dirt with my boot and hugged myself, feeling cold even though it was late spring. "I ... need more time. Until I can figure out what's happening to me. Please don't tell Seth."

Archer sighed. "Come on." He put his arm around my shoulders and we kept walking. "The formal's on Thursday night. You coming?"

I groaned. "No. It's the last place I want to go."

"Come on, Gracie. You ... in a dress. I'd like to see that."

I punched him in the ribs and he let go of me. "I hate dresses."

"I know! Which is why it would be priceless to see." He

smiled. "Abby will be really disappointed if you don't come."

"Fine … I'll think about it."

Archer was smart enough not to push the issue any further.

I was thinking about how weird it would be to wear a dress again—the last one I'd worn was my white gown that had turned black when I fell—when Archer stopped at the mouth of the path, grabbed my shoulders and pushed me behind a tree. Across the clearing Seth stood near the trampoline, and he wasn't alone. He was with Michael, and neither of them looked happy. No surprises there. Their lips moved, but I couldn't hear what they were saying, no matter how hard I strained.

What's going on? Archer thought, his hands tightening on my arms as he peered over my head from behind me.

I don't know. But it probably isn't good if it involves those two.

Seth pinched the bridge of his nose and anger flared in his eyes. The next moment, Michael orbed and was gone.

Any time Michael showed up there was always something about to go down. And from the way Seth had reacted to him, I wasn't the only one keeping secrets.

SETH
Tuesday night

Grace stalked across the clearing, Archer in tow, and I braced myself for the shouting, but when she reached me she said nothing. She glared at me and waited, her hands on her hips.

I was about to tell her it wasn't what she thought, but what did she think? And if I said that I'd be lying, because she knew I'd been holding something back. I was about to get all defensive when I realised I wasn't the only one in this mess. It wasn't only me who'd been keeping secrets. But standing up for myself would anger her more. Sometimes, backing down was the best thing to do.

"Well?" she said.

"I'm not having this fight with you, Grace." I headed towards the cottage so I could arm up for the night's hunt.

"Don't you walk away from me, Seth Brone."

I stopped and turned to face her. Grace's brow furrowed and her lips puckered, but she was, and always would be, the most beautiful angel I'd ever seen. Moving towards her, until I'd closed the gap between us, I reached up to touch her face. She flinched, and my hand lingered near her cheek, waiting before I tried again. This time she let me touch her, and she closed her eyes when I cupped her face in both hands.

When I leaned in her breath was warm on my lips, and I pressed my forehead to hers. I wanted to kiss her, but she was angry. I'd only make it worse.

"Please, stop fighting me. I'm not the enemy," I said.

"I don't know who is anymore," she said.

"You have to trust me." I slid my hands behind her head, twisting my fingers into her hair, and she lifted her chin, her eyes still closed.

"What did Michael want?" she asked.

I tensed. "He's causing his usual trouble."

Her eyes opened and her gaze bore into mine. She probed my thoughts, searching for a more solid answer. Her lips parted in another response, and this time I didn't hold back. I kissed her. Hard. And I didn't care if Archer stood there watching. I'd told Grace so many times I loved her, but it never seemed to be enough. Even the power behind those three words was not enough to explain how I felt about her.

Grace circled her arms around my waist and pushed her body against mine, then she broke free and stared at me again.

You're trying to distract me, she thought.

Is it working?

Archer cleared his throat. "Can we get going?" He stomped past us towards the cottage and slammed the front door once he was inside.

I rubbed Grace's nose with mine. "I better go."

"I'm still mad at you, even after that kiss."

I smiled. "I know."

I didn't want to leave her standing there, but I couldn't stay either. Maybe Michael was right, and I should ask her what she wanted, because she sure as hell wasn't going to tell me herself.

But there would never be a right time to tell her she had to die.

Once I was inside the cottage, I peeked out the front window and watched her walk back to the shed.

Archer was in the lounge, hidden behind the false wall that ran around three of the four walls of the room. Sounds of him rummaging around filtered through the open door, and I waited for him to re-emerge. He came through the sliding panel doorway and threw me a stake belt.

"You need anything else, get it yourself," he said.

"I'm good. I'll kill them with my bare hands if I have to."

Archer glared at me but didn't reply. He hit a button on the keypad and the door slid closed. I stared at it for a second, realising no one had ever told me the code.

I shrugged it off and followed Archer back to the clearing. He glanced at the shed as we passed and headed into the forest. We fell into step together, taking a path that twisted behind the shed and back towards the highway. Lately, the vamps had been hanging out around town, and we were sure to find a few cruising the streets before the night was over. I enjoyed listening to the sounds of the forest, waiting to hear the tell-tale rustle of something other than an animal, or the hum of a car on the road.

Archer seemed to be in a worse mood than he'd been in before he went to see Grace, and I wondered what they'd said to each other. I didn't often look at Archer's thoughts, but this time I was curious about how Grace reacted to him pushing her about hunting. From the way Archer was moping and grumbling under his breath, she obviously hadn't agreed with his point of view.

"You going to tell me what she said?" I asked.

"Trust me, you don't want to know."

It was all I needed to get Archer to think about the biggest thing that was bothering him, and he was right. I didn't like what I saw.

I stopped and stared at his back until he realised I wasn't walking with him anymore.

Archer stopped as well, his shoulders drooped, and he turned around.

"You read my mind, didn't you?" he asked.

I ignored his question and asked one of my own. "How bad is it?"

Archer ran a hand through his hair and grabbed it by the roots, gritting his teeth. "It's—"

"Duck!" I conjured a fire ball and threw it in his direction.

My fire sailed over his head, singing the tips of his hair and making it crackle. Archer hit the ground, falling on his belly. The chest of the vamp behind him exploded into flames. The vampire's screams resounded through the forest. Archer kicked the vamp in the knee and it stumbled backwards to the forest floor. I misted and landed next to the fiery mess, pulling a stake from my belt and finishing the vamp off. The cloud of dust extinguished the flames, falling onto the scorched earth. I put my hand out and Archer grabbed it so I could pull him to his feet.

"You really should pay more attention," I said.

"I would if you didn't distract me all the time." Archer ran a hand over his head. "I can't believe you burnt my hair."

"You'll live ... It's a good thing I've got your back."

"Yeah, but it should be Grace."

I didn't disagree.

We pushed through the trees and emerged onto the highway, heading towards Hopetown Valley High and the town. We'd fallen into a bit of a routine, never hunting where we'd been the night before, and never creating a recognisable order. Because there had been a rise in the number of vamps coming to the area, it was time to patrol the streets and hope no one was stupid enough to be out wandering around late on a weeknight. I didn't like our chances now exams were finished. All the year twelves would be taking advantage of their newfound freedom.

"You don't seem surprised," Archer said, "about Grace."

"I've known something's wrong since not long after the city. I've been waiting for her to tell me."

"How is it possible? She's an angel, for crying out loud," Archer said, throwing his hands up. "Why all of a sudden can't she heal herself?"

"It's possible," I said, stalling while I chose my words, "because the Council has decided to change the rules."

Archer scoffed. "Which ones?"

"Physics, science, biology—I don't know. Whatever makes an angel an angel."

"Can they do that?"

The road lit up with the glow of headlights as a car came around the bend behind us. I glanced over my shoulder but couldn't see anything through the glare.

I waited for it to roll past before attempting to answer Archer's question. Maybe if I told him the truth, he'd be less angry with everyone and more willing to protect his sister.

"Apparently they can do whatever they like," I said.

When we reached the school driveway, I stopped. Light from the dorms spilled into the darkness, and a few borders milled around the steps. Most of the year twelves were gone, but the rest of the school had to finish the term. I listened and tried to separate the chatter from anything unsavoury. All seemed clear, so we walked a little farther before jumping the wall and skirting around the school grounds towards the cemetery. If there were vamps around, that was where they'd be.

We kept to the shadows so no one would see us if they happened to be looking over from the school. The gate to the cemetery squeaked when I pushed it open.

Archer stopped and the gate clanged shut behind him. "Does your conversation with Michael have anything to do with what's going on?"

I put my hands on my hips and stared at the ground, pressing my lips together. "I can handle Michael."

"No one can handle Michael."

"Can we hunt and talk about this tomorrow?" I said.

Archer pulled a stake from his belt and adjusted his grip. "There's something you're not telling me." He shouldered past me and stalked down the centre aisle of headstones.

"Believe me, you won't like the truth."

He stopped and faced me, clenching his fists at his sides. "Try me."

"After we do some dusting." I raised my eyebrows.

"There's another one behind me, isn't there?" he asked. "Why don't they ever sneak up on you?"

Archer spun and threw a punch as he came around, connecting with the face of a slender girl vampire. She shrieked and stumbled backwards but didn't fall. Blood trickled from her nose and she dabbed at it with the tip of a finger. Another vampire blurred to her side, his lips pulled back in a snarl.

"Oh, scary," Archer said.

Sometimes I wished he wouldn't get so cocky. I was the one who had to make sure he didn't end up dead. He seemed to forget most of the time that superpowers aside, he was still human.

I misted and landed behind the two vamps, wasting no time in planting a stake in the guy's back. Sometimes it was too easy. The girl made to run, but I grabbed her arm. She cried out as my fingers dug into her flesh.

"Not so fast," I said. "Where are you from?"

"Nowhere," she said, trying to yank herself free.

Her mind told me a different story. The city vamps were trying their hand at the country life. They'd heard that Hopetown Valley no longer had a hunter. If they were careful, they could come and go as they pleased, feeding and using their glamour to make people forget.

If no hunter was here to stop them, they'd have a never-ending supply of blood without the risk of being staked.

Not if I could help it.

"You thought there were no hunters here," I said.

The vamp bared her teeth and struggled in my grasp. The next second she exploded in my hand, ash falling all over my arm. Archer tucked his stake into his belt. I huffed as I brushed the dust off.

"What?" Archer asked. "She wasn't going to tell us anything we didn't already know. It's a shame to have to kill the pretty ones though." He stood with his feet apart and crossed his arms over his chest. "Now. You were saying something about the truth?"

I stared at Archer for a long moment, wondering if I told him how long it would take for Grace to find out.

"How good are you at keeping Grace out of your head?"

"Pretty good," he said. "Why?"

I leaned against a tall headstone. The angel on top had its wings curled around its robed body. Its face wore a mournful expression.

"Because if I tell you this you have to promise to keep it from her," I said.

"I'm listening ..."

I hesitated once more before finally deciding to tell Archer the truth. "Heaven wants Grace back, but to get her there ... she has to die."

Archer's face morphed from confused to angry and back again in a matter of seconds. His eyebrows pinched and he bit his lip. "This is why you don't want her hunting ... and why she can't heal."

"Like I said. The Council changed the rules. But it

gets worse."

Archer threw his hands up. "How could this possibly get worse?"

"If I don't get her into a situation where she can die … if she doesn't return … I've got a one-way ticket to the In-Between, courtesy of Michael."

Archer grinned. "That doesn't sound so bad."

I ignored him and continued, "If Grace stays, I go. If she goes … no matter what happens … I'll lose her anyway. I can't lose her again, Arch."

He rubbed his face with both hands and shook his head, his mouth moving but not forming words. His mind was a jumbled mess, but the one thing I could read was that he didn't want his sister to die, but he also wanted her to be happy.

"What are we going to do?" Archer asked, his eyes glassy.

I shrugged. "That's a good question."

And one I didn't have an answer for.

I'd spent months trying to figure out what to do. I'd even asked around the fallen circle if anything like this had been seen before, if there had been any talk, but I hadn't wanted to draw too much attention to Grace's situation, so I'd backed off. If the wrong people had found out she could die, she'd have been gone already.

"I don't understand," Archer said. "Why don't they send someone to strip her? Surely that would be easier."

I scoffed. "Because Michael is using her to punish me."

Archer stared at the ground, his brow furrowing. "I think I hate him more and more every second. Who can we ask for help? Surely you have a contact somewhere

who knows about this kind of stuff, who's seen something like this happen before?"

"Who would you trust with Grace's life?" I clenched my fists.

Archer pressed his lips together. "What about Hope and Justice? They seemed … okay. We could ask them without letting on it's about Grace."

I raised my eyebrows. "And who would they think it was about?"

"We have to do something!"

Yes, we did, but I was at a loss as to what to do other than protect the girl I loved from whatever was coming. Every day I'd woken up hoping that it wouldn't be the day Michael showed up. Now he had, and he'd given me five days. If there *was* a way out of this mess, I intended to use every second I had left to find it.

GRACE
Wednesday morning

I woke to the sun pouring through the windows at the top of my room, and the feeling of Seth rubbing circles on my back with his fingers.

I rolled my head to the side and stared into his dark eyes. "Nothing's changed. I'm still—"

"Mad at me, I know. I would be, too."

I slipped my hand under my cheek and shifted from my stomach to my left side. "Why would you be angry with yourself?"

"I have a habit of doing things that warrant anger."

I laughed and swatted him on the shoulder. No matter how mad I could get with him, he always managed to make me smile some way or another.

"How was the hunt?" I asked.

"Usual," he said, but didn't elaborate.

Seth shifted closer, his arm draped over me. I stiffened as he pressed against my hip, glad his arm wasn't higher and near my wound. He leaned in to press his lips to mine, and my phone buzzed on the side table before announcing the call with its loud trill.

Seth grimaced, pulling away. "That's a bit much at this early hour."

I picked my phone up. "It's just after eight." I swiped the screen to take the call.

Abby's voice penetrated my eardrum from the other end of the line, asking where Archer was. "He's supposed to pick me up. He's fifteen minutes late."

"That's because he's probably still in bed, snoring," I said.

"Today is a big day. It's dress day."

I took a deep breath and held it. Why couldn't everyone have forgotten about the formal? Dances were not my thing. Sticking pointy pieces of wood into bad guys—that was my thing. Although, not so much lately.

"He's not answering his phone. Is he coming to get me?" Abby asked.

I sat up and flung my legs over the side of the bed. "Let him sleep a bit longer. He was out late last night."

Abby went silent, and I could practically hear her thinking at the other end of the phone.

"I'll be there in fifteen." I sighed and ended the call before she could answer.

I shimmied into my jeans and laced my boots. I didn't bother changing my singlet top because I didn't want Seth to see the patch over my wound. It would raise too many questions I didn't want to answer just then. He lay back on the bed, one arm behind his head and a smirk on his face.

"Today is going to be interesting."

"I'm not going with her," I said. "It's all Archer."

"What's the deal with them anyway?" Seth asked. "He getting any action?"

I grabbed my pillow and threw it at his head. "It's none of our business."

He laughed and chucked the pillow back at me. "You're not the least bit curious?"

I shook my head and dropped the pillow onto the bed, then walked to the door. The last thing I wanted to talk about was Archer's sex life, or mine for that matter. Seth had been such a gentleman in that department, and I'd managed so far to keep him at bay, but I wouldn't be able to forever, and I wasn't sure I wanted to go down that path with him. I'd told him I loved him, but the last time I got too physical with someone I cared about, it hadn't worked out. I didn't want to make the same mistake twice.

Seth wore a silly grin, and I chuckled before yanking the door open and heading into the hall. Soft snores came from Archer's room as I passed, and I was careful on the metal staircase not to make too much noise. It wouldn't be long before Abby subjected him to dress torture, so he could have a few more minutes sleep.

Outside, I unlocked the car and climbed in. My side ached when I twisted into the driver's seat. Maybe I'd tell Seth about it today and ask him what he thought. There had to be an explanation, but no matter how hard I racked my brain, I couldn't come up with one that made sense. I'd told Archer because I trusted my brother with my life, so why hadn't I told Seth yet? Surely I could trust him as well. I'd kept it a secret from him this long, but maybe it was time to tell him why I hadn't been fighting.

The Defender roared to life when I turned the key, and I headed down the long driveway towards the road. Ten minutes later, I parked in the Hopetown Valley High carpark and let the engine idle while I waited for Abby. She bounced down the dorm steps, golden hair swaying around her shoulders. I groaned at the sight of the huge smile plastered on her face.

Today was going to suck.

Abby yanked the door open and flew into the car in a flurry of blonde excitement.

"One more sleep," she said, clapping her hands. "All the senior borders have passes today. This is going to be so much fun."

How someone could get so excited over a stupid dance was beyond me.

I shoved the car into reverse and backed out of the car space, taking a deep breath and willing myself not to say something nasty. Abby and I had never really been friends, until she'd gotten caught up in my world and the fight in Wide Island. I could have gotten Josh to glamour her and make her forget everything. Michael would have done it, too, but I didn't want that for Abby. She was stronger than anyone gave her credit for. She deserved to remember, and Ryan deserved to have someone remember him, too.

"Abby, I told you. I'm not going," I said.

She did her best to keep the smile on her face. "I'm hoping you'll change your mind once you see the dress I got for you. You're going to love it."

"You shouldn't have bought me a dress." I sighed,

wondering why on earth she would do that.

"I didn't. Seth paid for it; I chose it."

"Great. That's just … great." The car bumped down the driveway and I pulled into the car port, killing the engine. "I'm not exactly happy with Seth right now."

Abby turned in her seat and faced me. "What is it this time?" She raised her eyebrows.

I couldn't help laughing. Lately, my life had been one big drama. I could have made a TV show out of it.

I told her about Michael and how Archer and I had seen them talking. "When I asked him about it, he shrugged it off." I stared at Abby. "If Michael is around, it can't be good."

"I don't know the guy." Abby twirled a lock of hair around her finger. "But based on the last time I met him, I'd probably agree with you."

I pulled the keys from the ignition and opened the car door, stepping out onto the damp grass. We didn't speak as we walked to the shed, and I tried my best not to listen in on Abby's thoughts, but her mind was so loud it was hard not to hear it. She looked at herself in a mirror, wearing her formal dress and pushing her boobs up so they sat right. It was nice—the dress, not her boobs.

Abby opened the shed door and waltzed in, tossing her purse on the couch. "You ready?" she asked Archer, who sat at the kitchen table with Seth, a spoon of cereal half raised to his mouth.

"I don't get why Grace can't take you," Archer said.

"I'm happy to go," I said, not actually meaning it. Dress shopping with Abby was the last thing I wanted to do.

Archer hid a smirk behind his hand.

You're teasing me! I thought.

He pressed his lips together, suppressing his smile. *And it's fun.*

"Grace can't take me because it will spoil the surprise." Abby grinned.

"But … what if it doesn't fit properly?" Archer dropped his spoon into his bowl, sat back in his chair, and draped one arm on the table.

I was going to strangle him.

"It will fit. Now can we go?" Abby stared at Archer, her hands on her hips.

I closed my eyes and tried to block out the perfectly formed image of my formal dress that floated into Abby's head. She was right, I did like the dress, but I didn't want to admit it. And seeing it didn't make me want to go to the dance any more than I wanted to stick pins under my fingernails.

Seth got up and came over to where I stood near the door. "You okay? You look …"

Like I'm about to throw up? I thought.

Seth laughed and rubbed my back. *It's not that bad. It's a nice dress.*

You saw it, too? You're not supposed to see it before the night.

We're not getting married. He pulled me close and pressed a kiss to my temple.

Archer opened the door for Abby and she went outside. My brother hesitated and looked at Seth.

"Don't let her—"

"Okay, off you go." Seth grabbed the edge of the door and pushed Archer outside. "You've kept Abby waiting

long enough."

I stared at the door after Seth closed it, trying to figure out what had happened. As usual, I couldn't get a read on Seth's thoughts, and when I tried to hone in on Archer's he was focused on Abby, and not feeling so good about the day ahead. That made two of us. But there was something Archer had been going to say before Seth had interrupted him, and I wanted to know what it was.

I faced Seth. "Don't let her what?"

"It's nothing to worry about."

"We both know that's not true."

"Grace, if it was important, I'd tell you."

"Would you?" I asked.

Seth folded his arms over his chest and leaned against the door. "If you had something important to share, would you tell me?"

I mimicked his stance, hugging myself tightly, my shoulder pressing into the wall. His eyes bore into me, but I refused to look away. I also didn't have an answer for his question.

"Didn't think so." Seth pushed off the door and went over to the kitchen sink, pouring himself a glass of water.

I followed, determined not to let him turn this around and make it about me. "Does this have something to do with Michael? What was he doing here? Why won't you tell me what's going on?"

Seth sat at the table and rested his hands in front of him. "Okay, sit. You want to talk about this? Let's talk."

SETH

G race stared at me for a moment before grabbing the back of the chair and pulling it away from the table. The legs screeched on the concrete floor and the sound echoed around the shed. She sat down and put her palms flat on the Formica surface, her gaze never leaving mine.

I wasn't sure how to read the expression on her face, and I couldn't figure out if she was angry, nervous, scared, or all of those things rolled into one. But she wanted to find out what Michael had said to me, which meant I had to think fast if I was going to keep lying.

Maybe I should've told her when I'd first found out she could die. I always had a way of making a mess of things.

"What was he doing here?" Grace asked.

"I ... was asking him for help." *Lie.* "The vamps are still out of hand." At least that part was true. "I can't protect Archer for much longer. One day—"

"Well, I can't protect him either." Grace went silent, her cheeks moving as she ground her teeth. "How is Michael supposed to help?" she finally said.

I rubbed the back of my neck and sighed. "Heaven wants you back. I think they want to reinstate you."

Grace opened her mouth, and a puff of air came out. She took some deep breaths and sat back in her chair, letting her hands fall into her lap. It wasn't a lie, but I'd hardly told her the whole truth either.

"Well ... that's ..." She stared at me. "Why didn't Michael come to me?"

"Grace." I leaned forward with my elbows on the table and stared at her. "Do you want to go back to Heaven?"

She shook her head. "No. But ... It's not that I don't want to. I want to be wherever you are."

I squeezed my eyes shut and pinched the bridge of my nose. How was I supposed to tell her that no matter what we did, that was never going to happen? It didn't matter if she stayed or if she went. We would never get to be together again, and all I wanted was to make the most of what little time we had left—less than five days— which was hard to do when all we did was fight and keep secrets from each other.

"One day, Archer is going to die," I said.

"I know. He's human."

"That's not what I meant. You've always protected him. If you go back, you'll be able to do that again. You'll get your healing powers back." Was I trying to convince Grace or myself?

"What are the conditions?" Grace asked.

I dropped my hand away from my face. "What do

you mean?"

"Oh come on, Seth. I know as well as you there are always conditions when Michael is involved. There has to be a catch." She stopped, and her eyes widened. "That's it, isn't it? He's offered you something, which is why he didn't come to me. He knew I wouldn't want to go back after everything that's happened. So he's trying to get to me through you."

Grace was too smart for her own good.

I leaned forward in my chair. "Michael could offer me the world and it wouldn't be enough to make me betray you."

"How do I know that if you won't tell me what he said?"

"Everything I've ever done has been to protect you. You have to trust me."

"You keep saying that!" Grace stood and her chair tipped over, crashing to the concrete floor. "Trust is earned, Seth. It isn't something you can expect me to give you on your word."

Please, I thought. But she was already gone, her black mist lingering where she'd stood seconds before.

I misted as well, guessing she'd headed for the family cemetery again. I honed in on her thoughts, searching for her essence because I had to catch her before she got there, otherwise I'd never find her.

I landed on a path that led deep into the forest. Grace was a few metres in front of me, and I watched as the cemetery shimmered into focus.

"Grace, wait! Stop running away from me."

She spun around and came towards me, a fire in her eyes so intense I thought she was going to hit me.

"Tell me what you're hiding."

"I love you, Grace. I would never do anything—"

"Please don't say to hurt me, because we both know that isn't true."

"You're one to talk." I glared at her, my blood racing so fast through my veins I thought it would burst through my skin. "You seem to have forgotten about Josh." The moment the words were out of my mouth, I wanted to take them back.

Grace's mouth opened a little. She let out a short breath then pressed her lips together. She clenched her fists at her sides. "You … were gone. And he needed me."

"Not in his bed!"

"I didn't think you'd stoop so low as to use that against me."

I ran a hand over my head, wanting to scream at her. She was right. What I'd said was a low blow. But here I was, thinking we'd gotten past everything that had happened. That Grace and I were finally at a place where we could lay low and be happy together. But I was beginning to think that day would never come, because time was running out. There would always be something standing in the way. And being the idiot I was, I'd only made it worse.

"You have to believe that when the time is right, I'll tell you everything," I said.

"What's wrong with right now?" Grace planted her hands on her hips. The sunlight shone off her dark hair and sparkled in her eyes. She'd always been so sexy when she was angry.

She scowled at my thoughts. "You'll let me hear you think something like that, but you won't tell me the truth."

"I'm trying to protect you," I said.

"From what? The monsters under my bed?" Grace scoffed. "I can protect myself."

"Are you sure about that?" I asked.

Grace shouldered past me and walked in the direction of the shed. I dragged a hand down my face and followed. Why did I always have to ruin things? I couldn't remember the last time Grace had looked at me and been genuinely happy.

I wanted her to be happy.

"I don't know what you want me to say," I said after we'd walked in silence for a while.

"I want you to open up to me." She kept walking, staring at her shuffling feet and hugging herself tightly. "When have you ever really let me in? Never."

"I'm not the 'letting in' type."

Grace let out a groan through clenched teeth. She stopped and stamped her foot, glaring at me. "If you want this to work, there's only one way it can."

I kept walking. I didn't want to play this game. If she couldn't see how much I loved her and that I wanted what was best for her, then I didn't know what else to do. "You're not exactly open with me all the time either."

"Okay then. What do you want me to tell you, Seth?"

I turned around and looked at Grace standing in the middle of the path with her arms out. Fuming.

"It's been months, and we still ..." I sighed and shoved my hands into my hair, grabbing it and pulling. I didn't want to confront her about her injury, because that meant I'd have to come clean about how I knew. She couldn't know the truth yet. I wasn't ready to see the look in her eyes when I told her, so I said something else. "We haven't talked about Josh since we got back from the city."

"Really? We're going to do this? Because you just shoved him in my face ... I can't believe this." Grace shook her head and stormed past me. "I am trying to move on from that, from everything. You tell me I have to trust you, when clearly you don't trust me." Her voice echoed through the trees.

"Can you blame me?" I stalked after her, wondering when we'd started fighting and why. It seemed like fighting was all we'd done for a long time. "You slept with him."

Grace spun on her heels. "What do you want me to say? I'm not sure exactly what you want to talk about. Do you want me to tell you the details? Is that it? Or are you searching for an apology? Because I'm not going to apologise. I'm not sorry I did it because I hurt you; I'm sorry because I hurt him."

I let out a long breath. "I'd hoped that I would be—"

"Talking about this will not change the past." She walked away again.

"Grace, where are you going?"

"Home. Don't you have somewhere else to be?"

I caught up to her, ignoring the spite in her voice. "Despite everything, my place is here, with you."

"No. Until you can tell me what's going on, and what you're hiding from me, I need some space. Don't you get it? Michael is involved, and he won't let anything rest until he gets what he's here for. God, Seth." She shook her head and misted, landing ahead of me along the path. "I can't breathe when I'm around you. Give me some room to breathe, please."

Are you breaking up with me? I thought.

Maybe ... leave me alone.

I clenched my fists and misted. When I landed, Grace stopped and stared up at me, her eyes glistening with unshed tears.

"I love you," I said. "I don't need room to breathe. You are my breath. I exist because you are the only one worth existing for."

"Prove it." Grace misted again, only this time she didn't land anywhere near me.

I screamed, and it echoed through the forest, bouncing off the trees and smacking into my heart like a hammer shattering glass. I punched the nearest tree. It seemed tree punching was becoming a regular occurrence for me.

I thought about following her and telling her everything right from the very beginning. My original deal with Michael, and how I'd planned to win her back. How that deal involved me growing and aging along with her in this incarnation, and in order to be with her forever she had to give me her heart, and if she didn't I'd end up in the In-Between.

She'd told me she loved me.

Only now the rules had been changed.

Heaven wanted Grace back, and there wasn't a damn thing I could do about it.

ARCHER

I swung the Defender into a park on the main street of Macquarie Cove. Hopetown Valley had one dress shop, but Abby said the dresses in there were not good enough. She had the perfect formal outfits on layby at some fantastic store I'd never heard of. No surprises there. The drive had taken almost an hour, and Abby hadn't been very talkative, which was not completely normal, but welcome. I had too much on my mind with what Seth had told me about Grace to be in the mood for chit chat.

"Everything okay?" Abby asked as I killed the engine.

"Sure." I smiled before getting out of the car and going around to open her door.

"You seem preoccupied." She twisted in her seat, but didn't get out of the car.

If only I could talk to her about Grace. But I couldn't do that until I'd talked to Grace about Grace. How was

I supposed to deal with the knowledge she could die? The best thing to do was focus on the moment, and right then that involved Abby and formal dresses.

"It's nothing we can't talk about later," I said.

"Grace will be okay, you know."

I furrowed my brow. "Abby, what—"

"I know you're worried. About her, and Seth, and Michael showing up ... I'm blonde, but I'm not stupid."

"You know about Michael?"

Abby shrugged. "Grace told me."

"Right ... And I never said you were stupid."

"I bet you've thought it on occasion." Abby jumped down from the car and smiled. "Ready?"

I did what I always did when I felt awkward or put on the spot. I made fun of the situation. "If you mean for food, then yes. I'm ready. If you're asking whether I'm prepared for flouncy dresses and other girly crap, then I'm totally not."

"Come on, this will be fun. And you can take your mind off things for a while." Abby linked her arm through mine and yanked me towards the shops that lined the street.

"Couldn't Claudia do this with you?" I pressed the button on my key and the Defender's blinkers flashed, the locks popping down. Why on earth I'd agreed to go with her to pick up formal dresses was beyond me.

"I want everything to be perfect for Grace. And you know her better than anyone."

"She is going to kill you. You know that, right?"

"She can't possibly say no when she sees the dress Seth paid for," Abby said.

I shook my head and laughed. "You do realise she

already knows what it looks like."

Abby's eyes widened as she pushed the door open into a small dress boutique, a bell above the door tinkling softly. "She wouldn't!"

"She would." I held the door until we were both through, letting it swing shut.

"Well, it's the formal. I don't care if she read my mind. She needs to go."

I raised my eyebrows. "Because you said?"

"Because she has to let her hair down and relax for once."

"I'm not sure Grace's idea of relaxing involves any form of dancing or socialising. Putting a stake in an angry vamp is more her style."

"See? That's my point," Abby said. "She needs to forget about all of that, even if it's for one night."

I laughed and shook my head. "You really don't know Grace at all."

Abby smiled her typical smile and went farther into the shop. My heart panged with guilt at everything she'd been through during the past few months. If someone had told me at the beginning of the year that I'd be friends with Abigail West, maybe edging closer to more than friends, I'd have told them they needed to be committed. I'd never liked Abby, but that was when all I could see had been her superficial exterior. Underneath the nail polish and perfect hair, she was pretty cool. After the fight in Wide Island City, she'd needed someone to help her not freak out, and I'd needed someone to not be Charlotte.

Abby turned and faced me, surrounded by frilly lace, and way too much silky fabric. She pressed her lips together and twisted her hands, fidgeting with her fingers.

"What?" I asked

"Thank you."

"For …?" I rolled my hand in the air.

She shrugged. "For, you know … coming with me. I know you don't want to be here."

"Are you kidding?" I chuckled. "I couldn't think of anything else … actually, you're right. I don't want to be here."

"Archer!" Abby whacked me on the arm, laughing.

The store was small, but it somehow managed to cram in more dresses than I'd ever seen in my lifetime. Racks lined the outer walls, filled with gowns of every shape and colour. More racks went down the middle of the store, and I stared at the ocean of flowing fabric.

"I feel like this place is going to swallow me whole. Don't let me get lost in here." The dresses rustled as I moved past them.

Abby pushed me towards a low leather seat that faced the change rooms lining the back of the store. "Sit."

She went to the counter off to the left and chatted to the sales lady in her bubbly voice. The lady was tall and slender, dressed in a tight black dress and stiletto heels that could do some damage if you pissed her off. If they'd been wood, they would've made good stakes. Her name-tag read Rebecca.

Rebecca ducked out the back and returned with two black clothing bags draped over her arm. She laid them on the counter and Abby unzipped the one on top. She squealed, and I cringed.

"I'll hang it in the change room and you can show your boyfriend," Rebecca said.

Abby glanced over her shoulder and I raised my eyebrows. The shop assistant could be forgiven for thinking we were a couple, but we weren't. We hadn't quite made it there yet.

"Um … I don't … he's—"

"It's okay, Abs. You can surprise me tomorrow night," I said.

Her lips twitched into a small smile before turning back to the assistant. "I'll try it on to check the fit, but can I see the other one first?"

"This isn't a surprise also?" Rebecca asked.

"It's for his sister. I want his approval," Abby said.

Who was she kidding? We'd be walking out of the shop with the dress regardless of whether I liked it or not.

"I'll put it on the mannequin for you." Rebecca picked up the gown bag and hung it on a hook outside the line of change rooms. She wheeled a mannequin torso out of the end change room and stood in front of it. Abby bounded over to me and blocked my view.

"Wait until it's on the model," she said, and every time I tried to look around her she moved so I couldn't see. "I want your honest opinion, okay?"

"Sure. But it's a dress. Aren't they all the same?"

"You did not say that, Archer Tate."

"Ready," Rebecca said.

Abby grabbed my hands and pulled me up, and we faced the mannequin together. She squealed and clapped her hands like an excited eight-year-old.

I had to hide my own excitement.

"It's … black," I said.

"That's all you've got for me?" Abby planted her hands

on her hips.

I shrugged.

What I really wanted to tell her was she knew Grace better than I'd thought. My sister had always been a romantic. She loved Shakespeare and that kind of stuff. I personally didn't understand it, but the black lace dress in front of me was something Grace would adore, even if she didn't want to go to the formal. I had a feeling she'd go just to wear that dress.

"It's really nice, Abs. Very Grace. Can we go now?"

"Right after I have my last fitting." She flounced into one of the change rooms with the other black bag in her hand. Rebecca re-bagged Grace's dress then went to help Abby. I got comfortable on the leather seat and listened to Abby's excited exclamations. I couldn't help smiling.

She took longer than I'd expected to try on a dress, so I pulled my phone from my pocket and swiped the screen. Ever since Seth had told me about Grace, I'd had a strong urge to do something about it, but what? I wanted to believe there was someone other than Michael who knew something.

Hope's name flashed past as I scrolled through my contacts. I thumbed back and stared at her number. She was good. She was what Grace used to be. Angels were supposed to be trustworthy. Maybe I could call and see how things in the city were going, and drop an innocent question or two while we talked. I pressed her number and put the phone to my ear, staring at the floor while I listened to the ring tone.

"Who you calling?" Abby said.

I quickly pressed "end" on the screen and pocketed

my phone. "No one. You ready to go?"

Abby smiled but didn't press the issue. I wasn't sure how I felt. She'd either stopped me from doing something stupid or finding answers. When my phone rang, I pulled it out and rejected Hope's return call, telling Abby it was Grace and that she was probably wondering how much longer we'd be. Abby seemed happy with my explanation, but I think she was too excited about the dresses to be worried about anything else.

In the car on the way home, Abby couldn't get the grin off her face, and it made me happy to see her so smiley. Happiness was something that didn't follow my friends and me around much, and Abby deserved it.

She'd changed, and I was the first to admit that the changes were for the better. She'd been Hopetown Valley High's princess, but lately she'd come down to earth. Especially after finding out her ex-boyfriend was a vampire.

None of us talked about Josh, and sometimes I wished I could read minds like Grace so I could find out if Abby was coping as well as she appeared to be or if it was all a front. I liked her, but we both had scars that hadn't healed, and making anything more of our relationship than what it was at that point could be bad for both of us. Abby missed Josh, even after he'd dumped her for Grace and then all the other crap had happened. I missed Charlotte, too, even though she'd made me angry as hell. Still, I didn't want what had been growing between Abby and me to turn into some rebound thing that we'd both regret.

Abby turned to me as we passed into Hopetown Valley. "Did it bother you what that sales girl said?"

I tightened my grip on the steering wheel. "What? No."

I shook my head. "It did look like we were a couple, so ..."

Abby looked at her hands, a blush creeping up her neck, then she stared out the window at the passing shops of the main street. We fell into an uncomfortable silence. I didn't have uncomfortable silences with Abby. I was usually too busy joking around with her.

"We should have a bet," I said to lighten her mood.

Abby looked at me from the corner of her eye and raised her eyebrows. "For ...?"

"Which one of us Grace is going to kill first." I grinned. "My money would initially be on you. But then I thought, she'd expect you to do something like this, so I'm going with me."

Abby laughed and tapped her temple. "Archer, you said she already knows about the dress."

"You're too smart for me."

"I'm not going to respond to that."

I rounded the bend past the school and headed for home. "She still won't want to go."

"I wouldn't be too sure," Abby said. "It's a killer dress."

The Defender bumped down our long driveway and I guided it into the carport at the back of the clearing. Abby jumped out and I helped her get the dress bags from the boot. The afternoon sun beat down as we crossed the clearing to the shed, and I braced myself for the onslaught of rejection and dress-hate-based comments Grace was sure to let fly.

Abby stopped in the doorway and I bumped into her. I had to grab her shoulders so she didn't topple forward. Grace stood with her back to us in front of the church pew that lined the shed wall. She had her top off, and angry lines marked her skin. They looked fresh. Grace hastily pulled her singlet over her head.

Our gazes met in the mirror that was propped up on the pew; her eyes were wide. She glanced over her shoulder, her cheeks wet with recent tears.

Grace? I probed her thoughts to see if she was okay, but she threw her wall up and blocked me out. I did the same. If I let slip I knew what Seth had been keeping from her, and if she knew he knew about the wound on her stomach, all hell would break loose. I hated being in the middle of things. Knowledge wasn't power. It was a curse.

"Are you okay?" Abby asked. "Your back ... are you hurt?"

Grace wiped her face with her hand, looking away from me. "I'm all good."

She was far from good. The wound on her stomach had been one thing, but the lines on her back? What else had she been hiding?

10

SETH

I walked around the forest for a while, listening to the sounds I'd become so familiar with. Eventually I arrived back at the shed, and I wanted so badly to go inside, to fix everything, but Grace had asked for space. If she wanted room to breathe, then I'd give it to her.

With one last look at the shed, I surrounded myself with my mist and headed for home, or what used to be home. My real place was with Grace, but I had to settle for my unit on the outskirts of Hopetown Valley.

I landed in the kitchen. After a few months away, the place was covered in dust. I'd never been one for possessions though, so all I'd need to do was wipe the table and change the sheets. If I could be bothered.

I grabbed the fridge door handle and waited, listening to the quiet of the apartment. Either Michael was getting sloppy, or he wanted me to know he was there. I ignored him. He hadn't done anything to warrant me treating him any other way. All he'd done was everything he could to make my existence suck.

"That's not entirely true." Michael stepped into the kitchen from the hallway.

The fridge door squealed in protest as I opened it. I peeled the six-pack plastic off the one beer left on the top shelf, and ignored whatever it was growing in the crisper.

"Took you long enough to come out," I said, opening the bottle and taking a swig.

"What do you think you're playing at?"

"I don't know what you mean, Michael."

"You had the perfect opportunity last night to get her fighting again, yet you didn't even suggest it."

"That's not going to happen," I said. "I did what you wanted. I told her Heaven wants her back, and like I knew she would, she said she didn't want to go."

"You didn't tell her everything."

"And I won't," I said.

"Tell her."

"No."

We stared at each other across the kitchen with its dingy black-and-white lino floor, like a giant chess board. It seemed fitting, since Michael and I had always danced around each other like we were playing a game of strategy.

A game I could never win.

He wanted me to ask Grace to do something she didn't want to do.

"You'll end up—"

"I know where I'll end up, Michael. You keep reminding

me. But *not* telling her is the better of two very shitty options."

"If you told her what's at stake, she'd go back in a heartbeat," Michael said.

I didn't doubt the truth in that, but I didn't want to be the reason for Grace doing something she didn't want to do. I didn't want to put any of this on her. She shouldn't have to suffer because of something I had done, or feel obligated to be with me because she knew what my fate would be if she wasn't.

"If I don't tell her, I go to the In-Between and she dies eventually because of what the Council have done." I pushed off the bench and stepped forward. "And if I tell her what's really going on, she'll insist on returning to save me. Either way, I lose her. So tell me, Michael, what would you do if you were about to lose the one person you lived for?"

Michael studied me, his brow furrowed and his lips pursed. "I would let her make her own decision. She already knows you're not telling her everything."

"What do you care?" I took another swig of beer.

"You don't know for sure what she'll decide," Michael said. "But she has to be the one to make the choice. You can't make it for her. And the only way she can do that is if she knows what's at stake. You can't protect her forever. Time is running out, Seth. I'd suggest you get a move on."

The thought occurred to me that I could call his bluff. Who knew if he was telling me the truth about anything? And why should I believe what he said? He would only tell me what he wanted me to know, or what I needed to know to give him the outcome he was after. He always had some sort of surprise up his sleeve or a hidden meaning behind his words.

"I don't understand why you're making it so hard. You could have told her everything yourself by now."

"Reinstating the fallen is not a simple process," Michael said. "There are aspects I can't get involved with."

I scoffed. "I bet that's killing you."

Sometimes I longed for the days when Michael and I used to be friends, before the war between us started. If only I could trust him again.

I tilted my head back and emptied my beer. The alcohol did nothing to calm me, and I set the empty bottle on the bench. "You gave me five days. I still have time, so I think we're done here."

Michael smiled. "We're far from done." He turned but stopped, rubbing his chin with his hand. "Oh, and to give you a bit of a hurry on, there's one more thing the Council wanted me to tell you. If you don't tell Grace the truth, the one she's supposed to die for will take her place. And it will be on you."

"Then tell me, who *is* she supposed to die for?"

The doorway filled with spinning orbs of light and Michael disappeared.

I closed my eyes and clenched my fists. What was he playing at? Michael kept dropping hints about what had to happen, but I was so angry I couldn't put the pieces of the puzzle together. Grace had to die for someone, but it couldn't be me—that would be too easy. Or maybe she didn't love me like she claimed she did.

Pain crunched through my knuckles as my fist hit

the fridge, denting the front of it. I hit it again and again, until the enamel cracked and my hand was covered in blood. Everything I'd tried to do for Grace had been in vain. How was I supposed to fix this mess when it had already been decided? Michael and the Council had everything figured out, and I didn't even know why they wanted her back. Why was Grace so important to them?

Michael had made another move in whatever game he was playing, and it was time I thought about making my own.

11

GRACE

Archer's face morphed from shock to confusion to anger in about five seconds. He pressed his lips together and narrowed his eyes as he walked into the shed.

"Tell me what's going on," he said.

I didn't understand what was going on, so how was I supposed to explain anything to him? I looked at my arms, and tears splashed onto my skin. My eyes blurred as I stared at the red scratches on the backs of my hands. I blinked and they faded, like they were coming in and out of focus. It was as if every cut and bruise I'd ever had was coming back, all at once.

"I don't know what's happening," I said.

Archer came and stood in front of me, his face fixed with a frown, and I leaned against the sink, avoiding his stare. "You're hurt."

I glanced up, and his eyes softened when a tear spilled onto my cheek. "I don't know what's wrong with me. What's happening, Arch?"

Abby went to the couch and laid two black bags over the arm. I squeezed my eyes closed for a moment because of what was inside them, and I didn't want to deal with it right then. I had worse things to worry about than the school formal.

"Gracie, we need to find out why this is happening."

"Does it have anything to do with being a fallen angel?" Abby asked.

"As far as I know the fallen can heal themselves, but not others," I said.

"Where's Seth?" Archer asked. "You two are usually joined at the hip."

I sighed and sat in one of the chairs at the kitchen table. "We had a fight. I told him I wanted space, and he went home."

"Does he know about this?" Abby sat in the chair across from me.

"I haven't told Seth anything," I said. "He's hiding something from me."

"I don't know." Archer stuffed his hands into his pockets. "Maybe he *could* help. He's been fallen way longer than you. Maybe he's seen this sort of thing happen before. You know … With the weird, scurvy-type-wound thing."

I wrinkled my nose. "Maybe …" My forehead creased as I stared at Archer, trying to figure out what he was thinking. "Get that wall down and tell me what you know."

He shook his head. "Some secrets aren't mine to tell."

"Not helping." I leaned forward and put my arms on

the table.

Archer took a deep breath. "You should call him and apologise, or make up, or whatever. Seth needs to be here."

I never thought I'd hear Archer say those words. Seth was one of his least-favourite people. Archer glanced at Abby, and she bit her bottom lip. I looked between the two of them, her thoughts shouting at me so loudly it was hard to ignore them. All she wanted was Seth and I to be a happy couple so we could go to the formal.

"Call him," Archer said. "We need to get everything on the table and figure this out."

"You call him." I folded my arms and sat back in my chair.

Archer scowled but pulled his phone from his pocket. I was mad at Seth and I didn't want to see him, but Archer was right when he said Seth needed to be there. Only I didn't want to be the one to ask him to come back. I was stubborn like that.

"Yeah," Archer said into the phone. "What we were talking about before. Looks like something else is going on."

I jumped to my feet. "What were you talking about before?"

Archer pocketed his phone and sat across from me. "Sit down. He's on his way."

I flopped back into the chair. He glared at me, and I resisted the urge to poke my tongue out at him. The door to the shed opened slowly and Seth came through—one of the benefits of being able to get anywhere you wanted to in seconds. I stared at him, and when I probed his mind I found it locked up tight. As always.

"Still not letting me in," I said.

The door clicked as he closed it. "You're the one who asked me to leave."

I dropped my gaze and looked at a spot on the table. "I'm angry at you, remember?"

Seth glanced at Abby and Archer. "Can I talk to Grace … alone?"

Archer took a deep breath and ran a hand through his hair. "I'm staying."

"Don't make me pick you up and throw you out," Seth said.

"Of my own house?" Archer got up and moved towards Seth. "I'd like to see you try."

Arch, it's okay, I thought. *I want to talk to him alone, too.*

"I want to know everything when I get back," he said. "Come on, Abs, I'll take you back to school." Then he took Abby's hand and led her to the door.

I raised my eyebrows. Since when had they become so friendly?

"Guess we'll try your dress on later," Abby said.

"Sure." I smiled, cringing on the inside. I didn't want to do the whole dress thing. I'd be more comfortable going to the formal in jeans and a singlet top, and wearing my combat boots. What was I saying? I'd be even more comfortable not going to the formal at all, but I was starting to feel the slight pangs of guilt because Abby had put in so much effort, and I didn't have the heart to tell her to back off anymore.

Seth made sure the door was closed, then came and sat across from me at the table.

"How bad is it?" he asked.

"Why do you assume it's bad?"

"I'm here, aren't I?"

Yep, he was. And the reason why was because things were bad. He knew me so well.

"I'm ... hurt." I didn't know how else to explain it.

Seth studied my hands which I had flat on the table. He frowned when a mark appeared across my pale skin. It turned red and angry. He ran his thumb over it and his touch made my skin tingle, distracting me from the dull ache I had begun to feel all over. Then the mark disappeared.

"Are they ... anywhere else?" He raised his head and locked his stare on mine. "Can I see?"

"You want me to take my clothes off?"

"Ideally the circumstances would be better, but yes." He let go of my hand. "I want you to take your clothes off."

"I'm still mad at you."

"I know," he said.

The chair scraped on the concrete floor as I pushed it away from the table. I turned around with my back to Seth and grabbed the hem of my singlet top, pulling it over my head. The motion stretched the skin around my middle, and I winced.

No sound came from behind me, and I shivered when Seth's fingertips touched my shoulders.

"How many are there?" I asked.

"A lot, but they're coming and going. Fading ... Why didn't you say something?"

I shook my head and wrapped my arms around my middle. "I was scared. I *am* scared. What's happening to me?"

Seth moved his hands down my back, touching the

scars left behind by scrapes, cuts, and wounds from years of fighting, put there by fingernails, tree branches, and rocks. I'd never noticed how bashed up I'd get after a hunting session. I'd always healed instantly, and now those injuries were coming back and disappearing again as if they'd never been there. My battle scars were coming back to haunt me.

Seth gently grabbed my shoulders and turned me around. My stomach didn't have as many scars as my back, but my arms were a different story. I hugged my top to my chest, hiding my bra and the patch on my side—the reminder of the last injury I'd gotten before I stopped hunting. He pushed the fabric of my top aside and ran his thumb over the white material. I tensed.

"Can I get dressed now?" I moved away.

Seth dropped his hand to his side. I pulled my singlet over my head then grabbed a cardigan from the church pew and slipped it on to cover my arms.

"We need to talk about this, Grace." Seth went to the couch and sat on the edge, resting his elbows on his knees. He stared at the floor and took a deep breath. "Things have changed. It's why this is happening to you. The Council are interfering."

"What do they have to do with marks appearing all over my body?" I moved to stand in front of Seth and folded my arms.

Seth raised his head and stared into my eyes. "They have everything to do with this, Grace ... I told you. Heaven wants you back. And it looks like they're playing dirty to get you there."

"And I told you, I don't want to go."

Seth rubbed his face, sighing. "They know you're stubborn, so they're testing you." Seth looked at the floor again. "You're not indestructible anymore. If you don't go back, you'll die ... for good."

"I can't die."

Silence filled the room like a dead weight, pressing down on us and squashing us into the floor. I'd been speculating when I'd told Archer if I could get hurt I could die. It wasn't supposed to be true. I'd been thinking out loud and trying to explain to him why I'd chosen to stop hunting. I didn't for one second believe that it could become my reality. Or did I? Did I somehow know it, but not know it?

"Like I said ... things have changed." Seth studied his hands.

I sat next to him on the couch, unable to stand on my wobbly legs. "You're lying."

"I can see why you'd think that, but I'm not."

I wrapped my arms tightly around my middle. He was serious. "This is what you've been keeping from me?" I wanted to deny it, but I would know when he was lying to me. Wouldn't I?

I could die.

The Council wanted me back, and to get me there they had changed the rules. Now I had another reason to hate them. If they thought making me mortal would make me want to go back, they had another thing coming. They'd chosen the wrong angel to test.

"Well, it's a sucky test. Bring it on. I'll just need to be more careful now I know."

"I don't want you to die," Seth whispered.

There was so much anguish and heartache hidden in those six words, and my anger softened. I knelt on the floor in front of Seth and pushed his knees apart so I could slot myself between them. His eyes remained downcast, and when I placed my palms on his cheeks to get him to look at me, his eyes glistened with tears.

"I don't want to go back," I said. "My place is here with you. I'm your breath, remember?"

Seth's lips curled up on one side and he pressed his forehead to mine. "All I've ever wanted to do was protect you."

I should have stayed mad at him. There was more than what he'd told me, there always was, but I was tired of fighting with him. We'd been doing it for far too long. The tender side of Seth was the side I loved the most, and I loved him more for wanting to protect me.

I brushed my lips over his in an apology I didn't have the words for. He pulled me closer, and for a few minutes I lost myself in him, pushing everything else to the back of my mind to deal with later. In that moment I didn't want to be angry, or scared, or injured, or mortal.

All I wanted was Seth.

12

SETH
Wednesday night

Archer picked his way through the forest, stepping lightly on the undergrowth to make minimal noise. We were in full stealth mode, which was more than I could say for the vamps we were chasing. They were either stupid, or from the city so they'd be used to noise and not having to cover their tracks. I was hoping for the former. Stupid seemed like a good enough excuse.

Archer held his arm out to stop me, and we crouched behind a mass of bracken fern. Two vamps were ahead of us, one of them crouched on the ground, feeding from a girl lying in the dirt. For a moment she looked like Grace, with her dark hair spread on the ground around her head like an inky halo.

I blinked a few times and frowned, wondering if Archer saw any resemblance between the girl and his sister.

I hate it when we find them like this, Archer thought, curling his fingers around the stake in his hand.

He knew I could hear him, but he couldn't hear me if I thought back. I nodded my agreeance. It was better when we could streak through the forest and off the vamps quickly, turning them to ash. When we had to save people at the same time, it made everything harder.

I wished Grace were with us; she was so much better at the compassion thing. She would have been in there already, carving them up and getting the victim to safety. I thought things through too much. Or maybe I was distracted, worrying about her, and my head wasn't in the game.

"Better get her out of there." I misted before Archer could reply.

I landed behind the vampire who wasn't feeding and shoved a stake through his heart. He didn't know what had hit him, and his dust billowed over his feeding friend.

The feeder let go of her prey and stood, glaring at me. She wiped the blood from her lips with the back of her hand and snarled. Archer raced past me with his stake drawn, but she darted to the left and he missed his mark, skidding in the dirt. I misted again and landed in her way, shoving her back towards Archer before going to check out the girl on the ground. Archer could handle one vamp on his own. He didn't need me watching over him every second.

I put my fingers to the girl's neck, checking for a pulse. It was weak, but at least she was alive. She blinked slowly as I ripped a piece of fabric from the bottom of my black T-shirt and pressed it to her neck. Now I was closer to her, she looked nothing like Grace.

Archer grunted, and I glanced up to see him getting punched in the face. I stifled a laugh.

"Not funny!" He ducked another punch.

"This one's feisty," I said. "Need to get this girl to the hospital. You good?"

Archer planted his feet and squared his shoulders, waiting for the girl vamp to run at him again before lifting his arm and ramming his stake into her chest. She exploded into ash all over him, and he brushed it off with a grimace.

"Am now," he said. "The girls always fight harder."

"Back in a sec." I misted and left the girl sitting in emergency at the Hopetown Valley hospital. She'd be fine as long as they got some blood into her soon.

When I got back to Archer a few minutes later, Grace was with him.

For a moment, all I could do was stare at her.

She had said she didn't want to hunt, and I hadn't pushed her to do so. We still had time before my deadline, and I wanted her safe as long as possible. I hoped she would come around and end up agreeing to go to the formal with me. All I wanted was for her to have one normal day, without all the crap that came with her life.

"I thought you were staying home," I finally said.

She shrugged. "What's the point? I have to face everything some time. Hiding won't change anything."

"Fighting won't either," I said.

"Fighting always changes everything."

"No, dying will change everything."

"Can we please not argue for once?" Grace said.

Archer scoffed. "As if."

She frowned. "Come on, we've got vamps to kill."

I raised my eyebrows at Archer, and he shrugged. She was coming with us. If we'd both learnt anything over the years, it was that we couldn't argue with Grace once she'd made up her mind. If she didn't want to fight, she wouldn't. If she did, well, then she would. End of story.

Grace stepped lightly through the forest ahead of me with Archer by her side. He'd hardly said two words to me since she'd shown up. He was mad about what was happening to Grace, and he thought it was my fault, which it was in a way, so he blamed me, which he had every right to do. I blamed me, too. If I'd never made my deal with Michael, we'd never have been in this mess in the first place, but neither of them knew that, and I wanted to keep that bit of information to myself for the time being.

As we walked through the forest, my senses were on high alert and I flinched at every sound, ready to defend Grace if I needed to. I couldn't have talked her out of hunting if I'd tried. It seemed now she knew she could die, she was more determined to put herself in danger.

I didn't get it.

She didn't want to go back to Heaven—she'd told me that much. She'd stopped hunting when she'd first figured out she wasn't healing properly, but now … it was like she had a death wish but for all the wrong reasons.

"Why are you doing this?" I asked, catching up to Grace so I could walk on the other side of her. "Archer and I can hunt without you for a while longer."

Grace glanced at me from the corner of her eye. "I'm

a hunter. That hasn't changed."

"Everything has changed," Archer said. He threw me a scowl.

"You said there were more vamps coming here. And I'm in the mood for some dust on my boots. Now can we try and concentrate?" Grace said. "I don't want to think about anything else."

The forest stirred with the unmistakable sound of vampire movement, and Archer jogged away into the undergrowth, the mat of leaves on the ground muffling his steps.

Grace stopped and tilted her head, listening. I took a moment to really look at her. Every time I did, it was like I was seeing her for the first time, even though she'd changed so much over the years. I had the overwhelming urge to wrap her up in my wings and fly her away from everything. If only doing that would help.

"How many do you think?" I asked.

"It's hard to tell."

"Don't do anything stupid. If you can't handle it, let me know."

Grace scoffed and put her hands on her hips. "I'm yet to meet a vampire I can't handle."

"You know what I mean." I put my hand in the small of her back and we kept going.

Archer's path led us to a clearing and into the middle of a dusting battle. I counted three piles of ash already, and he wasn't done. Two more vamps circled him, baring their fangs.

"Need a little help?" I asked.

"Nope, I got this." Archer kicked one of the vamps as it

came at him. The other one circled, looking for a way in.

"Hey, pretty boy," Grace said.

The vamp lost interest in Archer and headed towards us. Grace took a stake out of her belt and squared her stance, adjusting her fight-ready pose. I stepped in front of her and got my own stake ready.

Seth! Grace thought.

The vamp took a swing at me and I dodged to the left, bringing my knee up into his stomach. He doubled over, and I grabbed him by the scruff of his shirt and threw him into a tree. He got up quicker than I'd expected. Grace misted and landed in front of him, planting a punch in the middle of his face. The vamp's head snapped backwards and cracked the tree trunk, which made him angrier.

He lunged at Grace with his hands out, ready to throttle her. She brought her arms up and deflected his attack, but it wasn't enough to stop him barrelling into her. They fell. I misted and came back under Grace before she hit the forest floor. A rock dug into my shoulder and I clenched my teeth.

I forced the three of us into a roll to gain the upper hand. The vamp gnashed his teeth at Grace's neck, and I was beginning to think catching her had been a bad idea. I rolled us again, throwing the vamp off, then grabbed Grace by the upper arms and misted, landing far enough away so we could both gain our feet.

"What are you doing?" Grace asked. "I could've taken him."

I clenched my fists but didn't retaliate. We were not going to discuss my actions in the middle of a fight. I turned towards the vamp, ready to take out all my anger on him. He sized me up then tried to get around me, heading towards Grace. I shoved him back so we could get closer to Archer. When I was a few metres away, Archer finally managed to get his stake into the vamp he'd been fighting, and a cloud of dust billowed into the air before falling to the forest floor.

The vamp I had my eye on took a step back. It seemed he wasn't as eager to fight, being the only one left.

"Come on!" I really wanted to punch something.

Archer came to my side. *Mist behind him,* he thought. He knew I'd hear him, even though I wasn't able to talk silently back.

Archer moved forward, his stake gripped so tightly his knuckles were white. I waited until the vamp moved backwards again, then I misted.

"Boo," I said, and the vamp whipped his head around to look behind him.

Archer lunged forward, planting his stake in the vamp's chest at the same time as I drove mine into his back. When the cloud of ash had fallen, I stared into Archer's smiling face.

"Not bad," he said. "Seems we can work together on some things."

I snorted then looked around for Grace, but she was nowhere to be seen.

"Grace?" I called into the forest.

An owl hooted in reply.

"Where is she?" I spun in a circle, searching the trees for any sign of her.

Nothing.

"Did you see where she went?" Archer asked.

"Would I be looking for her if I did?"

"Maybe she went home." Archer searched the trees as well, sounding unconvinced. He furrowed his brow and called out to her with his mind.

"She answering?" I asked.

He shook his head. "No, but she's not close. I vote we look for her at home first. If she's not there, then we can panic." He stared at me with his hand out.

I raised my eyebrows. "What?"

"Take us back to the shed."

"You want to hold hands with me?" I goaded him.

Archer shook his head. "And here I was thinking you'd become more mature."

"Oh! So I'm the immature one."

"Would you shut up and take us home?" Archer extended his hand further. "I don't want to walk."

I chuckled and shook my head, then slapped my palm into his and misted us to the clearing.

"Don't make me hold your hand again." I walked towards the shed door.

"Was it as good for you as it was for me?" Archer wriggled his eyebrows.

I opened the door and Grace stood at the sink, leaning on the bench with her shoulders hunched. They quivered, and her body heaved with a sob.

Archer ran to her and put a hand on her back. She shook him off and walked to the middle of the shed, standing behind the couch. Tears ran tracks through the dirt on her face, and she hugged herself as if she were cold. The look she gave me would give the fires of Hell a run for their money.

"Grace …" I took a few steps until I got to the coffee table. "Don't cry."

"We'll figure it out," Archer said.

She squeezed her eyes closed then opened them and stared at her brother. "What's there to figure out, Arch? I'm useless. I can't fight anymore because for some reason, I'm mortal and I can die." She swatted at her cheeks, smearing the dirt on her face. "What good am I? How can I do my job? How can I protect you?" She turned her gaze on me. "How can you do your job knowing you have to look out for me?"

"Just for the record, hunting isn't actually my job, and it shouldn't be yours anymore either," I said. "You're a fallen angel, Grace. You don't have to answer to them anymore."

"Yes, I do, don't I? They're trying their hardest to get me to go back, and I know you're not telling me everything. If I don't go, there will be consequences."

Archer went to Grace and wrapped his arms around her. She buried her face into his chest and I ached to be the one comforting her, but I wasn't telling her everything. And I kept trying to convince myself it was because I refused to be the reason she made a decision she didn't want to make.

"Hey, you're forgetting that I can die, too. It's always been a possibility but it's never stopped me from fighting," Archer said. "Since when do you give up this easily?"

Grace pulled away and looked up into Archer's face. "You never had to worry because I was always there to heal you when you got hurt. Now I can't even heal myself." She walked around to the front of the couch and sat down, putting her face in her hands.

My skin itched to touch her and pull her into my arms. To make it go away and keep her safe.

I went and sat beside her, not sure how she'd react if I tried to hug her. She leaned into me and put her head on my shoulder.

"We'll get through this," I said, unable to really believe my own words.

"Will we?" She stared at me, her eyes glistening.

"Sure we will." Archer flopped into the big armchair and closed his eyes. He didn't sound very convincing.

I pressed my lips to Grace's hair, not wanting to say yes, because I couldn't promise we would. How were we supposed to come out the other side of this when all our options ended with the same result? No matter what happened, we wouldn't be together.

I slipped my hand into hers and gave it a gentle squeeze. "We have to hope that we will," I said. "Because what do we have if we don't have hope?"

GRACE
Thursday morning

I sat curled into the corner of the lounge, my copy of Shakespeare's Complete Works open beside me, waiting for Abby to burst through the door like a tornado. Archer had left a half hour ago to pick her up from the dorm, and I wondered what was taking him so long. The anticipation of dealing with Abby, dresses, and makeup was killing me.

Seth handed me a hot cup of tea and sat beside me on the couch.

"You don't have to go."

I looked at him over the top of my mug. "You're kidding, right? You bought me a dress. And Abby will be crushed if I don't."

"Since when do you care what Abby thinks?" Seth asked.

"Since she got dragged into all of this. I worry about her. I keep having to remind myself I'm not the only one with problems. She lost Josh and Ryan as well."

"Josh isn't dead."

"Technically, he is," I said.

Or he may as well have been. We hadn't parted on bad terms, but they weren't all that great either. The bottom line was I missed him, and even though I didn't love him like I thought I had, I cared about him.

Seth took a deep breath, and I held mine. I didn't want a repeat conversation or to deal with the jealousy.

"You have a suit, don't you?" I asked, getting back to the subject of the formal.

Seth smiled his crooked smile I loved so much. "Yep."

"That's all I get?"

"You'll have to wait and see."

"But you've seen my dress!"

"No ... I've seen an image of your dress in Abby's head. Not the same thing."

The door burst open and Abby charged in with a backpack flung over her shoulder, a silver case in one hand, and a shopping bag in the other. I cringed at the thought of all the things she had hidden in there, waiting to torment me.

Archer followed silently and made a bee-line for the fridge. Something was going on between him and Abby, but I decided not to look in on them. I wanted them to tell me in their own time, if there was anything worth telling me about.

"Please say you haven't shown him your dress," Abby said, pointing at Seth.

I glanced at him, then back at Abby, teasing her. Her eyes widened, and I laughed. "Relax, *I* haven't even looked at it. Seth knows nothing. But if you're thinking about it right now, you've probably given it away."

"No!" Abby dumped the case and shopping bag on the kitchen table and spun to face Seth.

He raised his hands in defence. "I promise not to peek in your head for the rest of the day." *Don't tell her I've already seen it,* he thought, smiling at me.

I closed Shakespeare and slid off the lounge, hugging the book to my chest. "Let the torture begin."

"It's not torture, Grace. This is going to be fun." Abby clapped her hands, grabbed the case and adjusted the strap of her backpack on her shoulder. She shoved the shopping bag at me and I almost dropped my book, then she headed for the stairs.

Archer stood in the kitchen leaning against the bench with his ankles crossed. He smirked. "Have fun."

I groaned and followed Abby. "Can I wear the dress and be done with it?"

"No way." Abby opened the door to my bedroom. "Full makeover for you today. When I'm done, every girl in year twelve is going to wish they were you. Or me." She giggled and went in, dumping the case and backpack on my bed.

I stood at the door and glanced down the stairs at the boys. "Don't go too far. I may need rescuing."

They smiled but didn't say anything.

"Get in here." Abby grabbed my arm and pulled me into the room, pushing the door closed.

I threw the shopping bag onto the bed and slid my book onto the low bookcase that ran the length of one wall, making sure I put it back in the right place. Abby tugged at my cardigan, so I peeled it off and tossed it onto my pillow. She sat me on a chair in front of the small mirror on my wall and gently unclipped the chain around my neck, putting in on the side table next to the bed. She ran her fingers through my short locks, gathering them together. The attention was a little unnerving.

Abby scrunched her fingers. "Up-do?"

"No way." I shook my head. "Can we leave it down, please?"

"But it sticks out funny. It's like it has a mind of its own." She patted and pulled at the strands in an attempt to tame them.

"I like my hair," I said.

"Fine, but your face is another story."

"I actually like my face, too."

Abby looked over the top of my head at my reflection, raising her eyebrows. "We're in damage control, Grace. We need to cover up those marks."

"Oh …" I stared at my face in the mirror. My skin was doing it again—old wounds resurfacing then disappearing. I sighed.

"Don't worry. With the makeup on, if they flare up no one will notice." Abby smiled.

"My dress is strapless. You can't paint all of me."

Abby frowned. "Probably not, but I have some fantastic cover-up, and I'm a wiz with a make-up brush … We'll figure something out."

She unzipped her backpack and laid a towel on the bed. For an hour I sat like a good little girl, gripping the sides of the chair while Abby painted my face with creams and other stuff. There were so many tubes and pots of makeup strewn over the bed, and I had no idea what any of them were for.

"Almost done." Abby dusted my nose and cheeks with a powder-laden brush.

She stepped aside and I blinked at my reflection. I looked like me, but not as pale. Angels had perfectly smooth skin already, so all she'd done was give me more colour.

"It's um ... great," I said.

"Never underestimate the power of makeup." Abby waved the brush. "Now, on to your eyes and lips."

"We're not finished?"

"Not even close."

I groaned, but closed my eyes when Abby asked me to, and for another hour she worked with more makeup items, pots of eye colour, pencils, and tubes of lipstick. I got to the point where if she'd asked me to pout one more time, I'd throw something at her.

"Can I look yet?" Despite not really wanting to wear makeup, I was curious about what she'd done to me.

Abby stepped away from the mirror. "Ta-da!" She spread her arms wide and tossed the makeup brush she'd been holding onto the bed. "What do you think?"

Before I could answer, a knock sounded at the door. "Are you decent?" Archer asked.

"Come in," Abby said. "But if Seth's there, tell him to get lost."

Archer came in with a plate of sandwiches. "Lunch is ... ready ..."

"Close your mouth, Arch," Abby said.

Archer stared at me in the mirror. "What did you do to my sister, Abs?"

Arch? Abs? Since when did they call each other by their

shortened names? I glanced at Archer, then at Abby. A grin spread across her face, and her eyes sparkled.

"Doesn't she look great?"

"She looks ... different," Archer said. "I mean good, different. But, you know Grace is beautiful without any makeup."

Abby scowled. I hid a smirk. She really had done a great job. My lips glistened with a deep pink gloss, and the dusty grey and dark purple she'd smudged around my eyes made them smoulder.

"I like it." I jumped up and took the plate from Archer.

"I better not be peeling Seth off you tonight."

I laughed. "I probably wouldn't let you."

Abby ushered Archer out of the room and we sat on the bed to eat lunch. After ordering me to eat carefully so I didn't smudge my lipstick, she chattered away about all sorts of stuff to do with the formal—who was going, the decorations, how much planning had been involved—and I listened, but at the same time I didn't. I was dreading going in the first place. All I could think about was putting on my dress. And I may have been exceptionally coordinated, but I wasn't sure if my talents included dancing.

"Grace." Abby snapped her fingers in front of my face. "What's wrong?"

"Sorry ... nothing." I shook my head and bit into my sandwich.

"Well, I need to make myself over now." She dusted her hands over the plate and jumped up.

"Um. Do you want ... help?"

Abby laughed. "I'm fine. You can sit and watch, and

think. Or whatever." She riffled through all the things on the bed and got started on her own makeup. "Or you can get the dresses out."

I eyed the black bags hanging from the hook on the back of the door. I'd been avoiding them, but I guessed it was time to think about undoing the zipper. I'd already seen what my dress looked like from the image in Abby's mind, but when I slid the zipper down, I wasn't prepared for how beautiful it was.

My fingertips slid over the soft folds of lace, and I stood for a minute, staring at the intricate details of the fabric. I grasped the hanger at the top and slid the dress out of the bag, holding it up in front of me. When I turned to Abby, she had that grin plastered on her face again.

"Do you like it?" She raised her eyebrows.

I leaned forward, gazing down at the dress. "It's really beautiful. Thank you."

Abby had done a great job of choosing something she thought I'd like, and she hadn't been far off the mark. The bodice was a corset with lacing up the front. It was strapless, and made from red satin, covered in black lace. A cute little frill decorated the top of the corset. The skirt was tiered layers of the same black lace, shorter at the front where it fell above the knee, but ankle-length at the back. Black lace gloves were pinned to the coat hanger.

"To cover my arms?" I held them up, and Abby glanced over her shoulder.

"Hopefully they'll be enough?" She grabbed the shopping bag I'd tossed on the bed earlier and pulled out a box, handing it to me. "Shoes."

I lay the dress on the bed and opened the box. "Abby,

they're really nice, but no way am I wearing these." I grabbed one red stiletto by the strap and held it up. "I'll break an ankle."

"But they go with the dress," Abby said.

"I think I'll wear my boots." I put the shoe back in the box and closed the lid.

"You can't wear boots with that dress!"

"I can, and I will."

Abby opened and closed her mouth a few times. "Oh, fine."

"You've gotten away with more than I'd let anyone else," I said.

I sat on the edge of the bed and waited as she spent another half an hour finishing off her make up. Abby pinned her hair in a messy half-up do, letting her natural waves fall around her face and over her shoulders. When she was done, she picked up my dress and held it out to me. I peeled off my jeans and top, careful not to smudge my makeup, and quickly checked the patch on my wound was still in place before I stepped into the layers of lace.

"Does it hurt?" Abby asked, staring at my side.

I pressed my lips together. "I'll be fine."

Abby offered me a tight-lipped smile then took my shoulders and spun me around. After some adjusting of the laces, she had my dress fitting snugly, but not so tight I couldn't breathe.

She applied the last touches to her own makeup, touched up my lipstick, and then pulled her dress from its bag.

I helped her step into the floor-length satin gown. It was also strapless, and the beautiful dusty pink fabric hugged her curves. The dress featured a ruched section across her stomach, accented by a sparkly flower brooch where the fabric gathered at her hip. A chiffon overlay fell in delicate waves over the bottom half of the dress. Abby asked me to secure a clip in her hair to hide the pins. It was lovely, and matched the brooch on her dress. She slipped little flower earrings into her ears and smiled. She looked stunning.

"You're missing something," Abby said, staring at my chest.

My hand went to my neck. Abby had taken my chain off before she'd started on my makeup. I retrieved it from my bedside table and fastened the small teardrop diamond around my neck.

"Perfect," Abby said.

I hadn't thought to ask Abby who was taking her to the formal, but as she checked everything in the mirror one last time, I caught a glimpse in her mind. I'd known before I checked that it would be Archer. When I thought back, the two of them had grown closer. I'd noticed subtle hints about their feelings for each other whether they'd intended them to be noticed or not.

She turned to me. "Ready?"

I nodded. "You're going to knock Arch off his feet."

14

SETH
Thursday afternoon

Archer stood in the kitchen of the cottage, leaning against the bench with a beer in his hand.

"It's a shame they won't let us drink at the formal," he said.

"We're two of the few who legally can." I took a swig of beer. "And the school can't have alcohol on the premises."

He chuckled and shook his head. "I didn't need you to explain it. I was making an observation."

We drank in silence, watching the clock. It had taken us less than half an hour to put on the suits Abby had organised, and another hour to figure out how to do our ties properly. The rest of the time we'd been attempting to talk to each other while we waited for the girls. It was almost time to go back to the shed.

Something inside my stomach stirred. I couldn't explain

it. I'd never felt it before.

"What's with the face?" Archer asked.

"What face?" I stared at him over the top of my beer.

"You're doing this funny grimacing thing." Archer smiled. "You're nervous."

"I am not." I shifted on my feet and set my beer on the bench. Admitting Archer was right was never going to happen. But I *was* nervous, and for the first time ever I got a taste of butterfly belly.

I itched to see Grace and how beautiful she'd be. I never thought in a million years I'd be getting worked up over a school dance, but the dance wasn't really what I was excited about. It was Grace.

"When will you admit there's something going on with Abby?" I asked in an attempt to take the focus off me.

Archer frowned and crossed his arms, resting his beer in the crook of his elbow. "I ... I'm not sure if ... Why am I talking to you about this?"

"Who else are you going to talk to? Grace?"

"Wow, we are both so messed up." Archer pushed off the bench and tossed his can in the bin. "I don't know if it's too soon after ... Charlotte."

"It's never too soon."

Archer headed into the lounge room and pressed the combination on the keypad to open the arsenal wall. The door slid aside and he stepped through. I followed him into the secret storage area that sat behind the plain wall of the lounge room.

We went straight to the bench where the stake belts hung, and I lifted two down, handing Archer his favourite. We strapped them on in silence, hiding them under our shirts. Archer also fitted his dagger to his ankle and covered it with the leg of his pants.

I glanced at the array of weapons and laughed to myself. Most of them were collecting dust. We made use of the stakes and daggers all the time, and occasionally the cross-bows, but the rest of it had been sitting there for years. Carrying an axe or a spear wasn't practical, and most of the older weapons belonged in a museum.

I checked my pocket for the black pouch I carried everywhere—the one with Grace's tear inside. My fingers brushed the hard stone, and I remembered the moment I'd caught it in my palm.

"Don't be a douche like me and let her go," I said. "You'll spend the rest of your life trying to get her back again."

"I'm not sure I'm good for her." Archer headed back to the lounge room.

"You're as good as anyone. And shouldn't Abby be the one to decide?"

"I guess." Archer shrugged.

"Stop thinking about it too much. You like her. There's nothing wrong with that."

Archer pressed the button on the keypad and the door closed, concealing itself and becoming the wall as if it wasn't there. I finished my beer and we went out to the clearing. The low afternoon light danced through the trees, the shadows tickling the edges of the grass. Inside the shed, Grace and Abby would be waiting.

Archer rested his hand on the door knob. "You ready?"

"Arch, we're walking into the shed. What's there to be ready for?"

He shuffled his feet and took a deep breath. I wanted

to tell him I was as nervous as he was, but being the tough guy and all, I stayed quiet. Archer swung the door wide. The girls stood in the kitchen with their backs to us, laughing about something. Grace turned, glancing over her shoulder, and the world stopped.

It wasn't the makeup or the dress that made her beautiful. It was her. She had a light inside of her that nothing could ever put out, and it was shining right at me.

Archer stood with his mouth slack and his eyes wide. I nudged him forward, and he stumbled over his own feet. Abby giggled and walked towards us.

I veered away from Archer and headed towards Grace. She hadn't moved from the kitchen, where she stood with a radiant smile on her lips.

"Hey you," I said when I reached her, taking her all in.

"Aren't you going to kiss me?" she asked.

My lips curled up and I leaned in.

"No!" Abby shrieked. "Don't smudge her lipstick."

Grace laughed and rested her hands on my chest. I leaned down to gently brush my lips with hers.

"It's a nice colour on you," she said when she pulled away. "Abby wants photos, so if you want more kisses we'll have to wait until later."

I would wait forever.

Then I remembered we didn't have much time left. I forced a smile and kissed Grace's forehead before we turned to face the others. Abby pinned a rose to the lapel of Archer's jacket. She wore a tiny pale pink bouquet of miniature roses on her wrist. I shifted on my feet and looked sideways at Grace. I hadn't gotten her anything.

"I'm not sure what's more fun," she said. "Trying to

figure Arch and Abby out … or watching you squirm."

"I um … didn't get—"

"Don't worry. Arch isn't that smart either. Abby took care of it." Grace went to the couch and picked up a small plastic box. "Apparently I like roses, too."

I took the box from Grace, staring at the flowers inside. "Your dress is really nice. It's very … you." I took the wrist corsage out of the box and slipped it over her hand. The roses matched perfectly with the red on the top half of her dress.

"And you are very handsome." Grace pinned a single red rose to my lapel and smiled.

I'd never seen her wear makeup before. I brushed her skin with my fingertips and she closed her eyes, pressing her cheek into my hand.

"I want to forget about everything tonight," she said. "No vampires. No fighting. Just you and me, and some time together."

"That sounds perfect." I slipped my hand down her neck and onto her bare shoulder.

She leaned in and I pulled her to me, wrapping my arms around her and tracing her wing scars with my thumb. She nuzzled my neck and breathed deeply, pressing her palms into my back. I rested my cheek on the top of her head, closed my eyes and concentrated on the rhythm of her beating heart.

I could have stayed like that for eternity.

"Stop smudging your makeup." Abby stood beside Archer with her hands on her hips. "You have to keep that face until well into the after-party."

Grace pulled away from me and got up. "There's an

after-party?"

"Of course there is," Abby said. "It's our year twelve formal. There's always an after-party. Now, come on." Abby hitched her dress and tottered to the door.

I glanced down at Grace's feet. "No heels?"

"Are you kidding? I want to be able to walk." She grabbed my hand and pulled me off the couch towards the door.

We followed Abby and Archer out to the car, and I helped Grace get in without catching all the layers of lace on her dress on something. Archer helped Abby into the front passenger seat.

"How many beers did you two have?" Grace asked once we were all in the car. She smoothed her dress over her knees.

"One," Archer and I said in unison.

Archer glanced over his shoulder. "I'm fine to drive, Gracie. Stop worrying." He turned the key and the Defender roared to life. Ten minutes later we pulled into the car park at Hopetown Valley High.

Abby squealed and clapped her hands, and I had to stop myself from rolling my eyes.

"This is going to be the best night ever," she said.

Grace glanced at me. "I don't think I'm ready for this."

Abby spun in her seat. "You are getting out of this car right now."

"Come on, Gracie," Archer said. "You can slay a vampire with your eyes closed. This is a school dance. When you walk through that door, no one will know what hit them."

15

GRACE
Thursday night

Archer killed the engine and turned in his seat to look at me.

"You okay?" he asked.

"Just peachy," I said, trying to smile.

He flung his door open, jumped out and went around to the back of the car to open the tailgate.

"Here," he said, flinging a stake belt over the back of the seat. "Put this on."

I stared at him, then at the belt. "Where am I going to put this? I'm not exactly dressed for combat."

Seth laughed and shook his head. "Give her a thigh belt, you idiot."

Archer scowled but dug around in the back of the car, fishing through the gym bag we kept in there all the time, and pulled out a strap with a single stake in it.

I took it when he handed it to me. "I only need one anyway."

I lifted my dress to strap it to my thigh, making sure it was high enough for the shorter layers of lace to cover it.

"Need help with that?" Seth asked.

Archer slammed the back door of the car and it shook on its wheels. Abby giggled and raised her eyebrows. "Is he always this over-protective?"

"You have no idea."

Abby's door opened and Archer helped her out of the car. I pulled my dress over my leg as Seth opened his door. He held out his hand and I scooted across to take it. When I dropped to the ground, Seth was at my side, putting his hand on the small of my back. Together we headed towards the school gates.

The car park was busy with cars and limos coming and going to drop off formal-goers. Girls in dresses of every colour and style stepped out in sparkly high heels. For once I was smiling, but my stomach rolled with nerves and I twisted my fingers together, searching the grounds for any sign of trouble.

For a moment, I wondered what the hell I was doing. Abby had shrouded me so tightly in her whirlwind of excitement, I'd forgotten who I was. Grace Tate didn't do things like this. I couldn't let my guard down, not even for a second.

Seth put his hands over mine and untwisted the knot my fingers had become. I was glad to have him there, but how was I supposed to try and have a good night if all I was doing was looking over my shoulder?

"Stop worrying," Seth whispered in my ear, then kissed

my temple. "We can both look over our shoulders."

I hadn't realised I'd let my guard slip, and out of habit I quickly put the wall back up inside my mind. I wasn't sure why I didn't want to let Seth into my thoughts. After all, he knew what I'd been hiding. Maybe it was because he still wasn't being completely open with me, so I wanted to punish him. Looked like I was being the queen of petty.

"Please don't do that," Seth said. "You don't have to be so guarded around me."

I stared up at him. "I could say the same to you. You let me in, and I might let you in a little more." He frowned. "Yeah, I didn't think so."

"Can we try to have a good night?" Seth ran a hand over his short hair. "We're not even inside yet."

I took a breath and nodded. I didn't want to spoil the evening before it had even begun.

We headed through the big gates and towards the hall at the back of the school. Abby had a Cheshire grin plastered on her face.

"I can't wait for you guys to see the decorations," she said.

I couldn't wait to get the formal over with. I pulled the edges of my long gloves up my arms and hoped I wouldn't break out in marks.

We followed Archer and Abby into the main yard. This would be the last time we had to set foot on Hopetown Valley High grounds. The thought made me sad, and I realised I hadn't contemplated what I wanted to do for the rest of my existence. Going to school and hunting vampires had taken up such a huge chunk of my time; what was I supposed to do now that I couldn't do either of those things?

I took another deep breath and clutched Seth's hand, deciding that I wouldn't think about anything to do with hunting or Heaven until tomorrow. It was about time I had some fun. *Maybe.*

Seth flexed the hand I was holding, then put his other one over mine and loosened my fingers. "Relax. You're tensing up."

I wanted to laugh. I didn't know the meaning of the word "relax".

We rounded the back of the cafeteria. Three waiters in black tuxedos wove in and out of the group in front of the hall, offering trays of finger food. Girls in glittery dresses and killer heels clutched the arms of their dates. Students from the younger grades were all over the place, milling around, sitting on the grass, and leaning against the wall. They'd come over from the dorms, especially the girls, to check everyone out. It was like a tradition with the borders. No one wanted to miss the formal entrance.

Seth and I stopped away from the crowd, and for the first time in my life I felt sick about something that didn't warrant the feeling. It was just a dance. Archer saw us hanging back and grabbed Abby's hand to slow her down. They came back to us, Abby's smile falling away.

"What's wrong?" she asked.

"Nothing, I ..." I let go of Seth and wrung my hands together.

"Grace Tate, these people are your friends. You have nothing to worry about."

I didn't believe her. What if something happen.. ⁴⁰

Archer and Seth wouldn't be out hunting. What if some vampires showed up and ruined the party?

If they do, we'll deal with it, Seth thought. *Relax.*

I tried to smile. *Please don't tell me to relax again.*

He hugged me from behind, folding my jittery hands into his rough palms. Then he nuzzled my neck and kissed my collarbone.

What are you doing? I thought.

Taking your mind off things. He squeezed my shoulders with his upper arms, and I pressed my back into him. *Working?*

Claudia, Abby's best friend, spotted us and came over. The two of them did some jumping up and down, hugging each other and oohhing and aahhing over their dresses. It was warranted. They both looked amazing.

"Wow, Grace. I love your dress," Claudia said.

I smiled my thanks and returned the compliment.

"You kept everyone out?" Abby asked.

"Yep, the hall is perfect. Wait till you see it, guys." Claudia's smile was bigger than Abby's.

I glanced around and my heart fell. "I wish Emma and Ryan were here."

Seth tensed behind me.

Careful, Gracie, Archer thought. *You need to focus a bit more.*

"Emma is here in spirit," Archer said, so everyone could hear. "But she would've hated this."

More than I do, I thought.

"Who's Ryan?" Claudia asked.

"Oh, some guy." Abby flipped her hand and a strained laugh bubbled from her mouth.

Claudia looked at me funny, and her gaze flicked to Seth.

"He's a friend of mine from the city." Seth smiled. "Said he might come and see us."

When I said relax, I didn't mean forget the details, Seth thought.

"Right!" Abby clapped her hands. "We should go and mingle. They'll be calling us inside soon."

The last thing I wanted to do was mingle, but Abby grabbed my hand and Seth freed me from his embrace, so I had no choice. As we reached the rest of the class, Mr Bruner stepped out and gave us a curt nod. He proceeded to round up the students who shouldn't have been there and sent them back to the dorms. Mr Gerard, the headmaster, and a small group of chaperones stood inside the door, scanning the scene, no doubt ready to pounce at the first sign of trouble.

I grabbed Archer's wrist to see what time it was. Almost six pm, which meant the formal was about to officially start. A waiter walked past, and I grabbed a spring roll. I needed something in my stomach to stop the queasy feeling. When another waiter came near us, I took a glass of sparkling—non-alcoholic of course—in the hope that the bubbles would settle me more.

Abby flitted around, talking to as many people as she could, all the while with a smile on her face. I wondered if her cheeks hurt. Archer stood beside me, a Coke in one hand and a funny little smirk on his lips.

"Have you kissed her yet?" I asked.

Archer looked at me sideways. "No, and I'm not going to."

"Yes, you are." I glanced at him.

"We're not talking about this, Gracie."

Seth touched my arm. "I think everyone's going inside."

Abby toddled over and linked her arm through Archer's. I was glad I'd worn my boots and not the three-inch heels she'd wanted me to wear. I'd be toddling, too.

"I want a group photo," Abby said. "The four of us."

I sighed and Seth squeezed my hand.

When we entered the hall there was no getting away from the photographer. He'd set up right where everyone walked in. The theme for the night was glamour, so the photography wall was draped in rich purple curtains flecked with silver. Strands of sparkling silver beads hung from the ceiling. They moved slightly from the breeze coming through the door, and shards of light danced across the walls.

We waited our turn then went through the motions of the photographer telling us to smile, turn slightly to the left, and so on. Abby and Archer moved into the hall, and Seth pulled me close.

"Don't worry about the camera," he said.

"That's perfect." The photographer's camera clicked. "Hold it there."

Seth stared into my eyes, and for a moment I let myself get lost in them. If only every moment could be like that, the two of us with nothing to worry about and no one to protect. He leaned down and gently kissed me.

"Get a room," someone said.

I pulled away and searched the line of people waiting. My gaze locked with Ivan's. Blake was right beside him.

"Ignore them." Seth kissed my cheek and led me into the hall.

Ivan and Blake were fallen angels, but they'd been stripped a long time ago. Still, they gave me the creeps.

Beautiful silver and white cloths adorned the tables. A vase of purple flowers sat in the centre with purple and silver confetti scattered across the crisp surface. The deep colour of the napkins matched the flowers perfectly. Everything looked wonderful, and I understood why Abby was smiling so much.

We found our name cards and took our seats with Archer and Abby. Claudia and her date joined us, along with two other couples from Abby's group of friends. I didn't know them very well. When I'd been with Josh, he'd kind of snubbed his group. The only one I'd grown close to had been Ryan.

Seth squeezed my knee under the table. He leaned over and his breath tickled my ear. "Step one. Make it through dinner."

"And what's step two?" I asked.

He leaned back in his chair and pursed his lips into a mischievous smirk. "Dance with me."

Dare I ask what step three is? I thought.

He chuckled and planted a kiss on my lips. *You could take a wild guess.*

"Would you two stop it? Dinner is being served," Abby said.

"You're jealous." Seth glanced at Archer.

"I'm not going to bite." Archer picked up his fork. "But I may stab you."

The other couples weren't quite sure what to make of our banter. When I listened to their thoughts, they weren't too impressed with Abby coming to the formal with

Archer, but they couldn't see she'd changed.

After being through what she had with us in the past few months, I was glad we'd become closer. No one could ever replace Emma, but Abby knowing about my world made it easier to cope with sometimes.

Our entrée plates were placed in front of us, and everyone got stuck into their meals. At first I wanted to get it over with so I could get out of there, but by the time dessert arrived I was actually having an okay time. Claudia was really trying to include us in the table conversation, and things were loosening up between everyone.

Maybe it wouldn't be such a bad night after all.

16

GRACE

Seth rested his hands on my hips and we swayed to the music. So far, the night had been uneventful, but something bad was bound to happen; it was only a matter of when.

I reached up and circled my arms around Seth's neck and stared into his dark eyes. If anyone could take my mind off things, it was him. He smiled down at me and everything else fell away. It was as if we were the only two people in the room.

See how much better it is when you relax? Seth thought.

I grinned in response and stood on my tiptoes so I could press my mouth to his. He parted his lips and kissed me back, heat radiating between us like an unstoppable fire.

The lights on the dancefloor flickered through the haze of smoke pouring out of the smoke machines. The music sped up. I pulled away and laughed as the throng of bodies lurched into more energetic movement. Seth laughed, too, and we moved in time with the crowd. He grabbed my hand and I spun away from him before he pulled me back to his chest, running his hands down my sides.

Pain shot through my stomach and it took all my strength not to double over and scream.

Seth raised his eyebrows. *Everything okay?*

I took a step away from him, my head spinning and my vision blurring. *I'll be right back,* I thought. *Bathroom.*

Before he could respond, I turned and pushed my way through the crowd covering the dancefloor. The bathroom door swung open as I burst through, gasping, using the wall for support. There were a couple of girls in there, but I didn't look up to see who. I made a direct line for the nearest stall and locked myself in, clutching my stomach and finally giving into the pain. My eyes watered and I squeezed them shut, sitting on the closed toilet seat and waiting for the wave to pass.

Lines appeared on my arms, and when I touched the angry red streaks, they hurt. Old wounds coming and going across my skin, flashing on and off like a light switch. I wanted to look at my side and see if the wound from the tree branch had opened more, but I'd have no hope of lacing my dress again properly. I stood gingerly, waiting for another wave of pain that luckily didn't come. There was no blood seeping through the material, so I assumed it was okay. Maybe it was hurting more because it was a bigger wound than the others.

What was happening to me? Seth said Heaven wanted me back and to get there I had to die, but he'd never elaborated on how. Maybe my past was catching up with me, and it would result in my death. *I didn't want to die on a dirty bathroom floor.*

I needed answers.

There was one person who could give me more answers than Seth would. I'd already been in the bathroom for too long, but I wanted to risk it, so I pressed my hand flat against the cubicle door and took a deep breath. I could explain my long absence to the others later.

The room was quiet, so I let my black mist surround me and headed for the shadows of the school cemetery, landing at the back amongst the big Moreton Bay figs. Hopefully, no one would be stupid enough to venture down there in the dark. Despite the warmth of the late spring evening, I shivered and rubbed my arms with my hands.

"Michael," I said to the trees, hoping he could hear me. My guess was that he could. "Michael," I said again.

A light breeze rustled the leaves above me and a thick branch illuminated with tiny spinning lights. Moments later, Michael sat on the branch and stared down at me.

"Shouldn't you be dancing?" he asked.

I pressed my lips together and propped my hands on my hips. "I want answers."

"What's the question?"

"Don't play dumb with me. I have a very strong feeling you know exactly what I'm talking about."

He folded his arms and swung his legs in the air, smiling that infuriatingly charming smile of his, and all I wanted to do was punch it right off his face.

"I saw you talking to Seth the other day. I want to know what you said to him."

"Maybe you should ask him," Michael said.

I closed my eyes and took a deep breath. "Why are you being such a dick? You used to actually care about me."

"I do care about you, and don't talk like that. You sound like Archer."

We stared at each other, and after a few moments it was clear he wasn't going to speak first. I'd get nothing out of him unless I begged.

That wasn't going to happen.

I turned and headed into the cemetery, hoping I'd get the result I was after. I smiled when I heard Michael's feet land in the leaves beneath the trees.

"Where are you going?" he asked.

"You won't tell me anything, and I should be dancing, remember?"

"Grace … wait." Michael jogged to my side, and I stopped to face him. "I never wanted things to be like this between us, but you make it so hard sometimes."

"I make it hard? You're the one keeping secrets."

"You're pretty good at hiding things yourself." He raised his eyebrows.

I shook my head. "I don't want to go back. Why are you doing this to me?"

Michael ran a hand through his messy hair. It was the kind of hair girls wanted to wrap their fingers around and never let go.

"When you finally find out the truth, believe me … you'll want to go back. But there's one thing I want you to remember." He touched my cheek with his fingertips so gently it was like a feather brushing my skin. "I didn't change the rules. It wasn't me who wanted it to end this way."

"End what way? Michael?"

"Seth hasn't told you the entire story."

"Then why can't you?"

"It's part of his punishment."

I didn't understand. Punishment for what?

"Can you at least tell me what's happening to me?" I held my arms out, but the marks and scars were gone. My skin was perfect and blemish-free. The pain had gone, too.

"Make the most of your time with Seth while you can," Michael said.

I stared at him, so many questions touching my lips but none of them able to form into words. By the time I figured out what to ask, Michael was gone, darkness filtering into the space where his light had been.

I stood in the shadows and thought through everything he'd said. Why wouldn't he give me a straight answer? Maybe he couldn't. Maybe the Council were involved in the whole mess more than I'd originally thought. If they wanted me to return home, they'd do everything in their power to make it happen, even if it meant making my friends my enemies.

Michael used to look out for me, a long time ago. I wondered if he still was, or if he was simply following orders. I'd have to find out the hard way.

When I landed back in the cubicle in the girl's bathroom, Abby was calling my name. She pounded on the door.

"Grace, come on. Are you in there? It's safe to come out."

I turned the lock and pulled the door back. Abby stood with her hand raised, ready to hit the door again.

"Calm down, I'm here." I stepped out into the empty bathroom.

"Where have you been? Seth sent me in here to find you." Abby frowned. "And I know this cubicle was empty a second ago."

"I was talking to Michael." I stared at my arms and the blemishes that were no longer there.

"Well, you've had us worried." Abby grabbed my hand and squeezed it. "Did you find what you were looking for?"

I shook my head. "I'm as confused as ever. He told me to make the most of my time with Seth, as if I didn't have long."

"Long for what?" Abby asked.

"Has Archer not told you? I'm supposed to die."

"Not on my watch you're not." Abby pulled me towards the door. "Let's go have fun. We can worry about everything else tomorrow. I'm not going to let anything ruin this night."

She didn't seem surprised, so I peeked in her thoughts to find that Archer and Seth had filled her in on everything while I was having my pow-wow with Michael. Now, she was determined to *make* me enjoy the formal, and I would let her.

She shoved the bathroom door open and yanked me into the noise of the hall. Seth and Archer were at my side in an instant, and I wished I was anywhere else but standing there while they stared at me like I was a naughty little girl.

What happened? Seth thought.

Gracie, where did you go? Archer bombarded my mind as well.

They both threw thoughts at me at once, and even though I could hear them loud and clear inside my head,

I couldn't think with all the noise.

I took a deep breath and broke away from them, sick of everyone trying to look after me and protect me. The pain I'd experienced before had completely gone, but I needed some distance from them—from Seth always checking if I was okay, and from Archer wanting to know my every move. I walked into the mass of people on the dancefloor and swayed to the beat with them. From the corner of my eye, I saw Seth and Archer look at each other, and Abby grabbed Archer's arm, pulling him in the opposite direction.

Seth joined me on the dancefloor. He tried to get me to look at him but I avoided his gaze, blocking him out. I let the music run through my body, becoming drunk on the constant hum and the vibration through the floor. Seth probed the edges of my mind, looking for a way in, but I blocked him. If he wanted to keep things from me, then he could. I didn't care. All I cared about was letting go and moving to the music, because I'd never felt so free in my life.

If I was going to die, then I was damn well going to dance a little before I did.

17

ARCHER

Abby's hips swayed beneath my hands. She'd finally relaxed once she'd seen everything for the formal was fine. She may have seemed shallow sometimes, but the formal was important to her. She'd spent the last couple of months engrossed in its organisation, and I was proud of her and what she'd managed to pull off.

She rested her hands on my shoulders and stared at me. The look she held was one I hadn't really seen before, and my palms got sweaty. I gripped her waist and hoped I wouldn't leave sweat marks on the silky fabric of her dress.

Abby's lips turned up into a seductive smile, and she blinked. The music, along with everyone else around us, faded into the background. How had I never seen her like this before? I'd known Abby for years, and not once had she ever made me feel this way.

I wanted to kiss her, but in spite of everything she

was making me feel, did I want to go there? There were more important things to be worried about, like vampires, and death, and protecting Grace.

Grace. What was I going to do with her? I glanced around the room and spotted my sister with Seth. She danced with him, but it was like she was in her own world. I'd never seen her act that way before, and it scared me. Grace didn't do carefree very well. She did serious and paid attention to every detail.

My gaze locked with Seth's across the dancefloor.

Keep an eye on her, I thought.

He nodded over the top of her head, but I couldn't hear his reply thoughts. Grace stopped dancing and turned around, scowling at me.

I'm a big girl, Arch. Let it go for a night, she thought. She started dancing again, waving her arms over her head and swinging her hips in a way that looked completely wrong on my sister. Who was she and what had she done with Grace?

Abby slipped her hands up to my neck and locked her fingers together. She pressed against me and stood on her tiptoes. Her breath tickled my ear.

"What's the matter?"

I pulled back to look at her and smiled, shaking my head to indicate nothing was wrong.

Abby pulled my ear to her lips again. "When are you going to kiss me?"

I chuckled and lifted a hand to her face, running my thumb over the contour of her cheek. I guessed one kiss couldn't hurt. We were at a school dance. Kissing was supposed to happen. I'd deal with the aftermath tomorrow, like I always did.

Abby smiled as I leaned in. Our lips touched briefly, then someone tapped me on the shoulder. When I pulled back, Hope stood beside me, frowning.

"What the hell are you doing here?" I said.

Abby's fingers gripped my arm.

Hope tilted her head towards the door and motioned for us to follow. The hunter from the city hadn't changed since the last time I'd seen her. Her long, straight hair shone under the flickering lights of the dancefloor, and she looked out of place in her black jeans and combat boots.

I took Abby's hand and led her to the front of the hall. I wasn't about to leave her behind. If Hope was there, then something was wrong. I hadn't tried to call her again and she hadn't tried to call me, but she must have had something important to say if she'd left the city, and that something probably had to do with vampires.

Abby and I followed Hope around the side of the hall, into the shadows and away from the small groups of students and couples making the most of the night. Justice leaned against the wall at the far end of the building, picking dirt out of his fingernails with the tip of a stake. His black coat hung to his knees, and the sight made me laugh. Hope scowled.

"You're not going to find what I have to tell you very funny," she said.

I pressed my lips together and tightened my grip on Abby's hand.

"What's going on?" Abby asked. "You're a long way from the city."

Justice pushed off the wall, twirled his stake and

slipped it into his back pocket. We may have been on the same side, but I didn't like him much. The guy was a tool.

Hope exchanged a look with her brother and they rolled their eyes at each other. I didn't like being out of the loop either. Where the hell was Grace when I needed her? Oh, that was right—dancing up a storm.

Hope smiled and raised her eyebrows. I hated that she could hear my thoughts but I couldn't hear hers.

"Josh is back." Justice stuffed his hands into his pockets and rocked back and forth on his feet.

"Have you seen him?" Hope asked.

"If I had, would I be standing here talking to you?" I glared at her.

"We need to get Grace." Abby squeezed my hand and stared at me, her eyes wide.

I shook my head. "I want to know why he's here first, before he goes anywhere near her. She's dealing with enough crap without this to add to it. What's going on?"

Hope studied me. Her eyes shone, and the corners of her mouth turned up. "That's why you called me?"

I bit my lip to stop myself from retaliating. If I wanted Hope to tell me about Josh, I had to play nice. And I might need her help, so that was another reason to not be an arse.

"Can we deal with one thing at a time?" I said.

"We've been keeping an eye on Josh since you left. So far, he's stayed out of trouble, and no one has bothered him." Hope looked around the darkness as if she were waiting for someone to jump out at us. "When he left the city a few hours ago, we thought it best to follow him."

"You left the city unprotected?" I asked.

"Things have been quiet for a while, thanks to you lot," Justice said.

I scoffed. "I wish I could say the same about Hopetown Valley. We have more vamps passing through than we ever have before. It's like they're wandering around trying to find the all-you-can-eat buffet."

"I think we should get Grace." Abby tugged on my arm. "She needs to know Josh is here. We can catch up with Hope and Justice later."

"Grace is busy letting her hair down," I said.

Hope stared at me. She was reading my thoughts. She opened her mouth to say something when a snarl pierced the night.

Justice pushed past me and scanned the shadows, tilting his head to the side, listening and staring out over the space that lay between the hall and the cathedral grounds. The only light down that far was the soft glow of the lamps at the cemetery gate.

"You should get Abby back inside," Hope said.

We were the only ones at the back of the hall, and I wasn't about to let Abby walk through the darkness alone.

"I'm not letting her out of my sight," I said.

"Suit yourself." Hope moved to stand next to her brother. "Just don't ..." The snarl sounded again, and a vampire stepped out of the darkness. "... get in my way."

I pulled Abby behind me as the shadows rippled, like they were being torn apart. Abby's fingers dug into my arm.

"Oh crap," I said. "This doesn't look good." I counted at least fifteen vamps. "Where did they come from?"

"I don't think it matters," Justice said.

"Archer, how many people are at this dance?" Hope

asked.

"At least a hundred."

"Great." She looked at me sideways. "You need to warn everyone."

"What am I supposed to say? 'Run, there are vampires outside'?"

The vamp in the lead stopped a few metres from the hunting duo and bared his fangs.

"Arch." Abby tried to pull me away, but I wasn't bowing out of a good fight.

I loosened her hold on my arm. "Stay behind me."

The front vamp made his move, launching at Hope, probably thinking she was the weaker of the two hunters. He was in for a shock. She jumped and king hit him in the face, sending the vamp flying back and crashing into his mates. Vampires scattered then regained their feet, rushing towards us. I wished I could disintegrate into mist like Grace and get Abby out of there.

Abby shrieked as three vamps honed in on us. I stepped forward to meet them, drawing my stake and slamming it into the chest of the closest one. She fell to ash at my feet, only to be replaced by the next attacker.

Another vampire raced towards us and I shoved Abby out of the way. I grabbed the vamp around the throat, jerking my arm to the right and snapping his neck. Hope took a big hit and flew towards us, landing next to the vamp as she hit the ground. She reached over, slamming her stake into the creature's heart, then jumped to her feet before the dust could settle.

Abby whimpered behind me and I helped her to her feet. Her dress was torn and her palms bloody from where she must have scraped them when she fell.

"I'm sorry," I breathed into her ear, "but you have to run."

"I don't want to leave you."

I took a breath and gritted my teeth, but before I could make her go something slammed into me from behind. Abby made an "oomph" sound as I landed on top of her, then her head hit the ground with a smack.

I struggled with the weight on top of me, trying to fight it off, before it disappeared and I was covered in dust. Hands grabbed my shoulders and yanked me off Abby.

"I told you to get her out of here," Hope said.

Feet scuffed the ground behind us and I glanced over my shoulder. Justice fought to hold the remaining vamps at bay, kicking, punching, and stabbing as they came at him.

Abby moaned.

"She's hurt," I said.

Hope put her hand on Abby's arm and light flowed into her, running under the surface of her skin like a faint blue glow.

"Get her inside. Then find Grace and tell her about Josh. We'll head for the cemetery ... Try to lead the vamps away." Hope raced back to her brother's side.

I helped Abby to her feet, and we ran towards the front of the hall. It was time to get my sister completely back in the game.

18

GRACE

The floor vibrated under my feet, and I was glad I wasn't wearing sky-high heels like most of the other girls. If I had been, I would've stopped dancing ages ago. Sweat trickled down my back, and I relished the feeling of letting go.

My neck prickled and I stopped dancing, spinning to face the front doors of the hall. There were people everywhere, moving in every direction, and it was hard to see who was who in the dim light. When the lights on the dance floor strobed, I could make out some faces in the crowd, but not the one I was searching for.

I'd know his presence anywhere, even in a room full of gyrating, sweaty bodies.

I searched the perimeter of the room, and my gaze fell on the person I'd been looking for. The crowd around us shifted, and there he was.

Josh.

Seth pulled me close. "What's he doing here?"

"Calm your testosterone. I have no idea." I freed myself from Seth's hold. *But I need to find out.*

The people around me danced in a tightly packed group, and it wasn't easy pushing through them. When I reached the front door, Josh was gone. I spun, scanning the hall, trying to find him over the sea of heads that filled the room. He was nowhere, and it didn't seem like anyone else had noticed him. I edged my way around the wall, trying to get a better look at the crowd. It was easier than moving through all the dancers again.

Seth grabbed my arm. "Grace."

"Where did he go?" I turned to face him.

Seth released his hold on me and I stared at him. He frowned. "I don't really care where he went."

I ignored him and kept moving. If Josh was here, then something was wrong. He'd never come back. Not in a million years, because there was nothing left here for him.

When I'd done a full circle and reached the front door, I scanned the hall again one last time before going outside.

Bumps rose on my skin from the crisp night air. As I rounded the side of the hall I ran headlong into Archer. Our collision made me stumble backwards and I lost my balance, falling to the asphalt on my butt.

"Gracie!" Archer leaned down and grabbed my hand, pulling me to my feet.

Abby stood at his side, clutching his arm, her eyes wide.

I glanced around, taking in the scene in the semi-darkness. Ash littered the ground in several places.

"What happened?" I asked.

"Vamps," Archer said. "I was on my way to find you."

"Josh is here." I stared at Archer and his brow pinched.

"I know ... Hope and Justice filled us in."

"They're here, too? Why? Where did they go? What do they want? What does Josh want?"

Archer shrugged. "Which question do I answer first?"

"All of them." I planted my hands on my hips.

Seth cleared his throat. "Shouldn't we be ... doing something other than arguing?"

Abby laughed, and the sound shocked me. There was nothing funny about the situation, and I was about to point it out when I noticed she wasn't entirely okay. Her laughter was bordering on hysterical, and tears drew streaks through her makeup. Archer put his arm around her shoulders and tucked her into his body. She stopped laughing and buried her face in his chest.

Seth rested his hand on my shoulder. "Come on, we need to go find Josh."

It was the last thing Seth wanted to do, but as usual he wouldn't voice his concerns about it until he'd reached breaking point, and then he'd explode. I didn't want him to explode. Not over Josh. Or near him.

I glanced around, searching for any sign of vampire activity. Apart from the ash strewn on the ground, I couldn't see any, but that didn't mean anything. Archer and I had heightened senses, but they could still elude us, and they were probably waiting it out and regrouping now some of the pack had been dusted.

"Josh was in the hall," I said. "He came out here. None of you saw him?"

"Too busy fighting off the bities," Archer said. "Hope and Justice headed towards the cemetery ... I think."

"Then we'll start there." I headed towards the shadows behind the hall and the path that lead down to the cemetery gate.

"Grace," Seth said.

When I turned he looked at the ground and shook his head. Josh coming back was hard for him. But I needed answers. To everything.

"He probably just wants to talk." I shrugged.

"Yeah, because running away is a sure sign of that," Seth said.

I ignored him and turned around, heading for the cemetery and all its gloomy darkness. I got about three steps when I heard a scream. I whipped around and someone ran into the light that spilled from the front of the hall, illuminating a small area of the yard. The girl screamed again, her chest heaving with heavy sobs.

"There's so much blood," she said, her body a silhouette against the yellow light.

Archer, Seth and Abby hadn't moved. They stood and stared at the girl as more people spilled from the hall. All I got from the distraught girl's mind were images of blood, but in one of those images was a face.

Claudia's face.

I stared at Abby, and a pang of pain ran through my heart. She didn't need this. She didn't need any more heartache.

None of us did.

Arch, it's Claudia ... in the bathroom, I thought.

"What's happening?" Abby asked. She spun away from

Archer to look at me. "What can you read in their heads?"

Seth, can you go and check out the inside of the hall? See if there are any vamps left in there, I thought. *I'll meet you in the cemetery.*

He nodded and fell back into the darkness.

"Where's he going?" Abby asked. "Grace, what's going on?"

Archer stared at me over the top of Abby's head. The crowd outside the hall grew, and people pulled phones from pockets. The teachers were trying to get everyone together and keep them where there was light and apparent safety. A siren blared in the distance.

I pressed my lips together. "If we have any chance of stopping this, we need to get out of here ... before the teachers see us and round us up, too."

Archer scanned the crowed at the same time as pulling Abby away and to the very back of the hall. Red and blue lights strobed through the darkness as an ambulance drove through the school grounds. It came to a stop as close to the hall as possible, and two paramedics got out, one carrying a case. They pushed their way through the crowd and disappeared into the hall.

"Come on." Archer gently tugged on Abby's hand. "We need to go. I'm not leaving you here." He wrapped one arm around Abby and grabbed my hand, raising his eyebrows. *Guess it's time to go find Josh.*

I took a deep breath, trying not to listen to the commotion, but I heard one distinctive phrase and it turned my blood cold.

"It's Claudia," the girl who had first come out of the hall screamed hysterically, and Abby froze beside me.

Archer's hand tensed in mine, and before either of them could speak, I misted and took the three of us to the rusty gate at the front of the school cemetery. If there were any vamps left inside the hall, Seth would take care of them.

Abby broke away from us and wrapped her arms around her middle. She sat on the low wall next to the gate and stared at the ground. I wanted to hug her and tell her everything was going to be okay, but I didn't do hugging, and I didn't want to make a promise I couldn't keep.

Archer sat beside her and wrapped his big hand around hers.

"Is she dead?" Tears shone in Abby's eyes.

I wanted to say no. I wanted to say something to fix it all, but I didn't get the chance. Seth appeared beside me in his cloud of black mist. I turned and pressed my forehead into his chest. His hand fell onto my back and rubbed circles on my bare skin. Warmth flooded me, and for a moment I wanted to forget about Claudia dying and Abby bawling her eyes out. I wanted to forget about Josh. I wanted to walk away from everything with Seth at my side, and never look back.

"We could, you know," Seth murmured into my hair, "run away, together."

I pulled away and tilted my head back, staring into his open face. "No, we couldn't." I sighed. "This is my life. It's what I do." Seth kept his hand on my back and continued to trace his fingers over my skin. "I don't run away. I might stray from the path every now and then, but I'm not a runner."

He kissed my forehead. "It's a mess in there. No sign

of any vamps though. Hope and Justice must have cleared them out. I saw them amongst the crowd. Damage control, I guess."

"No sign of Josh?" I asked.

Seth shook his head. "No idea where he went."

"How many ... dead?"

Abby sniffled and stared at her feet. The diamantes on her shoes sparkled in the moonlight.

"Not sure. I'd say about five." Seth furrowed his brow, and I got the feeling there was more to it than that.

"What is it? Now is not the time to hold out on me."

Seth ran a hand over his cropped hair, his jaw working as he ground his teeth. "They were all dark-haired."

"What does that have to do with anything?"

"I think they're looking for you."

Archer stared at me. "They know."

Seth clenched his fist and turned away. He yelled and punched the cemetery wall, chunks of stone falling to the dirt at his feet.

"They're looking for me?" I tucked my hair behind my ear. "How would they even know I can die? Who would've told them?"

Seth wrapped his fingers around the bars that lined the top section of the cemetery wall. "I'll give you one guess."

I shook my head. "Michael? He wouldn't ... would he?"

"I'm betting he would if it meant you'd go home," Archer said, scowling.

I sat on the lip of the wall next to my brother and pressed my back against the metal bars. I didn't understand. Michael had helped us when we'd gone to the city to find Josh. He'd fought alongside us and made Angelica pay for what she'd done to Seth. We'd not always seen eye to eye, but he cared about me. Like Seth, he'd always tried to protect me. Why was Michael being such a bastard now?

"I think he wants to see you go back to Heaven as much as the Council does." Seth turned his head and stared at me, his cheek resting against the back of his hand. "He loves you enough to fight to keep you safe."

"Well, we all do," Archer said.

"I need more girls in my life," I said. "The boys are trouble." I tried to smile at my own joke, but I didn't feel like smiling.

"Back to the subject of trouble," Seth said, pushing off the wall. "Let's go and see what Josh wants."

I glanced at Archer, needing him to come with me, but I didn't want to put Abby in danger. Who was I kidding? No matter where she was she would be in danger.

You need to protect her, I thought.

I'll do everything I can to keep her and you safe. Archer rubbed Abby's back.

She can't come with us.

"We can't leave her here!" Archer said.

"She'll be safer back at the hall." I planted my hands on my hips.

Abby stood up quickly and shook out her hands, flicking her fingers like she had water on them, and then wiped the tears from her cheeks.

"Grace is right. I'll get in the way."

"Want me to take you back?" I asked.

"I'll be fine. You go and do your thing." She smiled with closed lips.

Archer glanced towards the hall. "I'll take you," he said.

Abby nodded and steadied herself with one hand on the wall. She lifted her leg, slipping the strap of her sling-back stiletto under her heel. Abby repeated the same for the other shoe then hooked them onto her fingers.

"If I need to run, I can't do it on these," she said, glancing at the shoes.

"I'll catch you up," Archer said, putting his hand on Abby's back.

"Stay alive." She stared at me then turned and walked with Archer along the path towards the hall.

"Right then." I turned to Seth. "Let's go see what the hell my angry ex wants."

He scoffed, but he slid his hand down my arm and took my hand. The cemetery gate squealed in protest as he opened it and gently tugged me through.

19

GRACE

I was thankful I'd said no to the high heels and worn my boots instead, even if they weren't Abby's idea of the best fashion statement. Seth and I walked silently into the cemetery crossing from one row to another to find the shadows. We passed Emma's grave. Usually I'd stop to talk to her, but I was sure Emma would understand my missing our ritual tonight.

A few minutes later Archer arrived, slightly out of breath, and fell into step beside me.

"That was quick," I said.

"I run fast." Archer stopped halfway along one of the rows to look at something. We stood together, staring at the inscription on the headstone of Josh's mother's grave.

"He's been here," Archer said.

"He brought flowers ... how lovely." Seth folded his arms across his broad chest and frowned. His hair looked almost white under the moon's pale glow.

A single rose sat in the small receptacle in the centre of the marble slab. Its pink petals drooped, and there was something sad but very moving about that single flower. I could almost be the rose, ripped from my roots and left to die in a harsh world that had no further use for me.

"He must be close," I said. "And this shows he still has some compassion."

"What made you think he didn't?" Archer asked.

More sirens blared and two police cars drove slowly through the grounds, followed by another ambulance. I hoped it meant there were survivors amongst the injured.

I rubbed my arms to rid myself of a chill that wasn't really there.

"Hope and Justice will sort it out," Seth said. "If they're as good as you two, everyone will be safe."

"They can't make them forget though," I said. "Forgetting is what most people need."

I turned my back on the hall in the distance and searched the shadows of the cemetery. It brought back so many memories of my time at Hopetown Valley High. I remembered talking to Josh after Emma's funeral, and the pain was strong, as if she'd died only moments ago. The conversation I'd had with Josh that day came to the front of my mind. My boots crunched on the gravel as I moved to the middle of the row, heading towards the back of the cemetery. The Moreton Bay figs cast huge shadows over the back section, where I guessed Josh would be hiding in the trees.

When we neared, I held my hand up for the others to

stop. Josh stepped from the darkness into a small patch of moonlight.

He looked ... surprisingly good.

I blinked, not prepared for how seeing him made me feel. In a split second I hoped he was okay, wanted to ask him a million questions, hit him for coming back, and hug him all at the same time. Many emotions ran through me and competed for my complete attention. Happiness, joy, worry, and fear, but anger won out in the end.

"What are you doing here?" I asked, unable to keep my voice steady.

Josh studied us for a few moments, his gaze lingering on Seth the longest. When I didn't think he was going to answer, he finally spoke.

"I came to see if you were okay."

"I'm fine." I pressed my lips together.

"That's not what I heard." Josh took a step towards me, his hands balled into fists.

"You know I can take care of myself."

"Yeah, well you know I can, too." His gaze bore into me. "But that didn't stop you from coming to the city."

"So this is tit for tat now?" Archer said. "You should have stayed home."

Josh leaped forward. "You don't know! Those vamps in there ... they came here to kill her." He stepped forward again into Archer's personal space.

Archer moved until his nose almost touched Josh's. "And you thought you'd come and save her? Well ... we got it. So go home."

In a blur of movement, Josh shoved Archer in the chest with both hands, sending him flying backwards and into a tall headstone. He was on his feet in seconds and ready to retaliate until I stepped in front of Josh and faced Archer.

I shook my head. "Don't, Arch. You're making things worse."

"You ended it with him. He shouldn't be here."

"Well … he is." Why did I always have to stop the boys from wanting to kill each other?

"What I want to know," Josh said, stepping to my side, "is what you're going to do to help Grace."

Seth started laughing, and the sound was so foreign after all the arguing and yelling, it took me a few seconds to register it. I stared at him blankly, wondering what on earth he thought was so funny. As quickly as he'd started, he stopped, and his brow knitted together, his eyes dark and angry.

"The question I'm going to ask is what do you know, Josh?" Seth moved to join our little circle.

Seth, stop being so macho, I thought. He scowled but stepped back.

"What did Michael tell you?" Seth continued.

Josh kept his mouth closed, and jealousy glinted in his eyes. He didn't want to tell, but nothing could stop either Seth or I looking in his mind and finding out anyway.

Seth laughed again.

Josh, I thought.

He peeled his glare from Seth to look at me. *You can still connect with me?*

Seems that way. I guess because I forced you to hear me, you always will if I want you to.

His mind filled with thoughts of us and what we'd

had. It seemed like an eternity ago, and I was surprised to find it didn't hurt as much as I'd thought it would. I didn't love him. I loved Seth. I would always love Seth.

Josh's thoughts ran through what Michael had told him, and he seemed to have one thought that overwhelmed all the others.

My being able to die was Seth's fault.

I didn't see how it was possible. And I couldn't get a read on the exact words Michael had said to Josh, as if there were a foggy spot in his memory.

Seth shifted on his feet, turning sideways to me and slipping his hand onto my back. His palm was warm against my bare skin. I was grateful for his touch. It grounded me in the moment and reinforced my feelings for him. He would always protect me, even when I didn't want protecting.

"You can't believe the thoughts of a jealous man," Seth said.

"Maybe not," I said with caution. "But I can believe his actions."

"What does it matter that Michael told him?" Archer asked. "He knows, so now he can help us protect you from whatever and whoever is coming to kill you."

"You should listen to Archer," Josh said. "We need to stop arguing and work out what we're going to do."

A crow cawed in the trees and I listened, realising I couldn't hear many other sounds. There was a low background hum, like white noise, coming from the direction of the hall, but the wail of the sirens had ceased, and apart from the crow, the cemetery was eerily quiet.

Too quiet.

I turned a slow circle on the spot, taking everything in. Archer glanced around as well, following my gaze out over the grounds of the school. A breeze stirred the trees, but the relative silence covered everything until a distant sound penetrated it.

A faint scream.

A splash.

"Did you hear that?" I asked.

"The fountain in the vineyard?" Archer said.

We stared into the darkness of the grounds. Something was going on down there, only I wasn't sure if I wanted to find out what. Archer ran down the slight hill along the back fence line to the gate hidden in the trees. The rest of us reached it before him, since he couldn't mist or run quite as fast as a vampire. Archer tried the gate, but it was rusted shut from years of no use. I slipped my hand into Josh's and grabbed Archer's arm, misting us to the other side of the fence. Seth followed.

"I've got a bad feeling about this." Archer edged forward into the open paddock. He turned back and held his hand out to me. "Angel express to the vineyard please."

"It's probably a trap," Josh said.

"You heard the scream, yes?" Archer said. "We can't ignore it."

From this side of the cemetery it was harder to see the hall, but the faint glow of red and blue lights flashed through the sky meaning the police were probably still there. I wanted to go back and see if everyone was okay, but I also wanted to find out where the scream had come from. Ignoring Josh's plea, I stepped towards my brother and took his hand. Seth moved to my side, making sure he was between me and Josh.

Having Josh there complicated everything. Why did he have to care so much?

I could ask you the same question, Seth thought. He didn't look at me though, staring straight ahead towards the vineyard.

I sighed and slipped my arm through Seth's, then grabbed Josh's shirt so I touched all of them, and misted us to the vineyard.

The sound of running water grew louder as we neared the arbour, the splashes coming from the fountain that sat beyond the entrance. I wished it were the only sound we could hear. As we passed under the heart-shaped structure, the noise of combat reached my ears, but I couldn't see who was fighting or where through the darkness.

"They really need to install lights down here," Archer said. "The darkness is inconvenient."

I couldn't have agreed more.

The four of us edged forward, the moonlight providing enough light to see the cobblestone pathway with the fountain at its centre. When we reached the lip, I rested my hands on the edge and looked in. The others fanned out around the circle, the water a constant rush in front of us.

Something flashed to my right and Justice ran between a row of grape vines, a pack of angry vampires hot on his tail. I glanced around and more vamps ran towards us from the other side of the vineyard.

"This doesn't look good," Archer said, but he wasn't watching the vampires. His eyes were cast down towards the water in the fountain.

It was then I saw the body.

Floating in the fountain facedown.

The girl's dress billowed out around her. Her black hair did the same.

"Run!" Justice yelled.

Seth grabbed my arm and pulled me towards the arbour and out of the vineyard. Josh streaked past us in a blur and stopped about ten metres away in the paddock, his eyes scanning the scene unfolding around us.

I glanced over my shoulder and saw Archer not far behind. I misted to him and grabbed him, misting us away from the path of the oncoming vamps and landing where Josh stood in the middle of the open grounds. Seth appeared moments later.

Vampires poured out of the vineyard in a black wave of anger and snarls. Hope orbed and landed beside Justice, grabbing him before dissipating into a mass of blue light again. Seconds later, they were at our side.

Six of us against … I didn't know how many.

"Fancy meeting you here." Justice smirked at Archer. "Any idea what to do about that?" He pointed his stake at the vamps coming down the slope.

"Fight them?" Archer shrugged.

Seth stared at Josh. "Whose side is he on?"

Josh balled his fists. "I'm on the side that keeps Grace alive."

"Good. Just wanted to be clear."

"What are they doing here?" I wished the boys would calm their testosterone.

"Who has time to ask silly questions?" Justice steadied

his stance and faced the vamps. "I suggest you get ready to fight."

Hope mimicked her brother, standing tall and ready, flexing her fingers around the stakes she held in her hands. I wouldn't have been scared either, if I were her. She had nothing to lose.

But me?

I had my life.

20

ARCHER

The first line of vampires advanced towards Hope and Justice. Hope's wings exploded from her back with a whoosh, and the fighting duo pushed forward, forcing some of them back into those behind them. Dust flew into the air in puffs before raining down onto the grass and anyone who happened to be in its path.

Vampires spilled around us, and the fight became a blur. I focused on taking down one after another as they came at me. Most of them couldn't fight well, so killing them wasn't a problem. There were a few that managed to come in hard then get away, only to come back again for another go.

Light spheres and fire balls assaulted the mob of vampires. It sucked that I had to rely solely on my stake.

"Have we made a dent?" I asked.

Grace's wings expanded with a crack, covering the

moon with an ebony blanket. She yelled as she launched at a female vamp, pulling her arm back, her stake ready to strike. For someone so tiny, my sister could jump, and she swung downwards as she sailed through the air, planting the stake right into the vamp's chest. The vamp exploded into dust, only to be replaced by another vamp a few seconds later. Grace conjured a fire ball and hurled it. The vampire in front of her went up in flames, lighting the darkness like a burning funeral pyre.

"There can't possibly be more," Grace said, her wings fluttering at her sides. "We're fighting on a carpet of ash."

I readjusted the stake in my hand before ramming it into the chest of another vamp as he ran towards me. We had reduced the numbers quite a bit, but there were still enough fighters to keep us on our toes.

A siren wailed in the background, and I assumed it came from the hall. Right then it didn't matter; we were too busy with our own fight to worry about anyone else's. I hoped we were far enough away so that no one could make us out in the dark. I also hoped no one was stupid enough to venture down into the paddock. One girl had made the mistake of going to the vineyard, and she'd ended up dead. We didn't need anyone else getting killed.

Grace cried out, and I spun to face the sound of her voice. Blood covered her arm, thick and black in the moonlight, running from a gash that spread from her wrist to her elbow. She tucked her wings to her sides and cradled her arm to her stomach, glaring at the vampire standing in front of her. His lips curled into a snarl, and saliva dripped from his fangs. His gaze flicked from Grace's watchful eyes to the blood on her arm.

One guess what he wanted to do.

I took a step towards my sister, anger clouding my vision. She'd spent so long looking out for me; I couldn't let anything happen to her. But she was stronger than I gave her credit for. Grace pulled her good arm back and planted a stake in the vamp's chest.

"Archer, look out!"

I spun around at the sound of my name, with only a second to register Abby standing on the edge of the battle field. Someone shoved me from behind. My face bit the grass, and the body on top of me pushed my nose farther into the dirt. Strong hands clamped around my neck.

Abby screamed.

I fought my attacker, trying to break free of his hold and get to Abby before a vampire did. I'd managed to roll and get my legs free, so I kicked backwards into the vamp's shins while I tried to prise his fingers from my throat. Moments later they released, and I fell back onto a pile of ash. Hope stared down at me and offered her hand.

"Don't worry about me! Protect Abby," I yelled.

Hope orbed, and I rolled onto my belly. Abby stood in the same place she'd been when I'd first spotted her, her eyes wide, surveying the scene. A vamp blurred past and barrelled into Abby a split second before Hope made it to her. Abby screamed when she hit the ground, the vampire going straight for her neck. She screamed again. Hope staked the vamp in the back, the ash covering Abby in a thin film.

Why had she followed us? If she didn't die tonight, I was going to kill her myself.

I got to my knees and stumbled to my feet, trusting

Abby was safe with Hope.

Grace lashed out as another vampire advanced on her. She gritted her teeth, swinging her stake towards the enemy. The vamp grabbed her injured arm and dug his fingers into the wound, Grace's blood covering his hands.

I couldn't lose my sister.

Before I took another step, the vamp attacking Grace exploded into dust and Seth appeared when the cloud dropped. He grabbed for her, as if she were the only thing keeping him alive, his eyes full of desperation and fear. I stood, frozen, wondering when my position as Grace's protector had been demoted. I'd been replaced by *him*.

Archer, get Abby out of here. Grace glared at me, and I snapped out of my reverie.

Hope stood beside Abby, quickly scanning the darkness before settling her stare on me. The sounds of Justice and Josh fighting the remaining few vamps settled over us. I was as angry at Abby as Grace and Hope were with me.

Hope orbed and joined her brother, helping him finish off the vamp he was fighting. I took a few steps towards Abby who offered me a small smile. She fidgeted with the fabric on the front of her dress.

I wanted to hug her. Then something streaked through the darkness and Abby flew towards me, her eyes wide and glistening in the moonlight. She hit the ground before I could comprehend what was happening. The vampire on top of her tore into her neck.

I ran towards Abby, the whole scene blurring before me, but I couldn't get to her fast enough. Ash and blood drenched the battlefield. My boots slipped on the ash-covered grass, and I stumbled, falling to my knees at Abby's head. The vamp growled, his teeth covered with blood.

Abby's blood.

"No!" I fumbled for my stake, my voice pouring out of me like hot lava spilling from a volcano. The pain burned on the way out, and I wished I could throw it at the vampire and turn him to dust.

I heard the others yelling in the background, but I didn't care what they were saying. All I cared about was Abby and making sure she was okay.

She wasn't.

Grace misted and landed next to Abby, grabbing the vampire by the shoulders and throwing him off. He tumbled across the grass and stopped about twenty metres away. Grace may have been bleeding, tears streaking her face, but she was focused on the mission. She assumed her battle pose, stake at the ready.

I stayed where I was, my hands and knees deep in filthy ash, unable to get up. I fell sideways onto the grass, and I finally understood why Heaven wanted Grace back. Unlike me, she never gave up. She was always loyal to her beliefs, even if she was a fallen angel; she fought for good, no holds barred. And she fought until she couldn't fight any more.

"Get up!" she screamed at me. "Get up, Archer."

If only I could keep fighting like she did. But what was the point? We'd already lost so much.

"Don't be a dick." Seth grabbed me and hauled me to my feet. "You don't get to pack it in now."

My breath came in ragged gasps, and I raised my head to look around. Josh was busy fighting a vamp twice his size, throwing several punches to the vamp's face before getting his stake in the right place. When the dust had settled, his gaze met mine then he glanced at the ground. Realisation shone in Josh's eyes as they widened and took in Abby's prone body. Josh heaved breaths he didn't need and stared at the vampire with Abby's blood on his lips. The vampire snarled, and Josh moved to join Grace, but she held out her hand to stop him. He hung back, waiting.

Hope orbed to Abby's side, crouched and placed her hand on her shoulder. Light flowed from Hope's fingertips into Abby, but it went out as quickly as it had lit. Hope shook her head and stood, her mouth pressed into a thin line.

Grace stalked towards the vampire, breaking into a run. I had a moment to register that Abby was dead, lying blood-soaked on the ground, and another half a moment to act. I blocked out the image of Abby's lifeless body and followed my sister. A yell ripped itself from my mouth, searing my throat on its way out. Grace was fast and would get to the vamp before me. I pumped my legs harder.

Grace stopped.

The vampire reached her.

Grace held a stake in each hand, her fingers curled tightly around them. I was almost close enough to touch her, to push her out of the way and take down the vampire, then she was gone, a cloud of black mist left in her wake.

The vamp slammed into me, hitting me harder than anything had ever hit me before. The force should have sent me flying backwards, but I didn't move. I stared into the vampire's dark eyes, the moonlight reflecting off their blackness. A river of ice flowed through my chest. My hands lost feeling, and my fingers uncurled. My stake hit my boot as it dropped to the ground.

I tried to back away from the vampire. My feet shuffled backwards, but pain ripped through my chest and made me stop. The vampire smiled and the sight of his blood-covered fangs so close to my face made me sick.

Grace screamed, and I wondered what was wrong with her. Was she hurt again?

Arch, it's going to be okay, she thought.

I turned my head to the feeling of her mind. She stood a few metres away, her eyes wide and full of tears. Seth stood behind her, his hands on her shoulders, a deep frown on his face. Hope and Justice stood to the side, both of them covered in ash, their mouths agape. Josh fell to his knees on the grass and punched the ground.

The vampire snarled, and I turned my attention back to him.

"You have no idea how good it feels to finally kill a hunter," he said. "Even if it is the wrong one."

Pain ripped through me again and I looked down. The vampire's fist was buried in my chest up to his wrist.

How is this going to be okay, Gracie? I thought.

When I looked into the vampire's eyes again, he laughed, then he ripped his hand out of me and the pain went with it.

Grace's screams filled the air.

My body went numb.

Then nothing.

21

GRACE

Seth's hands were heavy on my shoulders. I stepped
forward, away from him, not wanting to acknowledge
what he'd done.

Archer swayed on his feet, stumbling to one side. I
misted and landed behind him, catching him as he fell.
The vampire smiled, one side of his mouth curling into
a crooked, wicked grin. He held up his hand, blood
trickling down his arm to his elbow before dripping onto
the grass at his feet.

He held my brother's heart between his fingers.

I couldn't look away from the grotesque sight. Archer.
A piece of his insides. The most important piece. On
display for everyone to see.

Bile rose into my throat, and my knees buckled.
Archer's weight sent me to the ground, and his body
landed on me. I couldn't keep him upright. He slipped

from my grasp and ended up on the dewy grass. The white of his shirt was soaked with crimson blood.

The vampire laughed, a deep, throaty sound. He threw Archer's heart onto the ground where it landed next to him with a squelch. The vampire licked his fingers.

I was numb. From head to toe, numb.

I stared at the vampire, then at the messy, bloody organ on the grass. Then at my brother. His face was pale. His eyes were open and staring at something I couldn't see.

It hit me.

Archer was dead.

The vampire laughed again.

I wondered why no one had staked him. Seconds after I'd had the thought, he exploded into a cloud of dust, filling the air with filth. When it fell away, Seth stood in his place, staring down at me with a look in his eyes I'd never seen before. Usually his eyes were filled with a certainty I couldn't explain. He was always so sure of himself. Now, it was as if he were lost.

I knew how he felt.

My body took an involuntary breath, and my chest heaved with a sob so vicious I thought my ribs would crack. When I opened my mouth, screams filled the night, ripping my throat raw.

My body shook, and when I looked at my hands I couldn't keep them still. They vibrated before my eyes like a tuning fork that had found water.

"Grace." Seth leaned down, and I lifted my arms to ward off his advance.

I didn't want him near me.

I didn't want anyone near me.

I rolled towards my brother, grabbing his arm and pulling myself onto my knees.

"No, no, no." I shook him then ran my hands over his chest and up to his face, patting his cheek to try and wake him up. "Come on, Arch. Don't do this to me." I shook his shoulders, and his head lolled to the side. "Wake up!"

"Grace, there's nothing you can do." Hope knelt beside me, putting her hand on my back.

I shrugged her off, flicking my wings to push her away, scanning Archer's face for any sign of the spark in his eyes. The spark I loved so much. I ran my hands over his chest again and blood slicked my fingers. They caught the edge of the tear in his shirt, exposing the huge hole in his chest.

"His heart," I whispered. "He needs his heart." I searched the grass and found the missing piece of my brother. "We need to put it back in." I grabbed the bloody mass and it slipped between my fingers. Everything blurred as tears streamed out of my eyes.

Seth grabbed me, covering Archer's heart and my hands with his. "Grace, you can't …"

"Don't tell me I can't!" I ripped away from him, struggling against his strong hold, lifting the heart to put it back into Archer's chest. He needed it. He couldn't live without it. "He's not dead. He's not … he's …"

Seth wrapped his arms around me from behind, and I screamed into the night. He was the only thing holding me up, the only thing stopping me from shattering into a million tiny pieces. Heat filled my face as if it were burning off. I reached for my brother as tears ran hot trails across my skin, dripping onto Archer and mingling with the blood covering him.

There was so much blood.

I rested my hands on his chest and hung my head over my brother's dead body.

How could he be dead?

It should have been me.

Why wasn't it me?

"Why?" I whispered.

I looked up to see Hope and Justice crouched across from me on the other side of Archer.

"Why?!" I screamed at the hunting team in front of me, the team that was still intact.

Hope flinched and looked away. Justice rubbed his stubbled cheek with his hand, his gaze never leaving mine.

"We can't answer that." His eyes flicked to Seth, and then he stood and turned his back, walking away until he became a dark splodge against the open paddock.

Josh sat on the grass and our gazes locked. I had the fleeting thought that I wished it were him in Archer's place. Anyone instead of my brother.

Seth held me tightly, his arms a heat source against my bare skin. I fell back into him, not enough energy left in me to stay upright. All I wanted to do was lie down and close my eyes, but the tears wouldn't let me. They came thick and fast, like a river breaking its banks and spilling everywhere. With the tears came a sadness so intense I didn't know what to do with it. It was like my soul was withering away into nothing, dying alongside my brother.

What would I do without him?

"He can't be gone." I stared at Archer, unable to look

away and hating myself because I hadn't been there to protect him. I hadn't had his back, and he'd paid the price with his life.

I took Seth's hands and loosened his hold on me, crawling forward and laying my head on Archer's chest. I didn't care that he was covered in blood, that *I* was covered in his blood. I folded my wings over us, sheltering Archer from everyone and everything. I put my hand over the hole in his chest, and listened for the sound that wasn't there.

I thought if I listened hard enough I'd hear it—his heart beating.

All I heard was silence.

22

SETH
Friday morning

I stood in the doorway to Grace's room and watched her sleep. Her face was so peaceful, and I wished I could do something to make her look that way all the time. All I wanted was for her to be happy, but it seemed as long as I was around, that would never happen.

Maybe it was time to tell her the complete truth—that way she'd return to Heaven and we'd go our separate ways.

"Isn't that what started the mess you're in?"

I glanced over my shoulder to where Hope stood at the top of the stairs.

"Let her sleep," she said. "We've got a lot to talk about."

Reluctantly, I pushed off the doorjamb and followed Hope downstairs. I ran my hand down my face as I passed Archer and Abby, covered in blankets on the cool concrete floor. We had to bury them soon, but Grace would want to be there, so we'd wait until she was ready.

Justice stood near the trampoline out in the clearing. I wasn't sure where Josh had gone, and I didn't care. He should have been dusted, like the rest of the vamps the night before. I'd have put a stake through his heart myself, but it would be one more thing that affected Grace. She was already broken enough.

I stopped when I reached Justice and stared at them both, waiting for one of them to talk.

Hope sighed. "After you brought Grace home, there were more."

"We spent most of the night fighting them," Justice said.

I toed the grass with my boot. There was something both of them wanted to say, but neither of them was saying it. Justice pinched the bridge of his nose.

"Don't worry," I said. "I won't look at your thoughts, because you're going to tell me what's going on."

"We can't protect Grace anymore," Hope said. "We've already interfered enough."

My jaw ached from clenching my teeth, waiting for one of them to continue.

"She has to go home," Justice said.

"Why?" I asked. "She doesn't want to. And Heaven is fine without her."

Hope pressed her lips together. "They want to reinstate her."

"So give her wings back! It's that simple."

Justice shook his head. "No, it isn't."

I stared at the ground, furious at everyone and everything. This was about something different entirely. I was missing something, and then I had a thought. My options from Michael were to let her die and lose her in the process, or protect her and keep her on Earth, and still lose her.

I glared at Hope. "They're doing this to separate us. Grace made her decision. She chose me. She gave her heart to me, and Michael isn't happy about it. He never thought it would happen, so he changed the rules. This is about him not wanting Grace to love me."

Justice laughed. "Not everything is about you, Seth."

"Then give me another explanation. Why the hell won't they leave us alone?"

Light appeared in the clearing, orbs spinning around themselves, getting bigger until Michael stepped out. "Grace doesn't belong amongst the fallen."

"Maybe not," I said. "But she belongs with me."

"Looks like you made a right royal mess of things." Michael raised an eyebrow. "You made a mistake saving her and letting Archer die."

"I've made a lot of mistakes."

Michael glared at me, a look I'd become familiar with over the years. If he was trying to rattle me, it wasn't working. Every time I was around him I had a strong urge to punch him in the face. If he was supposed to be the symbol of goodness, then I was the devil.

Michael took a step towards me, the trampoline between us. "I don't need to remind you your deadline is looming." He smirked. "Oh, look at that ... I just did."

"You're an arse," I said.

"See, you did teach *me* something."

"What deadline?" Grace stood at the corner of the shed, her face puffy from crying. She hadn't changed out of her formal dress, but she'd put a cardigan on over the top. She pulled the sleeves over her hands and wrapped her arms around her middle.

She looked so fragile.

I wanted to hold her, but I held back, knowing she didn't want anyone touching her. Archer had died because of something I'd done. His death rested on my shoulders, and I wondered if Grace would ever forgive me, or if it even mattered since my time was almost up.

Grace walked over to our small group. She stopped and stared at the trampoline, a tear rolling down her cheek, dripping from her chin. I wanted to catch it to see if she was still my soul mate, if she was the one I was supposed to be with, but I let it fall away to nothing. I already had one of her tears, tucked away in the black pouch in my pocket.

She pulled the sleeves of her cardigan up and held her arms out. Red lines marked her skin, as if she'd had a fight with a rabid cat.

"Why is this happening to me?" she asked. "Why won't any of you give me some answers?"

Hope flinched. Everyone stood, staring at Grace, her eyes wide and filled with tears. Her shoulders shook, and she fell to her knees, her chest heaving in powerful sobs I thought would rip her open.

I scowled at Michael. This was his doing. He was the one who'd started it. He shook his head, and I knew what he would say. He'd blame me, but I disagreed. He had the power to stop all of this.

I didn't.

I went to Grace and crouched in front of her. She hung

her head, her hair hiding her face, and she dug her fingers into the ground. I gently grasped her shoulders and pushed her upright, placing one palm on her cheek. She blinked and looked at me. She was in a state of shock that I wasn't sure she would ever recover from.

"You," she whispered, the sound of her voice vibrating into my hand. "You saved me." She blinked again and more tears dripped onto her cheeks. "It was supposed to be me … not him. Not Archer."

"Grace, I …" What was I supposed to say? Sorry? Sorry wouldn't bring him back. Nothing I said would fix this.

Grace shied away from my touch. She wiped her dirty hands on her dress, but it didn't matter. Her formal dress was already covered in filth. She got to her feet and I rose with her, never taking my eyes from hers.

"I would've died for him," Grace said. "He's my brother … was my brother."

"I'm sorry," I said, knowing it meant nothing. "I love you. I was trying to protect you."

Grace took a deep breath, and her lips quivered. "I know you love me, Seth. So much. Yet why is it you always manage to find a way to hurt me?"

My mouth moved, but I couldn't find the right words to come out of it. She was right. I did always hurt her, no matter how hard I tried not to.

"Seth," Michael said. "Time's ticking."

I spun on my heel and ran at him, glad I had something I could punch because I didn't think I could hold my anger in any longer. I misted over the trampoline then barreled into Michael. We crashed onto the grass. Before I could get a punch in, Hope and Justice grabbed my arms and pulled me off him.

"Fighting won't fix this," Hope said.

Michael got to his feet and brushed himself off. "Tell her the truth," he said before dissolving into his orbs of light and disappearing.

"I want to bury my brother," Grace said, her voice quiet. "Until then, I don't care about anything else."

All of us faced her. She stared at her arms and the angry red lines, running her fingers over the ones near her wrist. She hadn't gotten any answers from us, and I thought how unfair everything must look to her.

"Okay," I said. "Then we'll talk."

She looked up and straight into my eyes.

I'll tell you everything, I thought.

She blinked a few times, her arms hanging limp at her sides, before turning away and walking towards the shed door. Her mind was filled with thoughts of Archer, and with every image of him she saw, her heart broke a little bit more.

23

GRACE

Blankets covered the two bodies on the floor of the shed. I couldn't believe my brother was under there. He was going to walk through the door any minute, only he wasn't. I wanted him to. God, I wanted him to. But he was gone. I'd been repeating it over and over in my head since I'd woken up.

He's gone.

Archer was gone.

Seth rested his hands on my shoulders from behind, and it made me keep moving into the shed. I didn't want him to touch me. I didn't want anyone touching me. Archer dying was Seth's fault. If he hadn't have misted me out of the way, then that vamp would have buried his fist in *my* chest. He would have ripped *my* heart out, and Archer would be alive.

I was angry at Seth for saving me, but I didn't have

the energy to yell and scream at him like I wanted to. All my energy had flowed out with my tears, and I was a shell walking around, somehow holding myself up.

I shuffled over to where Archer and Abby lay on the floor and stopped at their heads. It sucked we couldn't give them a proper funeral. It always sucked. Why did I have to keep burying my friends? Maybe it would have been better if I hadn't had any in the first place. If I didn't love anyone, then I'd have no one to lose.

"I can take them … if you want?" Seth stood at Archer's feet.

I didn't look at him. I couldn't tear my eyes away from the lumpy blankets.

All I could do was nod.

"We'll stay here," Hope said, "in case Josh decides to show up."

I didn't say anything. Words were not something I could do right then. All I could think about was Archer, and my mind kept flooding with memories and images of him.

Ready? Seth thought.

He waited for me to go first, and I didn't think I could move, but I took a deep breath and closed my eyes, misting to the part of the forest where the cemetery hid. Seth arrived seconds later, landing in a crouch on the grass to my left, the two bodies beside him.

The wall to the cemetery shimmered into focus and I clambered over it, heading towards the mausoleum. At the back was a small storage shed, the door hidden behind the branches of the surrounding trees. I had to put my shoulder into it to push it open. It had stuck shut from the build-up of dirt and leaves at the base.

Seth appeared at my side and grabbed my hand before it could reach the shovel propped in the far corner of the small room.

"I'll do it," he said.

He took the shovel, a coil of rope, and two planks of wood, then went outside and didn't glance back. I wanted to tell him where to bury Archer, but he already knew I'd want him near Pa and my parents. When I went back out to the graves, Seth had started digging in the right spot.

I sat on the wall and watched as the mound of dirt beside him grew. Sweat trickled down Seth's brow and into his eyes, but he didn't wipe it away, and he didn't stop until he'd finished.

It was afternoon by the time Seth pushed the shovel into the dirt and left it standing at the edge of the mound. He'd also dug a second grave for Abby beside Ryan's. He pressed his lips together and walked to the wall, stepping over and going to the bodies we'd left on the grass. Crouching down, he touched Archer and Abby's shoulders, misting and placing them next to the freshly dug graves.

"Why are you doing this?" I asked.

Seth came and sat next to me on the wall. "What do you mean?"

"This." I waved my hand and gestured at the piles of dirt. "Why are you helping?"

"That's an odd question." He looked at his hands, picking his fingernails. "I … have to do something. I never wanted it to be like this."

"You should've never kept the truth from me."

"Now is not the time, Grace."

I jumped to my feet and spun to face him. "When is the time, Seth? Because the way I see it, you've had plenty of opportunities to talk to me and tell me what's going on. But for some reason you won't."

He rubbed the back of his neck. "I meant we should wait until we've finished burying our dead."

Seth stood and took a step towards me, but I didn't want to be near him. I was tired of fighting. Tears stung my eyes as I stepped over the cemetery wall. I needed a moment away from death and having to deal with everything.

"You want to know why I haven't told you?" Seth said.

I stopped but I didn't turn around. I was sick of looking at him. "Why haven't you?"

"Because if I do, it will make you do something you don't want to … I don't want to be the reason you make a bad decision."

"I've made plenty of those already. What makes you think you have so much influence?" I clenched my fists and kept walking. Leaves rustled in the forest, and I searched the trees for the source of the disturbance. Moments later Josh stepped out from behind a tallowwood.

"I've been wandering around for an hour trying to find this place." Josh ran a hand through his hair. "Thought I'd make noise so you'd hear me. Need some help?"

I glanced over my shoulder at Seth who stood with his hands shoved into his pockets. His face wasn't letting on how he felt about Josh being there, but I knew him well enough to know he didn't like it.

I looked back at Josh and nodded. "That would be nice. You and Abby were … You should be here."

We stepped over the wall together, and when I reached

the graves, I went to Abby first. She would be easier to bury because she wasn't my brother. If I went through the process with her first, I hoped it would ease the burden when it came to Archer. Or maybe I wasn't quite ready to put him in the ground.

I knelt beside Abby, pulling the blanket away from her face. She looked peaceful, apart from the gaping hole in her neck where the vampire had sucked the life from her. Blood and dirt smeared her skin. I blinked away more tears. We hadn't always been friends, but I would miss Abby. She'd helped me in ways I never thought anyone could.

Josh stared down at her, his jaw set. He stood perfectly still until I slipped the blanket back over Abby's face. We lifted her onto the timber plank Seth had put aside to lower her into the grave. He'd tied a rope to either end, so Josh and I grabbed hold and gently put Abby into the ground.

Seth grabbed the shovel from where he'd left it and started putting dirt back in. None of us spoke. When the grave was half filled, Josh went to Seth and held his hand out for the shovel. No words passed between them, but I thought I saw a flicker of understanding and it gave me hope. Seth and I watched as Josh filled in the rest of Abby's grave.

Burying Archer was harder. I couldn't see through the tears, but I insisted on lowering him in as well. This time Seth helped, and I let him.

I went numb and ended up on my knees at the foot of the grave, watching every shovel of dirt as it fell into the hole. I cried until I didn't have the energy to cry any more, and Seth lifted me into his arms to take me home.

"I don't want to leave him." I stared over his shoulder as he carried me over the wall.

I'm sorry, Seth thought.

And I knew he was.

By the time the three of us reached the shed, it was almost dark. Hope and Justice weren't there.

Seth set me on my feet near the trampoline. "It's time we talked."

I stepped onto the trampoline and bounced a little as I made my way to the centre, sitting with my legs crossed and my hands in my lap.

Staring up at Seth I said, "Okay then. Talk."

24

SETH
Friday night

Grace wanted me to talk, and I didn't know where to begin. She'd want to know everything, but how far back should I go?

I glared at Josh. "Can you not be here?"

He folded his arms and stared back. "I'm not going anywhere. I want to know she's safe."

"She's perfectly safe with me."

"Really? Was Archer?"

"Stop!" Grace said, getting to her feet. The trampoline mat moved beneath her. "Would you listen to yourselves? Stop fighting for once, please."

I don't want him here, I thought. *What I have to tell you doesn't concern him.*

Grace's face softened and she bit her lip, nodding. She looked at Josh and immediately he backed away, turning before Grace opened her mouth.

"Josh ... we need some time," she said.

"I get it," he said without looking back.

Grace and I watched him disappear into the forest, and she sat on the trampoline again, crossing her legs and waiting.

With a sigh I ran a hand through my hair, and paced the grass in front of her. I needed to start with the original deal I'd made with Michael. The deal that started all of this and set everything in motion.

"After I fell ... I made a deal with Michael."

"I thought as much," Grace said.

I spun and faced her. "Would you please ... don't interrupt. This is hard enough as it is."

"Sorry ... keep going. I won't say anything."

"When I fell, I landed at the gates of Hell. I was lost, and scared, but mostly angry. The gates tempted me and invited me in, but I refused. I thought it would be the easy way, and after everything that's happened, I think I would've been right."

Grace stared from the middle of the trampoline, her head cocked to one side, listening. I'd expected her to have interrupted again, but she waited patiently.

"I didn't want the easy way, because I wanted to punish myself. I instantly regretted leaving you, and being swallowed by the fires of Hell wasn't punishment enough. When I found my way back to Earth, Michael came to me. He'd been sent by the Council to strip me, but he'd decided I deserved a different punishment. He wanted me to suffer for what I'd done to you, for leaving you, so he branded me with this." I held out my arm to show

Grace my tattoo.

"I'd always wondered how you'd gotten that," she said.

"Michael said it would be my permanent reminder of what I'd done, who I'd defied, and what I'd left behind."

"Michael's been pretty harsh on you over the years, hasn't he?" Grace asked.

I nodded. "Nothing I didn't deserve." I stepped onto the trampoline and it bounced under my weight. When I reached Grace, I sat opposite her with my legs crossed, our knees touching. For a moment I watched the moonlight play with her hair, dancing off the ebony strands as they moved.

"That was the beginning of all this?" Grace tucked her hair behind her ear.

I pressed my lips together. "Yes, but the deal came later. Remember when I found you in the forest and I was … younger?"

Grace laughed. "I accused you of selling your soul for your youth, only you'd already sold it." Her laugh fell away, and she frowned then looked at her hands. She pulled the sleeves of her cardigan over her fingers and played with the hem.

"Well, you were pretty much right. Michael told me I had one generation to convince you to love me again. When you gave me your heart, I'd be set free, and he'd leave me alone. If you didn't … he'd come to take my wings and send me to the In-Between."

Grace looked up and studied my face. I could see her sifting through her thoughts and trying to find the right words. She reached out and touched my face, running her thumb over my cheek.

"But I've given you my heart. What do you still owe him?"

I closed my eyes and relished her touch. She was gentle, and I embraced the love she had for me. It was real and solid, and it hurt that it was something I'd never be able to hold onto.

"I don't think Michael ever expected you to forgive me. He told me how broken you were when I'd left, and I'm not sure *I* believed you'd ever love me again either. But you did, and you do, and Michael isn't happy about it."

Grace's hand dropped from my face and I caught it between my own, closing her small fingers in mine.

"Michael tried to look after me when you left," Grace said. "But I didn't want to know him. I was angry because he'd known what you'd planned to do." She hung her head and stared at our hands. "I blamed him for you leaving. I shut him out for a long time, and then I was sent on my indefinite mission."

I sighed, wishing everyone would stop blaming everyone else for their actions. The only one I blamed for everything that had happened was myself.

"You shut me out, too."

Grace looked up. "What does he want from you now? What are you not telling me?"

I took a deep breath, ready to launch into an explanation of how Michael had changed the rules, and he'd worked everything so that no matter what happened, Grace and I would never be together, but I didn't get the chance.

A police car came out of the driveway and into the clearing, its tyres crunching on the gravel. The driver stopped when he saw us and killed the engine, stepping out onto the grass. He left the headlights on so they shone into the clearing and lit up the shadows. His partner got out of the car as well. She walked straight towards us, and I helped Grace to her feet.

"Grace Tate?" the female officer asked.

This can't be good, I thought.

"Yes," Grace said. "Can I help you?"

The male policeman joined his partner at the edge of the trampoline. "I'm Officer Daly, and this is my partner, Officer Walker. We came to see if you were all right. You were seen at the formal last night at the high school, but we couldn't account for you. I assume you know what happened?" The officers gave Grace the once over, taking in her dishevelled appearance with a frown.

"No," Grace said. "We left early."

"Is everything okay?" I asked. Daly looked at me as if I had two heads. "I'm Seth Brone."

Pretend we don't know anything, I thought, squeezing Grace's hand.

Walker took a notepad from her breast pocket and consulted it. "Yes, you're on here as well. And your brother, Grace? Archer—where is he?"

Grace's fingers dug into mine, but she shook her head. "No, sorry. He was with Abby West. He didn't come home last night."

"And neither of you know anything about what happened?" Daly asked.

"Maybe you should tell us," I said. "It seems pretty important. There was a whole bunch of dancing, and maybe some kissing, but other than that, you've got me."

The two police officers exchanged a look. "You don't watch the news?" Daly asked.

Grace shrugged.

Walker raised her eyebrows. "Someone attacked some of the students. There were … fatalities. We're doing the rounds to make sure no one else is missing."

"Oh," Grace said, pulling her hand from mine and twisting her fingers together. "That's …" She glanced up at me. "I hope it's no one we know."

I put an arm around Grace's shoulders and tucked her into my side.

Daly stared at Grace's torn and dirty dress. Frowning, she surveyed the clearing, taking in the shed, the carport, and the cottage. "You kids all right out here? Where are your parents?"

"My parents are dead," Grace said. "And I'm eighteen. I'm fine."

"You don't look it. Show me your hands, please." Daly stepped forward.

Something sounded in the forest, like someone crashing through the trees and undergrowth. The police officers turned their attention to the direction of the noise, and Grace tensed in my arms. We knew what it was, but how would we explain vampires to the police, provided they didn't get eaten first?

A few seconds later, Josh burst into the clearing from the path that led into the forest. His eyes widened at the sight of the two officers standing at the edge of the trampoline.

"Great," he said, right before a vampire crossed the tree line and barrelled into him.

He dropped his stake as they hit the ground, forcing Josh to use his fists to fend off his attacker. Hope and

Justice came out of the trees, but they had their hands full with more vampires on their tail. They were on a mission, and I cursed Michael for telling the city vamps that Grace could die.

"Excuse me," I said to the police officers, misting over to Josh and retrieving his stake from where it fell.

Josh and the vampire grappled on the ground, both of them fighting for the upper hand.

"I'm one of you," Josh said. "Get off me!"

"You're protecting her," the vamp said. "Vampires don't protect hunters."

I sighed, wishing I was anywhere else but right there. When had my existence become so complicated? I stabbed the vamp in the back, and he covered Josh in a cloud of ash. Josh got up and shook it from his hair.

"Thanks ... I think," he said.

"Get over there and glamour those cops. They need to forget about everything that's happened tonight." I didn't wait for a reply, running to help Hope and Justice.

For every vampire we dusted, another one came out of the trees, like they were waiting in line for their turn. I didn't care. I would dust them all night if it meant keeping them away from Grace.

I pulled my stake from the chest of a girl vampire, and her ashes fell to the grass. Hope stood a few metres away, watching the forest and waiting for more to come. We'd hit a lull in the attack, and I hoped that would be it.

"Why are you protecting Grace?" I asked, walking over to Hope. "You know Michael wants her to go home, and I'll bet he's said you need to see it happen."

She glanced at me, her lips pursed. "How do you know

so much?"

I laughed. "I know Michael."

Hope shook her head. "We're protecting her because this is not the way it's supposed to happen. She can't just die. She has to die right."

"Yeah ... for the one she loves the most."

I rubbed my cheek and looked over to Grace and Josh with the cops. He shook their hands and the officers got into the patrol car. All of us stood and watched as they drove back down the driveway. Grace and Josh made their way over to where I stood near the carport. Hope and Justice paced the edge of the clearing, stakes at the ready.

Grace's gaze met mine. *They won't be bothering us again,* she thought.

Josh stood beside her, too close, a permanent scowl on his face. I should have gone over and thanked him, but all I wanted to do was punch him. I thought we'd been done when we left the city, but as I'd learned the hard way, things had a way of coming back and biting me on the arse.

Justice came to my side. "I think we're okay for now."

"Don't say that." Hope came over as well. "You should never say that."

I smiled. "Never let your guard down. It's what gets you killed."

Something flashed on the other side of the clearing, near the driveway, and it wasn't until Grace was on the ground that I realised a vampire had come out of the forest and tackled her. She screamed and kicked, but the vamp pinned her down. Josh grabbed the vampire by the shoulders and tried to pull him off Grace, but the creature had his hands clamped tightly around her arms. All three of them ended up in a mass of arms and legs, kicking and flailing, Grace trying to get free while the other two fought her and each other.

I grabbed Hope's stake from her hand and misted to where Grace was on the ground, Josh and the vampire grappling on top of her. She'd curled herself into a ball underneath them while they tried to punch each other. I grabbed what parts of them I could and dragged them off her. She disappeared in a cloud of black, reappearing near the shed door. Josh got to his feet, the vamp following, and their arms and parts of their bodies became a blur as they kept fighting.

Grace ran towards me, blood trickling down her temple. Seconds later, Hope was beside her, putting her hand on her arm to heal her. Justice and I circled Josh and the vampire, looking for a clean shot.

Don't hurt him, Grace thought.

As much as I didn't like Josh, I wanted to do as Grace asked, but they were moving too fast, fighting in a frenzy of anger. My gaze connected with Justice's, and he set his lips into a thin line. I agreed with what he was thinking, but it wasn't going to end well.

Justice grabbed the vampire around the waist, twisting him away from Josh. I pulled my arm back, ready to strike, looking for an opening. Josh went in for another punch, closing the gap, and I hesitated. The vamp broke free of Justice's hold and went for Josh again. I struck forward with everything I had, aiming for the crazy vamp's back. My stake went through his skin next to his left shoulder blade, right to the hilt.

Josh cried out, his eyes widening.

Grace screamed.

The vampire struggled, his body pinned to Josh's chest. Neither of them had turned to dust.

"Grace," Josh said.

Justice ran at the vampire and slammed his stake in beside mine. This time, the vamp exploded and his ash dropped onto Josh. Justice pulled his arm back and let it fall to his side, shoulders slumped.

Josh laid there, my stake stuck in his chest too close to his heart.

"Don't move," I said, putting my hands out.

When I looked at Grace, her eyes were like windows, and I stared through at her broken soul. She fell to her knees, her mouth open, and I knew if I pulled that stake out and Josh died, I'd never be able to be the one to comfort her when all I'd done was destroy everyone she loved.

25

GRACE

I stared at the stake sticking out of Josh's chest. He was millimetres away from dying.

I didn't want him to die.

"Don't move," I said, echoing Seth's words.

Seth stared at me. His expression showed he was sorry for what had happened. He never wanted to do anything to hurt me, but he kept doing it all the same. Were we cursed to continue on this path of destruction? Was he forever going to play a part in my sadness? Would I ever be happy with him?

I couldn't answer any of those questions.

Josh took shallow breaths he didn't need. His gaze flicked from the stake to me and back again. We had to pull it out. It couldn't stay there. I flexed my fingers, put everything else out of my mind, and walked to where he lay on the grass. I'd lost so much; I wasn't going to lose

185

Josh as well. The damp grass slicked my skin when I knelt beside him, never taking my eyes from his.

"I won't lose you, too." I wrapped my hands around the stake.

"Easy," Seth said.

I glared at him. I didn't need him telling me how bad the situation was.

"I can feel it scraping," Josh said. "You have to pull it the right way."

All I could do was nod. I gritted my teeth, adjusting my grip on the stake. The world around me held its breath. I closed my eyes ... and pulled.

The stake came away from Josh's chest, but I was too scared to open my eyes. What if he wasn't there? What if he'd turned to dust at my hand?

Fingers curled around mine, clutching the stake.

"Grace."

Josh's voice.

I opened my eyes.

He sat in front of me, a small lopsided smirk on his face.

I dropped the stake and threw my arms around him. Tears streamed from my eyes, and my body shook. He gripped my shoulders and pushed me away gently.

Josh got to his feet and helped me up, his strong hands holding my shoulders. My legs wobbled, my heart aching at the thought of almost losing him as well. I wasn't sure how much more I could take.

"I need you ... more than you know," I said.

"No." He kissed my forehead softly. "You need Seth."

Seconds later, he was nothing more than a blur between the trees.

It wasn't until Josh was gone that I realised how much he'd become a part of my life. After losing Archer and Abby, his leaving was a blow I didn't know how to take. He was alive, but he was gone. Would I ever see him again?

I turned to Seth. I wanted to be happy with him. He was all I had left. Everyone else I loved was gone. It was Seth and me, and despite everything that had happened, no matter how much he had hurt me, I needed to fight for him, to fight for us, because without him, I'd be nothing.

Slowly, I walked towards Seth, swiping the tears from my cheeks and standing tall. Seth didn't move. He regarded me with a cautious and serious expression, his lips pressed into a thin line, his hands at his sides.

I set my gaze firmly on his. It took all my strength not to fall to pieces in those few short steps. But when I reached him, I couldn't help it. The moment his arms wrapped around me I fell into the darkness that was sadness, and it consumed me completely.

"I'm so sorry," Seth whispered into my hair. "For everything."

I wanted to scream at him, but I didn't have the energy. All I could do was cry and let him hold me.

I've lost so much, I thought, not meaning to let him in. But I didn't have the strength to hold my wall in place. I was tired of constantly blocking him out. It shouldn't have been that way. With Seth, I should have been able to be open all the time. The past had made us what we were, and I wondered if what we were was right for each other.

You have me, Seth thought. *You will always have me.*

"Oh my God!" Hope said. "Will you stop lying to her? Tell her the truth right now!"

My cheek lay against Seth's chest, and I listened to the rapid beat of his heart. Hope stood a few metres away, her hands on her hips, her attitude reminding me of myself. Justice paced the grass behind her, and I wondered if he'd worn a cow-track in it yet. I wished both of them would go away and leave us alone, and I couldn't figure out why they were hanging around.

I squeezed my eyes shut. Seth hadn't told me everything. He'd been about to before the police had turned up and interrupted us.

Taking a deep breath, I pulled back and stared into Seth's dark eyes. "The truth ... please."

Seth took my hands and loosened my hold around his waist. He stepped away, keeping my hands between his.

"I told you I'd made a deal with Michael, and that I'd met the conditions of that deal." He paused, as if waiting for my confirmation. "What I didn't say is ... afterwards, he changed the rules. Heaven decided they wanted you back."

"I already know that," I said.

Seth squeezed my hands. "Let me finish. Yes, they want you back, and in order for you to go home ... you have to die. But there was another condition Michael added."

I moved my lips to form the word *what,* but I didn't voice it. I waited, staring at Seth with no idea what he was about to tell me.

"I was given a choice ... protect you and keep you on Earth. Or let you die and return to Heaven."

"You chose to protect me."

"Yes." Seth nodded. "I did. Because I know you don't want to go back there."

"Tell her the best part," Justice said, pacing and not

breaking stride.

My hands grew sweaty in Seth's grasp, but he didn't let go, and I didn't want him to.

"If you die and return to Heaven," Seth said, "I will go free. Michael will leave me alone and stop finding ways to punish me for what I did to you all that time ago."

Seth stopped, and there was something in his eyes I hadn't seen for a long time. They glistened under the moonlight, and a single tear spilled onto his cheek. Suddenly, I didn't want to hear what he was about to tell me. I'd seen Seth angry so many times, but this was the second time in all my existence I'd ever seen him cry, and I had the diamond around my neck to prove it. If whatever he was about to tell me made him this upset, I couldn't let him speak the words, because then it would make it real.

It's already real, Grace, he thought.

"If I fight to keep you here, then Michael will hunt me down until he finds me ... He'll never stop, and he'll send me to oblivion for eternity."

Even though my hands were the only part of me Seth touched, I felt smothered, as if he'd thrown a hot, heavy blanket over me and I couldn't get it off. It took a few moments for my mind to work out that no matter which way this went, I'd lose him. But it also meant there was only one choice I could make.

Seth shook his head. "No ... this is why I didn't want you to know. You can't make a decision because of me. You can't do something you don't want to do because of me."

"How could I do anything else?" I said. "I've lost everyone except you. And now you tell me I'm going to lose you as well, no matter what I do." I blinked the tears from my eyes. "I'm so mad at you for every reason possible, but it's better to lose you and have you be free."

Seth clenched his jaw, the muscles in his neck working as he ground his teeth. "You don't have to sacrifice what you want for me."

I laughed. "You did for me. Isn't that how this started?"

Seth reached up with one hand and touched my cheek, using his thumb to wipe away my tears. His other hand held mine tightly.

"I think you've left something out," Hope said.

Justice stopped pacing and stared at his sister.

Lights appeared at the tree line on the edge of the clearing. Tiny spheres of blue spun around themselves until Michael appeared. I hated how he always turned up at the eleventh hour.

None of us said a word as he sauntered over to the trampoline. Once upon a time I'd loved Michael like a brother. But now ... I wanted to be as far away from him as possible. He'd brought all of this on us, and even though I'd almost come close to forgiving him for not telling me about Seth's intentions, I could never forgive him for the pain he'd put me through since.

"Yes, you did leave out a vital part. You forgot to tell her who she had to die for," Michael said.

I pulled my hands from Seth's and wrung my fingers together, the sweat forming a thin film on my skin. I stepped towards Michael and gave him a piece of my mind.

"I don't care what you have to say. You cursed Seth because of what he did to me, but look at this." I spread my arms wide. "Look at what you've done to us. You've caused far more damage chasing after your own vendetta.

You've made my life miserable because of your hatred for Seth. And you call yourself an archangel ... the epitome of goodness." I took a deep breath and let my arms fall to my sides. "You're nothing but a hypocrite."

Michael shook his head. "You may have always fought for what *you* believe in, Grace. But so have I." He stopped and stared into my eyes, not blinking. "Do you choose to come home, or stay here?" His gaze flicked to Seth.

I relaxed my fingers and looked at my hands. Angry, red half-moons crossed my palms and blood smeared my skin. If I stayed, Seth would be gone, and I would die, because I couldn't see the Council giving me back my immortality if I decided to stay fallen. I looked at Seth, his face a mask of hurt and anger. Still, he stood tall and set his mouth in a thin line. If I chose to die, I'd lose him, but he'd be free.

"I'll come home." I looked to Michael.

He nodded and walked over to us. Michael knelt on one knee and lifted the leg of Seth's jeans. He unsheathed the dagger strapped to his ankle and stood again. Michael handed the dagger to Seth, hilt first. Seth stared at it but didn't take it.

"You have to be the one to do it," Michael said.

"What?" Seth took a step back. "No! You can't ask me to do that." He grabbed my arm and pulled me behind him.

"What does he mean?" I asked, unable to believe that Michael had asked Seth to kill me.

"She has to die for the one she loves the most." Michael's gaze never left Seth's. "Since he's now dead, it only seems fitting you be the one to finish this."

Archer was the one I was supposed to die for? But I

didn't love him any more than I loved Seth. He was my brother. It was a different kind of love, but no more or less intense. The bottom line was, Seth could have saved Archer *and* himself, yet he chose me. Yes, I was angry that Archer had died as a result, but Seth had sacrificed his own future because I didn't want to go back to Heaven. I didn't want to go back, but now I knew what would happen to him, it was the only thing I could do.

"You could've saved yourself," I said. "I could've saved you. All you had to do was let me die."

Seth shook his head. "I couldn't. I will always choose you ... no matter what the consequences."

I blinked away more tears. Michael held the knife in the same position, hilt facing Seth. I took it and pressed it into Seth's palm.

"I've watched everyone I love die or leave," I said. "I can't watch them take you, too."

Seth tried to resist me, but I grabbed his wrist and he finally wrapped his fingers around the hilt of the dagger. His eyes glistened in the moonlight.

"I'm still here," he said.

"But you won't be. Do it." I pushed the dagger towards him. "Kill me ... it will save you. You have to, otherwise this will mean nothing." I grasped the chain at my neck and the diamond tear on the end sparkled.

"I don't want to lose you." Seth blinked, and a tear touched his cheek. He stared into my eyes. "You don't want this."

"I don't want them to lock you up. I want you to be free." I adjusted my grip on Seth's wrist and angled his hand so the dagger's tip rested on my chest. "I would rather die than live with losing you forever."

For a moment it seemed the world held its breath. Michael stood a few metres away, unmoving. Justice stopped pacing, and Hope slid her hand into his. I hated we had an audience, even though it was small. I wanted my last moments with Seth to be ours, but I had to share it.

Kiss me, I thought, and he did.

His mouth was hot against mine. He tasted salty from the tears both of us shed, running down our faces and mixing on our lips.

I will find my way back to you. I promise, I thought.

I'll hold you to that. Seth pulled away.

The dagger was in place. Its tip broke my skin, and a trickle of blood ran down my chest. I wanted to make this as easy for him as I could. Seth didn't want to do it, and I didn't blame him. I couldn't have put a dagger through his heart if I'd been told to. I would have rather died as well. But I was the one who had to face death.

"I love you," I said, pushing myself forward as hard as I could.

I screamed as the knife slid into me. The pain was hot, like fire spreading through my chest. Then my arms went cold, and I closed my eyes.

Seth's face was the last thing I saw.

26

SETH

Grace's knees buckled, and I caught her before she hit the ground. My dagger stuck out of her, buried to the hilt. It seemed like a cruel joke, and she was the punchline. I hadn't been prepared for her to force my hand. I'd been trying to find a way for her not to have to die. In the end, she'd done it for me, and the selfish part of me was glad she had.

I touched her cheek, her hair, and her lips with my fingertips, trying to find comfort in the thought that she wasn't really dead. But she would be dead to me, because once she returned to Heaven I would never see her again.

My knees gave way, and I slid to the grass with her in my arms. I pressed my forehead to hers and closed my eyes, letting my tears fall and splash onto her cheeks.

"You need to pull it out," Michael said, standing over us. "The dagger."

I hated him more than I had ever hated him in the past. Grace was my everything, and he had taken her from me.

"She won't go until you pull it out." Michael waited.

I glared at him. Hope and Justice crept nearer to watch, and I wanted to scream at them to go away. Turning my gaze back to Grace's face, I touched her lips again, burning her into my memory as deeply as I could.

"I love you, too," I whispered.

I took a deep breath and wrapped my hand around the dagger's handle. Blood trickled over the pale skin of Grace's chest and onto the fabric of her dress, mingling with the blood, dirt, and grime that was already there. She looked so peaceful, like she was sleeping.

The dagger didn't move as easily as I'd thought it would, and I had to pull quite hard. More blood oozed from the wound, but the second the tip came away and no part of the knife was left inside her, Grace's back arched and her lips parted. I dropped the dagger and cradled her across my lap, holding onto what I was about to lose. Black mist poured from Grace's mouth, rising into the air in thin tendrils and dissipating against the night sky.

Her hand jerked and light exploded from the ring on Grace's finger, sending a blanket of blue spheres over us. They floated down and when they settled onto her body, they burned.

The celestial fire spread until it covered Grace in blinding blue light. It licked at my clothing, burning through until it reached my skin. The pain was intense, but I held onto her for as long as I could. The fire danced over and around us. I would have to let Grace go. I didn't want to let her go. Then she *was* gone, and I was left with an ache in my heart.

When I raised my head, tears streaked Hope's face. She clutched Justice's hand so tightly I wasn't sure if his grimace was because of that or Grace's death. Michael wore a blank expression, and I wanted to punch him. He could have at least expressed some sort of emotion. He held his hand out to help me up. I stared at it, remembering the last time he'd offered me the gesture, and I'd ended up with a tattoo branded onto my arm.

I pulled my legs under myself and got to my feet on my own. I didn't want or need his help.

I clenched my jaw and faced Michael, my hands itching to hit him. "Are you happy now? I have nothing left. Which is what you wanted, isn't it?"

Michael regarded me for a moment, crossing his arms over his chest. "I think you've been punished enough."

I shook my head. "It doesn't end here. This will stay with me forever."

Michael came towards me, and I balled my hands into fists, ready for whatever he was about to do. He relaxed his arms by his sides and stopped within touching distance, staring into my eyes without a hint of regret or remorse.

He offered me his hand again, and again I didn't want to take it. We were not friends, and I was done with politeness and niceties.

"Can we not part on good terms?" Michael asked.

I laughed, but I didn't think what he'd said was funny. "I don't think that's possible."

He shrugged. "I'm offering you a truce."

"Truce? You said you'd set me free."

Michael sighed. "For once, would you trust me?"

I wanted to spit in his face. "Trust is earned—"

"Shake my hand, you stubborn idiot," Michael said.

He raised his eyebrows, his arm outstretched. I looked from his face to his hand and back again, wondering what the catch would be this time. He'd changed the rules on so many occasions already, I was wary he'd do it again.

"I don't blame you for thinking I'll come up with some other way to torture you," Michael said, "but this time I have no ulterior intentions. Grace is home; that's all I wanted."

"What about what she wanted? Or what I wanted? Does that not count for anything?"

Michael thought for a moment, rubbing his chin with his left hand. "What if I said you could follow her ... would you go?"

"What are the terms?" I asked. "There are always conditions when it comes to your deals."

"You can see her again, but you can't actually *be* with her. You know love between angels is forbidden."

I scoffed. "Wouldn't that put us right back where all of this started? I think I'll leave it in Grace's hands. She said she'd find her way back to me, and I believe her."

Michael extended his right hand again, waiting for me to take it. "Okay then. Like I said, you should trust me. And from now on, you can."

I hesitated but finally took it, and when my palm connected with his, he grasped my hand tightly and pumped my arm once in a firm shake. But he didn't let go. Heat flowed into me, and even though he was holding my right hand, my left arm burned. I held it out and watched as the cross tattooed there disappeared. The knots that symbolised my never-ending torment unravelled before my eyes until the black mark was completely gone.

Michael loosened his grip and let go. "You're free, Seth. I won't bother you again."

I didn't feel any different, and there was no relieving weight lifted from my shoulders, because I may have been freed from Michael, but I would never be free of Grace. Her memory would haunt me for the rest of my existence.

Michael backed away towards Hope and Justice.

"What happens now?" I asked. "There's no one to protect Hopetown Valley."

"That's not for you to worry about," Michael said. "You're not bound to me anymore, so you can wash your hands of this entire place."

I looked around the clearing, at the shed, the cottage, the rusted farm truck and the Defender sitting in the car port. Everything around me had been touched by Grace. She filled every space in this world.

I wasn't going anywhere.

27

GRACE
Heaven

When the knife had slid into me, it had hurt, but then I didn't feel anything, only an empty void in my chest that should have been filled with Seth. I was missing the most vital part of myself, and I didn't know how to fill the space that had opened up in my heart.

The darkness surrounded me, and it took a while for the stars to come into focus. It was as if they'd been holding their breaths, waiting for me to let go of mine before they started to breathe with me.

The last time I'd been in the Outer Realm, Seth had been with me, and it made being here now all the harder. All it did was remind me of him, what he'd done, and what I'd done to save him. I hoped Michael had kept his promise to set him free, and that my sacrifice hadn't been for nothing.

"It hasn't," Michael said from behind me.

I beat the air gently with my wings and turned to face him. The two of us hovered in the darkness, surrounded by a sugary blanket of stars.

"You set him free?" I asked.

"I always keep my promises."

I had so many questions for Michael—the first, what was I supposed to do once I got back home? I'd been away from Heaven for so long it was bound to feel foreign. And how was I to act in a world where I didn't want to be? How could they expect me to slip back in so easily? Why did they even want me to?

"The Council is eager to see you," Michael said.

I pressed my lips together. "Wish I could say the same about them."

"Please don't make this harder than it has to be, Grace."

I wanted to laugh. It seemed making things hard was what I did. "Can we go?"

I fluttered my wings and turned, searching for the re-entry star. It was the brightest star in the sky and would take us back to Heaven. My wing-tips flicked, and I noticed something I hadn't before. They were black, and when I craned my neck, stretching my wings out to the sides, they were not white like I'd expected. I was still fallen.

"Why?" I questioned Michael with my eyes, gesturing towards my wings.

"You haven't been fully reinstated," he said. "All in good time."

Michael took my hand, and I had to resist the urge to pull away. After everything he'd done to separate Seth and me, I didn't want to touch him. But I put up with it and let him guide me towards the star.

"I'm not happy about any of this," I said. "I did it for Seth. There's no other reason I'm here."

"I know," Michael said.

When we reached the star, it pulled us through and everything turned white. The brilliance surrounded us completely, and I should have felt safe, but all it did was suffocate me. I didn't want to be there, and the more I told myself that, the harder it was to accept what was happening.

Cloud dust formed around our feet, but we stood on solid ground. The whiteness changed to include shades of soft grey-blue, and the surface we stood on rose upwards until we emerged into the departure area of Heaven. Memories from the last time I'd stood on the departure pad came rushing back. It was when I'd been sent to Earth to start my mission with the Tate family. My heart lurched thinking about Archer, and again I wished I was anywhere but where I was. I wanted to be back in Hopetown Valley with Archer and Seth and Abby. I wished Emma and Ryan were alive, and I wished that Josh had never been turned into a vampire.

I blinked to clear the tears forming in my eyes and focused on my surroundings. The cloud dust moved around us like I remembered. It was soft and lapped at my ankles. When the departure pad came to a stop, Michael tugged my hand and led me off. I wondered where Daniel was. He'd always been there without fail whenever I'd left or arrived back from a mission. Not seeing his smiling face saddened me, and then he came into the room and took his place behind the arrivals desk.

"Sorry, Michael, I wasn't expecting you back yet," he said. "Hello, Grace."

Daniel smiled, and I couldn't help smiling back.

Michael led me to the desk that serviced the departure pad and also acted as the arrivals centre for anyone returning from a mission. Daniel produced a clipboard and pen, laying it in front of me.

"Sign your life away," Michael said.

I picked up the pen and scanned the document on the board. It had the usual reinstating details, like it had every other time I'd returned, but this time it didn't specify where I was being reinstated to. Instead, it said *UNDER REVISION* in big, red letters. I wondered if I'd get my white wings back when I touched the pen to the paper.

I didn't.

I dropped the pen on the counter and stood back.

"What now?" I asked.

"Now … we see the Council." Michael headed towards the exit. "Follow me."

What choice did I have? I was a fallen angel in Heaven. There was nowhere I could go where they wouldn't find me.

I gave Daniel a tight-lipped smile. "I'll see you soon."

He came around to my side of the desk and wrapped me in a big hug. "It's good to have you back, Grace. I've missed you."

I tentatively hugged him, not used to seeing him show much affection other than his bubbly smiles and greetings. I thought it best not to say anything, and he gave me a final squeeze before letting go.

"Look after her," Daniel said as I passed through the door with Michael.

Michael waved over his shoulder but didn't respond in any other way.

I followed him along the corridor I'd walked so many times before, but we didn't head towards the path that led to the cloud field. Instead, we turned left into a small room where Michael stopped. I'd never been into this room before, and I wanted to ask where we were. Before I could, the wall of cloud in front of us parted and an elevator door opened. Michael gestured for me to step in and he followed.

Once the doors closed, he pulled a card from his pocket and swiped it over a silver panel, punching in a number.

"Let me guess ... this elevator I've never seen before goes straight to the chambers?"

"You guessed correctly," Michael said.

"We could have taken the stairs."

"There are lots of things we *could* have done." Michael looked at me sideways and I faced the door, wishing I was anywhere but under his scrutinising eye. Yes, there were a lot of things I could have done differently—like everything since the start of school this year.

"Now you're getting all judgy on me?" I said. "When I have nowhere to go and no one to defend me?"

"The Council's job is to judge. I'm merely taking you there."

With those words, the elevator dinged and the doors opened. We stepped out to an all-too-familiar setting. The marble door of the Council's chamber stood before us, already in view as if they had been expecting us.

"They *have* been expecting us," Michael said. "You can open the door ... I presume you remember how."

I scowled. Of course I remembered how. I stepped forward and ran my fingertips up and down the marble. It was cool to touch, and I shivered. I couldn't remember it being cold in the past. The marble vibrated before the slab separated, and the two halves slid open. Michael pressed his hand into the small of my back and gave me a nudge into the room.

Suddenly, I was very aware of my appearance. I wore my ruined formal dress, covered in dirt, grime, and blood. My wings were grey, edged with black, and I was like a dirty mark on a white sheet.

The cloud dust floated around my ankles as I moved to the middle of the room. The twelve thrones were as I remembered them, lining the circular wall of the chamber. They were empty, or at least they seemed to be. I'd never seen a council member in person.

"Welcome home, Grace," the collective voice boomed. When the Council spoke it was as if one voice was speaking, yet it also sounded like many voices. It was disorienting.

I didn't respond. What was I supposed to say? It was nice to be back? Well, it wasn't. I didn't want to be there. I wanted to be with Seth, and with every passing moment I wondered if I'd made the right choice.

"It took a bit of work to get you here," the Council said.

"I don't believe in rewarding anyone if they don't put in the effort," I said.

The room was silent for a moment, and Michael rubbed his face, shaking his head slightly. If he thought I was going to lie down like a good little puppy and roll over, he was mistaken.

"We also see you haven't lost your attitude," the Council

said.

"And you haven't lost your ..." I looked around the room, "... starkness."

The cloud dust in the room swirled, as if the Council were taking combined breaths.

"We need to address your status," they said. "You may have noticed that you are still fallen, and returning here has not given you back what you threw away."

"I did not make that decision lightly." I moved farther into the room. "You forced my hand, pushing me to make a decision I should never have had to make."

"It was not your decision to make in the first place," the Council said. "You were ordered, and you directly disobeyed us."

I turned and glared at Michael. He stood with his hands clasped behind his back, staring at the floor of the chamber. I wanted to swat him, because there was no one else in the room in a physical form who I could swat. I wanted to argue my case now I was standing directly in front of the Council, but anything I had to say would land on deaf ears. They saw things in black and white. There were no shades of grey or colour in their world. Something either had to be done or it didn't. People were either good or evil. There was no questioning, or arguing. There was only what they said should be. Seriously, why had I come back?

Seth.

He was why, and again it was proof that what the Council wanted was what they got. Someone needed to give them a reminder of what the word "good" meant, and not everything was as plain as black versus white.

The world was full of colours they never knew existed.

I took a deep breath. "I have always stood up for what I believe in—even if it's not what *you* want me to believe."

"Grace Tate, do you want to be fully reinstated?" the Council asked, ignoring me. I hated how they always did that. They only answered or acknowledged things that suited them.

"I'm here because again, you forced my hand. If I had a real choice, I'd be on Earth with Seth. I want no part of this life anymore. I made my decision, and I stick by it."

I may have become fallen, but I fell for a good reason. I'd fallen for love, not only because I'd been in love with Josh at the time, but because I loved my friends, and I believed in protecting them. I'd fallen for Charlotte, because I would not kill her. I'd seen the good in her and I'd believed she could be saved. I never regretted falling, but I did regret not saving those I fell for.

It didn't matter anyway. I couldn't change anything. All I could do was deal with it.

"We will ask you this once more ... do you want to be fully reinstated?" the Council's voice echoed around the chamber.

"No," I said. "I do not."

Michael sighed beside me, and I wondered when he'd moved so close.

"Take her away," the Council said. "We'll see what she has to say tomorrow."

Michael grabbed my arm and pulled me towards the door.

"What, that's it? Where are you taking me?" I tried to free myself from Michael's hold.

DIE FOR ME

The Council didn't respond, and neither did Michael. He ran his fingers down the marble door when we reached it, then yanked me through after it opened. The chamber fell into the clouds around us as soon as the door slid shut, and I was left standing in the whiteness, Michael clutching my arm, and staring at me with a look that could set Hell on fire.

28

GRACE

I yanked my arm from Michael's clutches and headed
for the stairway that led to the cloud field. To say I was
angry with him and the Council would be an understate-
ment. The deal was, I died and returned to Heaven—I
never thought to ask if it included getting my status back.
I'd assumed that was a given. Obviously, I'd thought wrong.

"Where are you going?" Michael asked, orbing and
appearing next to me.

"Anywhere you aren't."

The cloud dust plumed into the air as I passed through
it, the turbulence mimicking my mood. I clenched my fists
and tried to mist away from Michael, but it didn't work.

I stopped and turned on him. "You've taken my powers
as well?"

"We can't have you flitting around like you own the
place."

I wanted to stamp my foot like a child; Michael made me so mad. What was I supposed to do? Be a prisoner?

"All you had to do was agree to be reinstated," Michael said.

"But I don't want to be." I folded my arms over my chest. "I assumed that would happen when you made Seth kill me. I didn't think you'd give me the choice."

"Well … you've been asked to choose."

"And I told you no. I didn't want this. I'm here because you played dirty. I'm here for Seth so you wouldn't lock him up for eternity."

Michael took a deep breath and let it out slowly. "And like I always said to Seth … your choices are your own."

"Can I go?" I asked. "If I look at you any longer, I might throw up."

Michael regarded me for a few moments, then brushed past me and headed down the staircase. "You have restricted access." He orbed and disappeared in a mass of blue spheres.

Restricted access? Great. So I was stuck in a place I didn't want to be, and I had no idea where I was allowed to go. There was only one way to find out. Since I couldn't mist anywhere, I went down the stairs intending to go to the cloud field. I didn't particularly want to see any of the angels I used to be friends with, but I was hoping I could find someone who I might be able to talk to.

As far as I knew, I was the first fallen angel in Heaven, and I didn't know what that meant or if there was anything special I should know. I needed someone to tell me, but I wouldn't get any answers from Michael. Maybe Daniel could help me.

I'd been walking for what I thought was a reasonable amount of time to reach the cloud field, yet I hadn't made it there. I stopped and glanced around, trying to find anything familiar so I could get my bearings. All I could see was white, and it stretched on forever.

I sighed, wondering if Michael was playing tricks on me.

I'd no sooner had the thought than the gate to the field appeared between the clouds. I went up to it and ran my fingers up and down its seamless centre. The silver was cool to touch, like the marble of the chamber door had been. I couldn't remember it being cold before— usually everything in Heaven was warm.

The gate opened, and I walked through. Angels milled about, talking to each other, while others came and went on whatever missions they'd been assigned. The movement within the field was constant, but it wasn't until I'd reached the centre that I realised not one angel had looked at me or tried to speak to me.

I stopped and turned in a circle, trying to make eye contact with someone, anyone. But none of them would look at me. They were supposed to be my friends, but they acted like I didn't exist. I held my hand in front of my face. It looked solid. I pinched my arm and winced at the sharp pain. I looked at my torn and messed up formal dress. Why couldn't anyone see me? I stuck out like the only mountain on a flood plain. I was black, and they were white.

There was something not letting them see me, and I didn't understand what it was. If Michael and Daniel could see me, why couldn't the rest of the angels?

I walked farther into the field, gasping when Annie passed

by. She looked at me, but when I went to talk to her she had no recognition in her eyes. She stared straight through me. I hadn't seen her since she'd been released from her ring during the fight in Wide Island City, and she was one of the last angels I wanted to talk to anyway, but still.

The movement in the cloud field continued, and I'd never felt so alone in all my existence. I reached out to touch a passing angel, someone I'd never spoken to before, and although my hand brushed her arm, my grip slipped and she kept walking. The angel didn't acknowledge me, and I was even more confused as to how I could have touched her without her feeling it.

The cloud dust spun around my feet as I twisted and turned, searching for the gate and my way out of the field. I couldn't take it. My breath shortened and my chest tightened. How could I have ever liked being there? I wanted out, but I didn't know which way to go. I stumbled in the direction I hoped was right, my gaze cast downwards to my feet so I didn't have to look at all the angels ignoring me. I wanted to curl into a ball and disappear, but to them I was already invisible.

I chanced a look up and finally spotted the gate in the distance. All I could think about was getting beyond the cloud field limits and back into the open space. Without realising what I was doing, I ran towards it, but it didn't get any closer.

Cloud dust exploded in front of me, and I stopped. It rose into the air like a fountain spout. When it settled, Michael stood before me. He fixed me with a serious stare, his brow pinched and his lips pressed into a thin line.

"What's happening?" I asked, unable to hide the

quaver in my voice. "Why can't they see me? Why can't they see you?"

"I'm an archangel. I'm seen only when I want to be. And you're fallen." Michael balled his hands into fists. "They have no reason to acknowledge you. You're not one of them ... one of us."

"Then why am I here? Why did you bring me back?"

Michael's jaw tightened. "You belong here."

It was my turn to clench my fists, and my nails dug into my palms. A moment ago I'd been disoriented and scared. Now I was bordering on angry. I was tired of Michael manipulating me and telling me what was supposed to happen. I didn't belong anywhere I didn't want to be.

"That's not a good enough reason, and you know it." I glared at him, standing as tall as I could. "I only belong here if I want to be here. So I'll ask again ... why did you put me through Hell to get me back to Heaven? Why is the Council so secretive?"

Michael's jaw worked as he ground his teeth. He was the angriest I'd ever seen him. The way he stood with his fists balled so tightly made the muscles on his arms stick out, and the fire in his eyes burned into me, like he was trying to set fire to my soul.

"You needed to be removed," he finally said, his voice even. "You were becoming a liability ... making too many bad decisions."

"Didn't you tell me my choices were my own?"

Michael's stare never left me. "You'd lost sight of the mission."

I shook my head. "No, Michael. I've never lost sight of what I believe in. I kept fighting even after Heaven threw me away like a broken toy. I fought for love, and friendship, and the goodness I could see when everyone else refused to look." I took a step forward. "I fought until you wouldn't let me fight anymore. Until *you* took away everything I had that was worth fighting for."

Michael glared down at me, and I couldn't help wondering if what he was telling me was nothing but an excuse to hide the real reason they'd wanted me to come home.

It was Michael's turn to take a step forward. "You think you're the only one this is about? The universe does not revolve around you, Grace." He took another step, and he was close enough to tower over me, but I wouldn't be intimidated.

"I'm not scared of you," I said. "I never have been. And I learnt a long time ago not everything is about me. The universe? It's a big place, and we *all* need to do our part to keep it together. I don't care what my status is. In the scheme of things, it doesn't matter. What matters is how we treat the ones we love."

Michael stared down at me. "As an angel, your status is what defines you."

"No." I shook my head and placed my hand on his chest, over his heart. "What's in here is what defines you."

Michael closed his eyes and bowed his head. His hair fell across his forehead, and I resisted the urge to brush it aside.

"You went rogue," he said quietly. "At first I thought the Council would let it be. After all, they let me help you in Wide Island. But when I returned, I was given a choice … I chose you." Michael opened his eyes, and the fire in them had dimmed.

My breath puffed from my lungs, and I gasped to take another, stepping back. "What choice? Tell me."

Michael licked his lips, and a little of his anger fell away. His face softened. "Bring you home … or strip you."

I took another step back. Michael's presence was so immense he made me feel claustrophobic. The other angels in the field closed in on me, too, and I looked around for the gate.

I needed to get outside the gate.

"If you don't accept the Council's offer to be reinstated, I will have to take your ring."

I looked at my fingers. The ring I'd worn ever since I was created had never left my right hand. If it came off, my wings would be gone, and Michael would have the power to send me to the In-Between or kill me.

I'd already died once, and I didn't want to do it again. I'd promised Seth I'd find a way back to him, and I planned on keeping that promise.

"I need time," I said. "The decision is mine, isn't it?"

Michael took a few steps back. "I'll come for you again soon. Make sure you have an answer for me." He turned and walked towards the cloud field gates.

"What? When? How long?" I asked, but he didn't look back.

When I blinked, I stood outside the field and the gates clanged shut, the sound echoing into the expanse of whiteness that surrounded me. Michael and the Council were trying their best to force me to comply, but I couldn't make this decision. How was I supposed to choose between Heaven and oblivion, when neither of them was my first choice? Seth would always come first.

29

SETH
Saturday night

She'd been gone a day, and my world had fallen apart the moment she'd left. I couldn't believe Grace was dead, and I'd been left to pick up the broken pieces that didn't fit together.

I'd spent the day in a mind-numbing stupor, moving from the couch to the kitchen to Grace's bedroom, not sure exactly what I'd been looking for. Whatever it was, I wasn't going to find it.

The shed door clicked closed behind me, and I strode across the clearing towards the cottage. Michael had said I didn't need to worry about Hopetown Valley, but this was my town. I'd been here as long as Grace had, and I wasn't about to walk away from the only place I knew as home.

My boots clomped on the steps up to the veranda and

I opened the door to the cottage, flicking the light on as I went inside. If I was going to do this, I needed more weapons now I didn't have Grace and Archer to fight with.

I stood in the lounge room and stared at the wall, then ran my palm over the smooth surface around where the keypad should have been. A small hole opened when I found the right place. Now all I had to do was figure out the code. Grace and Archer had never told me. I tried the obvious choice of Grace's birthday in a few different orders. Then I tried Archer's. I also tried their names, but nothing worked. I looked more closely, and discovered there were some numbers where the black ink in the little grooves had worn away. I tried another few combinations with the worn numbers, but again, nothing.

I pressed my forehead to the wall and racked my brain for something, anything I thought Grace would use as a code. They could be letters instead of numbers. I pulled my phone from my pocket and called up the dial screen. Each number had three or four letters beneath it. I rubbed my face and considered giving up and going into the forest to fight the vampires with my bare hands. Then I had a thought. Grace and Archer had probably used a name, so I ran through all the names of the people who were important to them. There were three I could think that had four letters in them. Emma, Ryan, and me—Seth.

First I tried my name, and I had to admit, I was disappointed when it didn't work. My next bet was on Emma, so I punched in 3-6-6-2, and the door to the armoury slid open. I shook my head and smiled.

I'd been inside the walls of the cottage several times since I'd starting fighting with Grace, but I'd never taken the time to look closely at what was in there. Grace was everywhere. She was in the organisation of the weapons that lined the walls, in the neatly stacked diaries on the small table, and in the beautifully scripted handwriting that filled them. She was all around me, in everything I saw, and I wanted more than ever to be able to reach out and touch her.

I strapped a stake belt around my waist before crouching down to take the dagger sheath off my ankle. The dagger that had killed Grace was inside it, her blood dried on the blade. Now that it had taken her life, I didn't ever want to use it again. I set it on the table on top of the most recent book which lay open at the last log.

There were plenty more daggers, and I took the closest one from a peg on the wall, weighing it in my grip before strapping it to my ankle. I had everything I needed so I locked the armoury and headed back to the clearing.

The forest was dark with the promise of vampires to kill. I hated Michael for taking Grace away from me, and if I couldn't take it out on him, I'd take it out on the vamps instead. Even though we'd dusted a lot of vamps on the night of the formal, there would be more lurking out there. All I had to do was look for them.

The leaves and debris on the forest floor crackled beneath my steps as I headed along the path from the clearing. I curved around to the left and headed towards the school. There was a lot of forest between me and the school grounds, but it seemed like a good place to start. If I ran out of luck and didn't find anything, I'd punch a tree instead. It usually helped me release the anger a little.

The forest filled with night noises from scurrying

animals and birds in the trees. I listened as I walked, honing in on anything out of place.

After I'd been walking for about ten minutes, someone started to follow me. I kept going and doubled back to get behind them.

It seemed odd that a vampire would stalk me. Usually they came out swinging, so I figured I wasn't being followed by any of the undead.

I stopped and glanced around. Peering through the semi-darkness, I took a stake from my belt and held it at the ready.

It didn't take long for me to spot my stalker. Hope stepped out from behind a tallowwood.

I let my arm fall to my side. "What are you doing here?"

"I could ask you the same thing." She walked towards me, the filtered moonlight bouncing off her dark hair.

"What does it look like I'm doing? I'm hunting."

"Michael said you didn't need to worry about Hopetown Valley."

"Yeah, well, Michael isn't here. And I need something to distract me."

Hope and I eyed each other for a few moments. I probed the edges of her thoughts, unsure what I was looking for, but it didn't matter. She had them locked up tight.

The trees above me rustled and Justice landed a few metres away, his boots crunching on the forest floor. "How's that working out for you?"

I narrowed my eyes, wondering why they'd come back. It couldn't have been out of the goodness of their hearts. I figured the hunting duo was up to something, but I had no idea what. My first guess was that Michael wanted to keep an eye on me, and he didn't want to do it himself.

"You two are checking up on me," I said. "Shouldn't you be back in the city by now? I thought you were heading home when you left with Michael."

"We've been ordered to stay until everything dies down," Hope said. "There's also a certain vampire still in the area."

"Keeping an eye on you is a bonus." Justice grinned, and I wanted to punch him. How anyone could be smiling after the past few days was beyond me. But then again, he hadn't lost the one angel he existed for. I'd like to see him smiling the day it happened to him.

"No wonder you never said goodbye," I scoffed. "And Josh is still here? Why?"

"Probably the same reason you are," Hope said. She smiled. "Everything is covered in Grace."

I turned and walked away from them. I wasn't in the mood for more chit-chat, or smart-arse comments. What I was in the mood for was finding some vamps and dusting their sorry arses.

"It won't make you feel better," Hope said.

I stopped but didn't turn around. "Really? Then what will?" Sweat slicked my palms and I wiped one hand on my jeans, adjusting the grip on my stake with the other.

"She's safe, you know." Justice came and stood beside me. "Michael will look after her."

It took all my strength not to shove my stake into him, even though he wouldn't turn to dust. "That's what I'm afraid of."

I kept walking, and they kept following. Knowing my luck, Michael hadn't actually set me free, and there were some strings attached to my lack of imprisonment, such as dragging Hope and Justice around with me.

After about ten minutes, I'd had enough.

"Michael!" I yelled into the forest. An owl took flight, the flap of its wings disturbing the tree it left, making the leaves flutter. "Come here! I want to talk to you." I stood on the path, my fists clenched into angry balls.

"He won't come," Hope said quietly from my side.

"No," I said. "He won't. He already has what he came for."

Something stirred amongst the trees, and I was glad for the distraction. The situation I was in sucked more than a hungry vampire. Now was a good time to put a stake in one of them.

"You should let the professionals handle this." Justice stepped forward and twirled a stake between his fingers.

I had to resist the urge to snort. "I ran with vampires for decades. I know how to kill them."

"You sure about that now you're not Grace's sidekick anymore?" Justice sprang forward and tackled the vampire as it blurred through the forest. They slammed into a tree before hitting the ground and ending up in a tangle of arms and legs. Another vampire blurred past, and then another. In seconds we were outnumbered two to one.

I didn't have time to be angry with Justice's remark. If anything, I wanted to prove I wasn't anyone's sidekick. Although I didn't know what that would achieve. It would keep my pride intact, I guessed.

A vampire tackled me from behind and I sprawled onto the ground, sliding through leaves and bracken fern, cutting up my palms. I reached behind me and grabbed the vamp's head, giving it a quick twist to snap its neck. By the time I stood, there was one vamp left. Justice had the girl by the throat and pushed up against a tree.

"She isn't here anymore. She's gone," he said. He threw her to the ground. "Go and tell your friends to leave or you'll end up dust."

The girl vamp scrambled to find her feet, then took off through the trees.

Yes, Grace was gone, and for the first time since she'd made me push that dagger into her heart, I let myself feel it. All it had taken was for someone else to say it. I fell to my knees and tilted my head to the sky, staring at a hole in the canopy where the stars shone through. My roar filled the forest, and it felt good to let it out.

There had to be a way I could reach her, and I hoped she could somehow hear me, or at least feel me in her heart, because she was in mine.

I stared at Hope. "How can I get to Heaven?"

Her mouth dropped open and she hesitated. Pressing her lips together, Hope worried at her bottom lip. "You can't."

She was lying—otherwise it wouldn't have taken her so long to answer. If Grace could get back after becoming fallen, then I could, too.

"I think I can." I held her stare. The coldness of the forest floor seeped into the knees of my jeans. "And you're going to help me."

GRACE
Heaven

Everywhere I went looked the same. I couldn't remember Heaven being that way. It used to feel so warm and cosy, like home. Now I was a complete stranger walking through the house of someone I didn't know. Nothing was familiar. I couldn't see all the beautiful and organised commotion I remembered. No angels walked the clouds with me, and I wondered if the Council had taken everything away from me in the hope I'd accept their offer of reinstatement because I was lonely. They should have known by now that I was stubborn. I didn't want to accept their offer because they wouldn't let me make my own decisions, and do what I thought was right. It was their way or no way, and I wasn't sure I wanted to go back to that. I refused to crack under their pressure.

They manipulated us until we bowed to their will. I

was not one of their puppets anymore. In their eyes they were doing the right thing, and they were the epitome of that goodness. But for those of us who had spent any time on Earth, we saw things differently. I knew what the real world was like, and it was very different to the idealised illusion the Council showed us. Those who were fallen were fallen for a reason, and not all of those reasons were evil.

I ran my hands through the cloud dust as I walked, not knowing where I was going and not caring either. Thinking was something I didn't want to do. I needed to clear my head of everything that had happened in my recent past. I'd been through so much, and I was scared that if I thought about Archer, or Abby, or Josh … or Seth, I'd crack and break until I couldn't be put back together.

I concentrated on the feel of the clouds on my skin, walking with my stare fixed on nothing in particular, because there was nothing to look at anyway. I reached out in front of me and ran my arm back and forth, stirring the dust until it swirled upwards. When it settled, I stood face to face with Charlotte.

My instant reaction was to gasp, but then my mouth opened to say hello, only she wasn't looking at me. She passed by without a word, and I faltered. She couldn't see me either.

"Charlotte," I said to her back as she slowly moved through the clouds.

She turned her head and glanced around, but she didn't reply. It was something though, and maybe if I tried hard enough, I could get her to hear me.

I followed her through Heaven, concentrating on her

mind to see if I could get in and talk to her, but even though I could see her, I couldn't feel her presence. Every time I tried to touch her my hand would slide off, but a couple of times she glanced at her arm and it gave me hope.

We reached a staircase, and I followed Charlotte down to the next level. She moved to the centre of the massive open space and slid to her knees before stretching out onto her stomach. She parted the clouds with her hands and stared through the hole she'd made.

We were on the reflection level, and it brought back memories of the last time I'd been there, sitting with Angelica and listening to her tell me Seth wasn't worth it. She'd told me if he'd loved me he never would have left. But it was because he loved me that he'd left.

I lay down beside Charlotte and made my own window in the clouds. I stared at the earth below. Hopetown Valley looked so different from the sky, and I wondered where Seth was. I so badly wanted to see him, but the Council would never allow it. Still, I searched for his presence until my eyes went blurry.

"Where are you?" Charlotte said from beside me.

I glanced at her, wondering who she was looking for. "You too, huh? Something tells me we won't find what we're looking for from up here."

Charlotte turned her head until she stared at me. This time I saw something in her eyes other than a blank, distant glaze.

"Is someone there?" she asked, slowly looking around.

I moved my arm so I could lay my hand over hers, and when I touched her this time, I felt her skin beneath mine. She looked at her hand and frowned.

224

"I'm here," I said, hoping she would hear me, but unsure how to tell her it was me if she couldn't.

Charlotte pulled her hand from under mine and sat up, crossing her legs. She stared through her window in the clouds, and I wondered what she was looking at, or if she saw what I saw.

"I know someone's here with me," she said. "I don't know exactly who, but I can't see you down there anymore, so I'm hoping I'm right. I miss you, Grace. I miss your courage, and bravery, your love, and especially your loyalty. You were the only angel I knew who fought for all those things. Who didn't follow the rules because you were told you had to." Charlotte paused. "I thought coming home would set us both free, but it hasn't. I'm not home. This may have been my home once, but now it feels like an empty void, and I'm too small to fill it."

Charlotte took a deep breath, and I wanted to hug her and tell her I was there and I understood, even if no one else did. I took a moment to really look at her, and she looked tired, like the sadness had taken root in her soul and covered it with a blanket.

"If that *is* you, Grace, then don't let them win. They may have created us, but we were given free will for a reason, and that reason doesn't always have to be bad."

I resisted the urge to laugh, and I smiled instead, pulling myself up and sitting opposite her with my legs crossed, too. "You know me. Always fighting for what I believe in."

Charlotte looked at me, really looked at me, and our eyes met across the veil that hid me from her. I froze, hoping that what I saw in her was recognition, and not a trick of the light.

"Can you see me?" I whispered.

Charlotte nodded, and a small smile touched her lips. "I couldn't before, but now I can."

She held her hand up with her palm facing me and I mimicked her, like she was my reflection. When our palms touched, I felt warmth for the first time since I'd returned to Heaven.

"You can see me!" Tears of happiness streamed down my face, and I sat there staring at her smile as my shoulders shook from sobbing. "I've been so alone since I got back. No one has seen me ... but I don't understand how you can."

"I guess it's because I want to," she said. "The other angels have no reason to acknowledge one of the fallen. But I have every reason to acknowledge you."

I entwined my fingers with hers and squeezed. She squeezed my hand back and we smiled at each other before I returned my attention to the hole in the clouds, searching for Seth. But I couldn't find any trace of his presence. My heart ached, and I realised if I spent one more second searching for him, I'd break ... more than I already had. If I was going to be where I was, even if I didn't want to be there, I was going to have to focus on something else. On something that wouldn't remind me of what I'd lost.

I swept one hand over the cloud dust, closing the hole and obscuring my view.

Charlotte stared at our linked hands. "I have so much to tell you, but I don't think we have enough time."

"We have all the time in the world," I said.

She shook her head. "If you're here, and you're still fallen, they'll make you choose. And if I know the Council, they won't give you long."

I pressed my lips together and took a deep breath through my nose. "I don't understand why they want me back so badly."

"There are many things we will never understand about the Council."

Charlotte moved her gaze from our hands to me, and her eyes locked onto mine. She was drowning in sorrow, and I wanted to reach in and pull her from the torrent. She needed saving as much as I did, only I had no one left to save me. Everyone I loved was gone, but I realised Charlotte was the same. She was right when she'd said we were more alike than I'd thought.

"I know what I'm going to tell them," I said, "and they won't be happy."

Charlotte got to her feet, still clutching my hand, and then pulled me up, too. "There's something I want to show you."

We walked through the cloud dust, and it swirled at our feet as we moved. Charlotte took me through open fields of whiteness and along narrow alleys with cloud walls two storeys high. After a while, I was even more lost than when I'd come out of the cloud field. Nothing seemed familiar, and I wondered again if the Council were doing it on purpose to make me feel this way. If their ultimate aim was to convince me to take their offer to be reinstated, they were going about it the wrong way.

Charlotte finally stopped and let go of my hand. She reached down to touch the clouds with the tips of her fingers, and a wall rose up in front of us. It extended left and right into the distance as far as we could see.

"A dead end?" I asked. "Where are we?"

"This is the soul level," Charlotte said. "It's where the important souls come to wait to be reborn."

"Only the important ones?" I raised my eyebrows.

"The ones the Council plan on sending back to fulfil their purposes. Most of them were fallen angels who've spent their time in the In-Between and can now be reinstated. Others are from Earth, and they either died before their time, they're in a mission cycle, or their life was taken in such a way it warrants sending them back."

"How do you know all this?" I asked.

Charlotte smiled. "I've spent a lot of time here since I got back. The Council wouldn't send me to Earth again because ... you know. So they asked me to oversee the arrival of souls. Not all missions are down there. We have plenty to do up here as well."

"But you're not happy? You don't want to be here, just like me?"

"At first it was okay. Then I started to miss my freedom. In Heaven, you're always being watched."

"It's the same on Earth," I said. "Only you can run farther, and there are trees, and stuff to throw at people. Up here there's nothing but clouds." I glanced around; the only sign we were somewhere other than the cloud field was the wall in front of us. "Why did you bring me here?"

Charlotte trailed her hand down the wall and a split appeared, forming a double door. "There's someone I thought you'd like to see."

The doors opened, and I stared through at a huge void

of whiteness. There were no clouds or pieces of sky poking through, only white. And it stretched on forever. Small orbs of light floated in the void, sometimes bouncing off each other, but mostly they hovered, moving slowly. Watching them was calming.

"See if you can find him," Charlotte said. "When he came here, I knew something was wrong. And then I couldn't find you, and now here you are. Look." She pointed through the door and into the whiteness.

I followed the line of her finger and stared at the floating lights. They all looked the same, and I didn't know how to tell them apart. Charlotte touched my back and gently pushed me through the door.

I would've known his presence anywhere, and I couldn't believe it had taken me so long to sense him. My breath caught in my throat.

Archer.

"What does this mean?" I took another step forward.

Charlotte's eyes sparkled with unshed tears. "It means he has another chance."

My heart filled to bursting point with happiness. The Archer I knew during my time on Earth may have been gone, but not completely. He hadn't been sent to rest for eternity; he'd been sent here. I had so many questions but no words to ask them. My mind was a jumbled mess of thoughts, and my body filled with feelings I couldn't cope with. I'd had my fair share of emotional turmoil, but this was far worse, and I thought that maybe it was what complete happiness felt like.

I focused on Archer's soul and smiled. It moved slowly towards me, floating through the whiteness like a piece of glowing glitter. When it reached us, the orb stopped and hovered in front of me.

I may not have wanted to be in Heaven, but having Archer there with me made it feel like I really had come home.

31

SETH
Early Sunday morning

I sat on the couch in the shed while Justice guzzled a glass of water at the sink. Hope paced in front of me, her arms folded over her chest, her eyebrows knitted.

"You're not going to like it," she said.

"Try me."

I leaned back into the couch and waited. If Hope didn't want to help me, she would have gone by now, but her and Justice were still around, which meant I had a fighting chance of getting them to help. I wasn't sure if it was a good or bad thing because I had trouble reading Hope most of the time, but like I kept telling myself, she was still there.

"I've already told you, I shouldn't be doing this ... helping you," she said. "You're fallen."

"So?" I shrugged. "Leave. I'm not forcing you to stay."

Hope stopped pacing and faced me. She took a deep breath. "I can't … leave. I want to help, but I'm not sure you trust me enough to do what I'm going to ask you to do."

"Why don't you start with why you didn't run back to the city when you were supposed to? Then I'll decide if I trust you or not."

Hope pressed her lips together. I clasped my hands behind my head and raised my eyebrows, waiting.

She hesitated, her eyes darting from my face to the floor and back again.

"Because … I know what Grace has gone through. I might not agree with every decision she's made, but I can see why she's made them. And Michael hasn't been nice to her. He says he cares, but if he does, why doesn't he want her to be happy? She deserves you … You deserve each other." She glanced at the floor again. "And I wish I had with someone what you have with her. And the only way to make things right is to make sure you're together."

I sat forward and leaned my elbows on my knees, clasping my hands to rest my chin on them. "So you're living vicariously through me." I smirked. "And Michael is a bit of an arse."

Hope picked up a cushion from the armchair and threw it at me. I dodged and it glanced off my arm, falling to the floor.

Justice set his glass down on the sink and came over. "Cut it out, Seth. You get one chance at this." He looked sideways at his sister.

"Okay then. What's the plan?"

Hope began pacing again. She chewed her fingernails

between sentences and avoided eye contact with me. The more she talked, the angrier I got, because the plan she was laying out seemed to be one-sided and totally in her favour.

When she'd finished, I stood up and balled my fists, trying to contain my anger. "Tell me how that's any different to what Michael would've done if Grace stayed."

Hope squared her shoulders, but she took a step back when I moved towards her. "The difference is I'll let you out," she said.

"How do I know that?"

"You have to trust me."

"Well, I have trust issues," I said. "If you're going to trap me in my ring, I need more than your word."

We stared at each other. I couldn't believe she expected me to hand over my ring and let her strip me. Who knew what she'd do once I was imprisoned? She could send me to the In-Between or kill me. It could be part of a plan she'd already concocted with Michael to get rid of me. Michael would have to assume I'd fight for Grace, but I couldn't do that if I was dead.

Hope pressed her lips together. "My word is all I can offer you."

I ran a hand down my face. "I don't think that's true." If I was going to do this, then she had to give me something to hold onto that she'd want back. "You give me your ring and we have a deal."

"No." Justice stepped between us.

Hope's expression stayed neutral, and she stared at me, past her brother.

"How would that work?" she asked. "I need my wings

to get into Heaven."

Yes, she did, but I was betting on her playing the angel-in-distress card. Thinking quickly, I formed a plan of my own, hoping it would be possible. If we went to the Outer Realm and found the re-entry star, we could make the trade as we were travelling through. I opened my mind and let her hear my thoughts.

Hope frowned. "There wouldn't be enough time."

"Yes there would," I said, "if we worked quickly."

"Enough time for what?" Justice asked.

"Do we have a deal?" I asked, ignoring him.

Hope nodded. "I hope you realise what I'm risking for you."

I didn't respond. I knew exactly what she was risking. I'd already lost it a long time ago.

"What the hell?" Justice said. "What's happening?"

"Seth and I are taking a little trip to Heaven. I'll be back as soon as I can." Hope walked towards the door and gave Justice's hand a squeeze on the way past.

"I don't get a say in this, do I?" he called after her.

When Hope didn't answer we both followed her out to the clearing, the three of us stopping in the middle. The sky above was pre-dawn dark; the stars shone like glitter. Hope looked at me, her eyes questioning, and I nodded.

She clasped her hands in front of her and light emanated from her ring. It swirled around her, covering her in a gauze-like veil. Then, *crack*. Her wings exploded from her back and blocked out the stars behind her. Her feathers shimmered white in the moonlight.

I followed suit, releasing my own wings, only mine didn't shimmer against the sky. They blended into the darkness like a shadow.

Hope kicked off the ground and after a second's hesitation, I followed. When I glanced down, Justice stood in the middle of the clearing staring up at us. Hopetown Valley spread out below my feet, the school and town growing smaller and smaller as we rose into the darkness of the sky.

The Outer Realm was accessible by anyone who could fly high enough to reach it, and up there, the only ones who could see us were those paying enough attention in the first place. We wouldn't have much time before someone, presumably the angel on duty, alerted the Council of my presence. A fallen angel in the Outer Realm was not a common occurrence.

I followed Hope as she twisted and turned through the black sky, passing between millions of tiny stars. After a few minutes she stopped and hovered, pointing into the distance at one star that shone more brightly than the others. If I had been alone, I would never have found it. There were a lot of things fallen angels were not supposed to see.

Hope took my hand and guided me towards the re-entry star. The last time I had seen it was so long ago. My heart lurched at the memory of holding Grace in my arms right before I'd renounced everything and fallen. The thought of returning home made me anxious, especially since I wouldn't be welcome.

"Stop," I said before we got any closer. "We have to make sure we do this right."

"I think it will be faster if you give me your ring now, before we go in." Hope hovered in front of me; she had hold of my hand. "Seth, you can trust me."

I took a deep breath. Trust was not something that came easily for me, no matter whom it was with, but what other choice did I have? As far as I could see there was no other way to get Grace back. Getting into Heaven was the only option, even if it meant risking my existence for it. I would do it for Grace. I would do anything for her.

Hope stared at my hand, the one she wasn't holding. I let go of her for a moment and grasped the ring on my finger. The last time it had been taken off, things didn't go so well. Losing my wings had hurt, and I braced myself for the pain that would come.

Slowly, I slipped my ring off my finger and grimaced, clenching my teeth against the sting at my shoulder blades. My wings turned to mist and I cried out. Hope caught me before I could fall out of the sky. She held her hand out, and I set my ring onto her palm.

"Now is when you say 'tricked you'!" I said.

Hope frowned. "You really do have trust issues. Come on." She tugged me towards the re-entry star.

"As soon as we're in you give me your ring," I said.

"Get your dagger ready." Hope looked at me. "I'm going to need some of your blood."

We stopped briefly in front of the star so I could pull my knife from its sheath. I gripped it tightly and nodded. Hope moved forward and the whiteness wrapped around us like a blanket. We didn't speak. I guess we'd said everything that needed to be said. All I had to do now was trust Hope would set me free on the other side and get me to Grace.

Hope stared into my eyes, and her gaze flicked to my

dagger. I let go of her long enough to cut my palm. She held my ring over it ready to smear the stone with my blood, and I clamped my hand into a fist and raised my eyebrows. I understood her hesitation at taking off her own ring, but I wasn't about to let her waver.

Hurry up before the star spits me back into the Outer Realm and you end up in Heaven without me, I thought.

Hope yanked her ring from her finger and tucked it into the pocket of my jeans. She winced at the pain, but didn't cry out like I had. She moved quickly, pulling my hand towards her and prising my fingers open. I watched as she smeared blood onto my ring, not quite believing I was letting an angel do this to me voluntarily.

The last thing I saw were Hope's eyes staring into mine before my essence dissolved and I was sucked into nothingness.

32

GRACE
Heaven

The orb of light twinkled like a star, its edges shimmering silver against the white of the void. I reached up with my palm out, hoping Archer would land on it. I wanted to touch him, and to feel our connection more deeply. The light hovered over my hand, radiating warmth onto my skin, and I smiled.

"Stop!"

I spun around. Michael stood behind Charlotte.

"You're not permitted to enter the Void," Michael said.

The smile fell from my face and I spun back towards Archer's soul. He was no longer there, and loneliness washed over me. I took a deep breath and faced Michael.

"You never told me where I couldn't go."

"She shouldn't have brought you here." Michael switched his glare from me to Charlotte.

"Why? What's so bad about me seeing my brother?" I said.

Michael shook his head. "There's so much you don't understand."

I stepped out of the doorway, and the door slammed shut behind me. The noise made me jump, furthering my anger. What I wouldn't give to feel completely happy and be able to shake the anger from my soul like a dog shook water from its coat.

"That's because no one has taken the time to help me understand," I said. "I was sent to Earth because I was too broken after Seth left. I had to pick myself up without anyone's help, and you wonder why I fought so hard. I fight for myself, because no one ever fought for me." I stopped talking, realising quickly we were about to have the same fight we always had, only with slightly different words. I was tired of fighting.

"You need to come with me." Michael turned and walked away, leaving me standing there with Charlotte.

I glanced at her, and she pursed her lips. I didn't want to go with Michael. I didn't want to leave her after just seeing her again. We'd had such a rough time when we were both on Earth; I was hoping we could get to know each other better.

"The only way you can do that," Michael said, reading my mind, "is if you accept the Council's offer." He didn't turn around when he spoke, and I stared at his back, not knowing what to do.

"Come on." Charlotte linked her arm with mine and gave a gentle pull. "You need to tell them your decision one way or the other."

I let her guide me, and we followed Michael through the cloud dust. We walked on and on, and I wondered where we were going, or what we were passing through, because it was not how I remembered Heaven.

"You exist differently here," Michael said, stopping at the bottom of a staircase. "You are fallen. You don't belong in Heaven, so everything is different even if you think some things are the same."

I had so many questions, but I didn't ask them because I didn't want to give Michael the satisfaction of seeing me unsettled. I was stronger than that, and I could deal with anything he threw my way.

We went up the stairs. They spiralled around and around, reaching into the clouds until I couldn't see them. I wanted to ask why Michael didn't orb us to the Council chambers, but I bit back my words, deciding to go with the flow and see what happened. If everything was different, as he'd said, then I had to accept it. When we reached the top of the stairs, they opened onto a landing. Michael led us through a doorway, and we stopped with a huge expanse of low-lying cloud dust spread out before us.

Michael stared at Charlotte. "You can leave us now."

I clung to her arm. "No. I want her to stay."

Michael regarded me with a stern look. His eyebrows furrowed, and his jaw tightened.

Before he could speak, I said, "Please. She's the only one who can see me other than you ... and Daniel."

"And the Council."

"Yeah," I said. "That makes me feel so much better."

Michael took a deep breath. "Very well."

He turned his back and held out his hand. Cloud dust

rose into the air until it reached his palm, then it went higher, forming a wall in front of us. He opened the door to the Council's chamber the same way I'd seen him do it many times before, and the three of us stood staring into the circular white room.

Michael moved to the outskirts of the chamber, and Charlotte hung near the door after it closed. I felt trapped, but I made myself walk towards the middle.

"You went to a lot of trouble to get me here." I raised my chin, speaking directly to the Council.

"It's time for you to decide," Michael said.

I looked around the room, taking in the twelve empty thrones, wishing I could put faces to the Council. It would make talking to them a whole lot easier.

"You don't need to see us, Grace," their collective voice boomed.

"Not being able to see you makes me trust you less," I said. If I trusted them at all.

"What do you choose?" They ignored my protest.

"Why don't you look in my head to find out?" I turned in a circle, taking in the entire chamber. The emptiness infuriated me.

"You are weak, Grace." The floor shook with the strength of the Council's voice. "Quick to anger and emotional in your decisions."

I scoffed. "If you think you know me so well, then tell me what I've decided. Tell me what my choice is!"

I walked over to Michael and stopped a metre away from him, daring him with my eyes to speak his mind, because I knew he wanted to. It radiated off him in waves.

"Go on," I said. "You can get inside my head, too. Tell

241

me what my decision is."

Michael narrowed his eyes, and probed the edges of my thoughts.

"I can't say what it is," he said.

"That's because I won't accept my reinstatement until you give me a good enough reason to stay." I moved away from Michael and farther into the room, until I stood near the middle of the line of thrones. "Why would I want to be here when all you've done is reprimand me for my actions? I have nothing to come back to, so tell me. Why should I choose to stay?"

The silence hung in the chamber like a wet blanket, draped over everyone, pulling us down. Michael glared at me, his arms folded over his chest. When I glanced at Charlotte her face was unreadable, as if she'd switched off so she didn't have to listen to the fight we both knew was coming.

That was what I did.

I fought.

And I'd never stop fighting for what was fair and right.

"You bring me here … no! *Force* me here, and you can't give me a reason to stay," I said. "My reason for everything is not here. He's on Earth, living with the fact he slid a knife into my heart because *you* said it was the way it was supposed to be. You sit up here on your empty thrones, where no one gets to see you and can only talk to you when you see fit. You have not seen the true face of evil. You don't know what it's like down there. There are beings you consider to be bad, but if given half a chance they can be something wonderful, if only because someone loves them. All I ever wanted was to be able to love freely, on my own terms. Not on the terms of some faceless entity in the sky, who has no idea what it really means to love or be loved. Our lives, the lives of everyone on Earth, are not black and white. They're filled will a million shades of grey that your narrow-mindedness will never be able to see. And inside that grey is a rainbow waiting to be released."

No one replied, and I faced a room of not only empty thrones, but empty silence as well. I was tired of the Council saying jump and then questioning how high they expected me to go.

I was about to open my mouth again to tell them how belittling they were, when the cloud dust beneath me parted. I expected to peek through and see the ground below, but instead the open space filled with images of my past. Every moment that had led to where I stood played out before my eyes.

Seth leaving; our constant fights over the decades; Josh; Charlotte; my fall; the battle in Wide Island; and the death of my brother and friends.

It was too much all at once.

My heart raced, and I wanted to get out of there. The walls suffocated me, and I closed my eyes to block out the images and take a few deep breaths.

"Is this some cruel joke?" I asked. "Why are you showing me this?"

"This is why we wanted you to come home," the Council said.

"Yeah." I opened my eyes and glared at Michael. "Because I was becoming a liability."

His lips twitched as if he were about to speak, but he stopped when the door to the chamber slid open. Charlotte jumped at the sound, and my heart went out to her. She'd changed since I'd last seen her on Earth. The Charlotte I knew would never have been afraid of anything. She was strong and a fighter. Heaven had turned her into a quiet and submissive wreck.

We waited for whatever was going to happen. I stared at the empty doorway and the fog of cloud dust on the other side, with no idea if anyone would step through, and if they did, who it would be.

The dust parted and Hope ran into the chamber, stopping beside me and turning to look back through the door as if she were expecting someone to follow. Her white dress billowed around her before settling against her legs.

Michael unfolded his arms and strode to where Hope and I stood—one white angel and one black one.

"No one is chasing you," the Council said. "We gave you safe passage to the chamber."

I wanted to point out that all angels should be safe in Heaven, then I realised I was an angel, and I was in Heaven, but I wasn't safe. It seemed status was everything to the Council.

She spun back to face me, and I had a hard time hiding my surprise. I raised my eyebrows and stared at her.

"I'm so glad you're here," Hope said.

She had one hand balled into a fist as if she was clutching something tightly in her fingers, and that was when I noticed something missing.

"Where's your ring?" I asked.

Hope looked at her hands, her fingers moving around whatever it was she held. Something was going on that I knew nothing about, and when I looked to Michael he held no answers in his expression, but I'd become used to his poker face over the years. He was good at hiding what he knew. I returned my gaze to Hope. She had something to tell me, and I waited for the Council to call her on it, but they didn't. They must have summoned her for a reason, but I couldn't imagine what it was. Hope and I had no connection other than fighting in Wide Island together, and recently at the formal.

"The Council didn't call me here," Hope said, reading my thoughts.

Michael frowned, the only indication he gave that said he wasn't pleased with Hope being there. I studied his face. He locked gazes with Hope, and something passed between them. She gave a slight nod, and Michael relaxed a little. Had they spoken to each other? Was he putting on an act? I pushed into his thoughts, but he shoved me out and I stepped back. Being a fallen angel in Heaven didn't allow me to force my way into another angel's mind.

Michael didn't take his eyes off Hope. "You're here now, so get it over with."

"Get what over with?" I asked, staring at her.

"I knew if I got here they wouldn't turn me away," Hope said. "Because technically I'm in trouble, and I need help."

"What are you talking about?"

Hope looked at her hands again. She slowly uncurled her fingers, and when I saw what lay on her palm, I took another step back. Then I wanted to tackle her.

"That's Seth's ring!" I moved towards her. "Why do you have it?"

"Because he has mine," Hope said.

I stared down at the ring, and my breath caught in

my throat. The tiny flicker of Seth's soul moved inside the black stone. He was here … in Heaven.

Hope had brought him to Heaven.

Why? I didn't understand if she was trying to help me or rub it in my face. From what I could read in her expression, she looked happy, not controlling or menacing. I had to believe she was there because she'd made some kind of arrangement with Seth. At least, that was what I wanted to believe. I also hoped Michael had played a part in getting Seth to Heaven. It would make him less of an arse.

"Hope. I'm very disappointed." Michael stood over us with his arms folded.

His words were not as angry as they had been, and his tone had changed slightly. Maybe he *was* on my side, and he was trying to play by the rules while breaking them at the same time, but I couldn't be sure because he wouldn't let me in.

"Why?" Hope faced him. "Because I thought it was more important to help my friend rather than be a good girl and always do as I'm told?"

Oh, she sounded so much like me.

I stared at Seth's ring. All I wanted was for Hope to set him free so I could see him again. So I could hold him and never let him go.

"You will be punished for this," the Council said.

Hope stood tall, her hand open, Seth's ring on her palm. "Look inside my heart and tell me I haven't acted out of love. Isn't that what we were made to do?"

I smiled. Michael's shoulders relaxed and his features softened. Why did he listen to Hope when she talked about love, but I had to argue until I was blue in the face?

Charlotte moved away from the door and joined our group in the centre of the chamber. Three angels who had broken the rules for love, and one too stubborn to agree that love was always the answer.

I held my head high and glanced around the room, wishing for the millionth time I could see the faces of the Council members.

"We were created to love, and protect, and cherish. To defy evil and raise all that is good up onto the highest pedestal. Why then do you try and make us stand in the dungeon when we don't belong there?" I asked.

"You. Are. Fallen!" they boomed. "You have no power or right to argue the case of good versus evil."

I shook my head. They hadn't listened to a word I'd said. It was like banging my head against a brick wall, one that separated me from them.

I smiled at Hope, and she nodded.

Hope bit the tip of her finger, drawing blood, and smeared it onto the stone of Seth's ring. The soul inside bounced around from one side to the other before black mist rose from the shiny surface. It poured out in waves, falling to the floor and mingling with the cloud dust. When it stopped, the mist formed the shape of man before solidifying and turning to flesh.

Seth propped himself up on his hands and raised his head. His gaze locked with mine, and I knew that no matter what happened from that moment on, we were both finally home.

33

SETH

Grace was the first thing I saw. Nothing else around me mattered apart from her. I kept my gaze on hers as I slowly got to my feet, vaguely aware of others standing in the room. Once I was up, I chanced a look around.

Hope stood near Grace, and when our eyes met she grinned. She had stayed true to her word and brought me to Heaven. Michael stood with the group but he wasn't quite a part of it. His face held his usual scowl—the one he'd come to use only when looking at me. Charlotte was also there, and even though I was happy to see her, I turned my attention back to Grace.

She smiled.

And my heart exploded.

Hope stepped forward, and I looked at her again. She held out my ring. I'd forgotten about hers, so I fished it out of my pocket, clutching it in my fist. I closed the gap between us and opened my hand for her. She plucked it from my palm with her free hand, but when I went to take mine, the room shook with the bellow of the Council's voice.

"Stop! You must not give it to him."

Hope glanced around the chamber, a place I hadn't been inside for a very long time, and she shook her head.

"It belongs to him, not me. I have no right to hold it."

"He is fallen," the Council said. "You have every right to take it from him."

Hope ignored the Council and pushed my ring into my hand. I slid it onto my finger and felt its power flow into my body. It ran up my arms and legs to my chest, forcing my wings to burst free. I cried out as their crack resonated around the chamber.

Hope also slipped her ring on, and her wings returned but again she didn't cry out like I had. They shimmered, pearly white against the dull lustre of the cloud dust.

Michael pinched the bridge of his nose, as if it was all too much for him. Grace moved until she stood close enough for me to slip my arms around her waist, but I dared not move. She touched my cheek with her fingertips and tears welled in her eyes.

"Why are your wings still black?" I asked, reaching up and clasping her wrist so I could press her hand flat to my cheek.

"I refused to accept their offer to be reinstated."

"It wasn't automatic?"

She shook her head. "Apparently they can't force me. I have to make the choice of my own free will."

"No one can force you to do anything."

"I told you I didn't want to come back."

249

K. A. LAST

"But you did it to save me," I said.

"Anything to keep you from the In-Between." Grace stroked my cheek with her thumb. "You don't deserve that. You deserve so much more than you have and more than what I can give you. You deserve to be free."

Michael scoffed. "That's exactly what I'd given him before he pulled this stupid stunt."

Grace stared at Michael, her eyes wide.

"Yes," Michael continued. "I'd set him free as I'd promised. But now, everything has changed. You should never have come here, Seth. You relinquished your freedom the moment you entered the place where you don't belong."

Grace clung to me as if the very thought of us being separated again would kill her. But I had killed her, and even that hadn't kept us apart.

"Michael," the Council said, "see to it that Seth is sent back—"

"No!" Grace said. "He belongs with me."

Michael grabbed my arm and pulled me away from Grace. Her fingers trailed along my skin as I was yanked free of her grasp. I struggled, wrenching my shoulders to try and slip through Michael's fingers, but it was no use. Michael was and always had been stronger than me.

Grace's knees buckled, but Hope caught her before she fell to the floor. A sob escaped her delicate mouth, and she clung to Hope, her eyes never leaving mine. Grace righted herself and stood tall, taking Hope's arm from around her waist and clasping her hand.

Michael and I reached the door, and as he lifted his hand to open it, Charlotte spoke.

"What is wrong with you?" She didn't only look at

Michael, but around the room, addressing the Council as well. "How can you condone something like this? Grace has never acted out of malice. She has nothing but love in her heart. A heart which *you* have shattered into a million pieces on more than one occasion."

"You are not fit to comment," the Council said. "The situation does not concern you."

"Then why am I here?" She turned a circle, taking in each throne one by one. "Was I not one of the reasons Grace defied you in the first place? Did she not see the good in me and then fight to keep me safe? I should never have let my brother kill me. I thought I was doing the right thing … returning home. Letting someone else fight the battle I was tired of fighting. But I would have been better off staying and fighting with Grace, because at least she isn't blinded by hatred for something she knows nothing about."

The chamber fell silent. No one spoke. I locked gazes with Grace, trying to fill her with my strength. *I love you,* I thought.

Her lips parted, but I shook my head. I didn't need a reply.

Hope stood beside Grace, holding her hand. While Charlotte's expression was angry, and she looked ready to give the Council another mouthful, Hope's lips were set in a line of determination. She was on Grace's side, even if she wasn't completely on mine. It seemed everyone in the room was defying the Council in one way or another— all of us except Michael.

How do you think you got here? Michael thought. *If it wasn't for me, you'd be floating in the In-Between.*

I glared at Michael, furious at his intrusion into my mind. Then I registered his words. I was smart enough to know not to reply. The Council would be able to hear my every thought, so I concentrated on Grace again.

Her voice was almost a whisper, but I heard it from across the room. "You once told me not everyone who's in Heaven's good graces wants to be there." She let go of Hope's hand and walked towards Michael and me. "Are you one of them, Michael? Are you doing all of this to prove to yourself that you're not? Because I thought we were friends, and friends don't betray each other."

Grace stopped a metre away from us and clenched her fists.

Hope stared directly at Michael and said. "If I were you, I'd listen to her. Everyone should have the opportunity for a second chance, even those who may not deserve one."

34

GRACE

T he moment the door closed with Seth on the other side was the moment I thought *that's it*. Would I ever see him again? It seemed I'd already had my second chance.

Hope and Charlotte came to my side. Their faces held all the words I knew they wanted to say, but sorry wasn't good enough. It would never be good enough. Being free was the only thing that ever would be, and as long as I was in Heaven, freedom would be a luxury.

"Have you come to a final decision?" the Council asked.

I shook my head. "I will not let you persuade me one way or the other. I don't choose this." I swept my arm around the chamber, and the cloud dust swirled between my fingers. "And I don't choose Hell. I choose Seth."

"That is not an answer."

"It's the only answer for me," I said. "Even if it's the

one *you* don't want to hear."

The door opened with a whoosh and Michael stepped through. "Charlotte, Hope ... can you leave us, please?"

I'd been waiting for this to happen. Take away my support network in the hope I would crumble and bend to their will. I was not their puppet, and no matter what they said or did to me, I had made my decision.

"A decision not to decide is not a decision at all," Michael said.

I squeezed my eyes closed and took a deep breath. Getting used to having my thoughts read all the time was hard. As a fallen angel, I had no mental defences in Heaven.

Hope and Charlotte left the chamber and the door closed, sealing me in with Michael and the Council.

"What did you do with Seth?" I asked.

"He's being detained until we can figure this out."

Michael pressed his palms together and put his fingers to his lips. He walked to the centre of the room and the cloud dust parted in a circle around him. The images of my most recent past appeared again—a ring of memories, some of which I would be happy to forget.

Michael glanced up, his eyes questioning. When I didn't speak he looked down again, taking in the visions one by one. He stopped on the night Archer died, and I forced myself to look away. I didn't need to see it in the chamber floor. It was fresh in my mind and constantly at the forefront of my thoughts.

Michael put his hands on his hips and sighed, hanging his head. "What would it take for you to be reinstated?"

"I've already told you—"

"No! Grace. You don't seem to understand." He stepped

towards me, his eyes wide, and the fire in his pupils burned. "It's this ... or the In-Between. If you don't say yes, you'll float in oblivion forever, and your soul will never be restored."

I shook my head and scoffed. "You think I'm scared of the In-Between? I've lost everything, Michael. I don't care. At least in oblivion I'll know Seth's there with me."

Michael didn't reply. He walked to the door and opened it, orbing as he passed through. Seconds later, he returned with Seth at his side. The door slid closed again as he man-handled Seth to the centre of the room. I watched as he pushed him to his knees and bound his hands in front of him with celestial fire.

Seth held my gaze, and I couldn't look away. He didn't speak, and I was too afraid to, not knowing what Michael was about to do.

"What if Seth's existence was on the line?" Michael asked. "Would you say yes then?"

Seth still didn't speak.

"You freed him. You can't touch him," I said.

"I can do whatever I want!" Michael stepped towards me, his fists clenched. He went back to Seth and grabbed his hands, prising his fingers open. "I'll strip him and kill him if you don't say yes."

My breath rushed out of my lungs, and I fell to my knees at the edge of the images of my memories. I'd returned to Heaven against my will to save him, and now Michael was going to take him from me anyway.

I couldn't watch him die.

Seth still said nothing, and when I stared into his eyes they were vacant, as if he looked through me.

I leaned forward, my hair hanging over my knees, and clenched my fists in the cloud dust. There was nothing solid to hold onto, and everything was slipping through my fingers. Had all of this been in vain? How could Michael do this?

When I looked up, his fingers wrapped around Seth's ring ready to pull it off, I saw something flicker in Michael's eyes. The fire burning in them had dulled, and there was something in the way he stared at me. I wanted to believe he wouldn't do it.

"Get up and make your decision," Michael said.

My arms and legs were cold, and I wasn't sure if I could stand, but I pushed myself up off the chamber floor. "I will not let you force me to do anything. If you want Seth's death on your conscience, be my guest."

As soon as the words were out of my mouth, I regretted them. I had died for him, but I didn't want him to die for me even though I knew he would. I didn't want the Council to win either.

From the look I'd seen in Michael's eyes, I'd hoped he was bluffing. Calling him on it was one of the hardest things I'd ever had to do.

"I died for Seth," I said. "I know he'll do the same for me."

Michael closed his eyes for a moment, then began to pull at Seth's ring.

"Stop!" the Council's voice boomed. "You won't get her to change, Michael. We go through this every cycle." They paused and I frowned, wondering what the Council was talking about. "It's time."

"Time for what?" The cloud dust closed over the images

of my memories that lay at my feet.

Michael let go of Seth's hand and the rope of fire broke, his arms dropping to his sides. Then he dissolved into a cloud of black mist. But we couldn't mist in Heaven. I opened my mouth to ask what had happened, but the words wouldn't come out properly.

"Is he ... what ... where did he go?" I stepped towards Michael, but stopped when he glared at me.

"Why does it always have to come to this?" Michael ran his hand down his cheek. "If you say yes, this will all be over."

"What will be over?" I stared at him, then glanced around the chamber. "What are you talking about? Either tell me where Seth went, or send me to the In-Between and get it over with."

Michael folded his arms over his chest. The corners of his mouth drooped, and he blinked slowly, shaking his head. "You're not going to the In-Between. That threat is always the last resort. And it never works."

"Michael," the Council said, "start the process, please."

"What process?" I turned a circle, taking in Michael's solemn face and the thrones filled with nothing but cloud dust.

Michael tilted his head back and looked at the ceiling. "Do I have to explain it to her again? I'm tired of this. Why won't you let it end?"

"Would you tell me what's happening? Stop talking like I'm not in the room," I said.

Dust swirled around the thrones, and wind whipped my hair into my eyes. I tucked it behind my ears and waited.

"You are being punished," the Council said. "The cycle will not end until you make the decision to accept your wings. Then, and only then will you be free of the relentless repeating of events."

What were they talking about? Repeating events? I didn't understand. So many questions filled my mind but one came to the forefront.

"What am I being punished for?" I asked.

Michael stuffed his hands into the pockets of his linen pants. He held my gaze for a moment, then he looked at his feet. "You don't remember ... because we made you forget."

"What?" I stepped forward, and now we were close enough to reach out and touch each other. But I didn't want to hug him. I wanted to slap him.

Michael raised his head and his eyes locked onto mine. "You and Seth have always been in love. Right from the very beginning. You were drawn to each other in ways none of us could understand, and you were forbidden to be together, but you both did it anyway."

"We separated you by taking the memory of your love from you," the Council said. "But not from Seth."

"You made me forget that I love him?"

"It hasn't stopped you eventually finding each other again," Michael said.

"So doesn't that tell you something?" I clenched my fists. "How could you do this to us? How could you make us go through all the heartache and the pain, over and over again, all because we love each other and you don't like it?"

"Your love is destructive," the Council boomed. "You were an archangel, Grace. You sat beside the Council, higher than any other angel in Heaven."

I stumbled backwards. They were lying; they had to be. I had never been an archangel; I would have remembered something like that. Michael nodded slightly to confirm what the Council had said.

"If it's true, then why didn't Seth tell me?"

"Because they wouldn't allow it," Michael said.

I wondered what else we'd been made to forget, and if my memories were even real in the first place. What had they done to us?

"You think it changes anything?" I asked. "You think I'll say yes now, because I used to be the most powerful angel in Heaven? What is power without love?"

"You must learn your lesson," the Council said, "and take your rightful place at our side."

"I do not want to be by *your* side … and I will *never* change my mind."

"Michael, erase her memories. Send them back, and we'll see what she has to say next time."

"Wait!" I said. "Seth. If you're going to make me forget him, I'd like to see him one last time."

The air in the chamber thickened. It closed around me and I drew short, shallow breaths, waiting for their answer. Everything was happening too quickly. It was a lot to process, but surely they would let me see him. They were supposed to be good and kind.

I waited.

"Very well. Take her."

I let out a long breath and relaxed my hands which I'd knotted together. Michael strode to the door and ran his fingers over the marble. It slid open and he turned to me, gesturing for me to follow. He waited until I had passed through, then joined me on the other side. The chamber wall fell into the mist and we stood surrounded by nothing but cloud.

Michael held out his hand, but I didn't take it. As much as I wanted to forgive him for the way he'd treated me, I couldn't. There was still so much I didn't understand.

"I've only ever wanted what's best for you," he said, sighing.

"What's best for me is what *I* choose. It doesn't matter if I make mistakes. They're my mistakes, not yours, and they make me who I am."

"I've made mistakes, too. And I'm doing my best to fix them." Michael reached out and squeezed my hand, and I let him. "Come on. I think there's someone who wants to see you."

I tugged my hand from Michael's and said, "Wait. Please, tell me why you've done what you've done? We used to be friends. I don't know what's been taken away from me, but I miss that. I miss the Michael I knew all that time ago, before Seth fell. Where has that angel gone?"

Michael ran a hand through his hair then gently pulled my arm until I fell into step beside him. "You've missed a lot while you've been on Earth. I … used to think following the rules was not always the right thing to do. But I'm an archangel. I have to follow the rules. I have to do what the Council tells me."

"Even when you don't want to?"

"Especially then." He stopped and faced me. "You have to understand … I'm only trying to protect you."

"Well, that gets old very quickly when everyone's doing

it," I said.

Michael pressed his lips together, touched my arm and orbed, surrounding us in his light until we had dissolved to nothing. We landed in a small room with walls, floor, and ceiling made of cloud. When I ran my fingers along the wall, it was solid but covered with a thin veil of dust.

"I can't leave," Michael said, moving to the corner.

It didn't matter. Seth stood at the window, his back to us, staring at the blue sky beyond. I went to him and slipped my arms around his waist, resting my head on his back. He covered my hands with his.

We stood like that for a while. It was nice that we didn't need to speak, and we could exist together in comfortable silence.

It's not good, I finally thought so Seth could hear me.

He let go of my hands and spun in my arms to face me. I locked my fingers together in the small of his back and gazed up at him.

What happened in there?

They tried to convince me, but I still said no.

What does that mean for us then? he thought.

I took a deep breath. *It means we have to do this all over again. I don't fully understand, but apparently we've been stuck in a cycle for a long time, and they plan to make us do it until my decision changes.*

I'm not sure what you're saying.

I stood on my tip toes and pressed my lips to Seth's in a chaste kiss. *They're going to take our memories.*

"What?" Seth pulled away, anger flaring in his eyes.

His gaze flicked to Michael and his jaw worked as he ground his teeth. Michael didn't flinch as Seth ran at him with clenched fists, and when Seth drew his arm back to strike, Michael let him. Michael's head snapped to the side and blood sprayed from his nose into the whiteness of the room. He straightened up and held Seth's stare, but he didn't react or respond in any other way.

Seth turned his back and walked over to look out the window. I moved to stand beside him, leaning into his side and resting my head on his shoulder. He didn't put his arm around me, but he didn't move away either. Seth clenched his fists and rested them on the windowsill. I stared through the hole in the clouds at the blue sky beyond, wondering where and when we were looking at. I wondered if this kind of detainment was designed to make you a little crazy, always wondering what lay beyond the expanse of nothing.

"This isn't fair," Seth said out loud, even though Michael would have been able to hear one way or the other. Seth hung his head, then turned it and rested his chin on his upper arm, staring into my eyes. "If they take our memories … they take us away from each other. And that means they've won."

I shook my head. "No. They can never take you from me. My heart knows you, and I trust that we will find each other again. Apparently we have before."

The silence hung between us, and I waited for the next question. I already knew who it would be about, and I was prepared. Or I thought I was. But hearing his name undid me all over again.

"What about Archer? You'll forget him." Seth stared out the window again.

A shaky breath passed over my lips. "If we are stuck

DIE FOR ME

in a cycle like the Council says, then I'll see Archer again."

"I can't believe you're so calm about this."

I wanted to laugh. If Seth had seen me moments before in the chamber, calm would have been the least accurate description for my emotions.

"We can't fight them anymore, so I guess we have to hope this time will be different. I love you, and I will go through all of it a hundred times more if it means there's a chance to find a way to end it." I gently pulled his arm and lifted it over my head so I could nestle into his side.

Seth wrapped me in his strong arms and kissed my hair. "I don't want to forget you."

"I don't want to forget you either. But don't think about that," I said. "Just think that when we get through this, it means we'll have nothing but the future waiting for us."

35

SETH

Michael spoke from the corner of the room. "It's time to go."

I raised my head and looked into his eyes, holding his gaze and refusing to look away. He knew exactly how I felt about him and everything that was happening. I didn't have to say it out loud.

Grace slipped her hand into mine and gently pulled until I walked with her towards Michael. When we stopped, she tilted her head to stare up at him.

"How does this work?" she asked. "And what happens after?"

Michael chuckled, and the sound gave me another reason to want to punch him.

"What happens after is up to both of you," he said. "As for how it works ... we erase your memory of every-thing that's happened from a certain moment, and you'll

be sent back to begin the cycle again."

"What moment?" I asked.

"I can't tell you that."

Grace's hand clenched mine. "I don't understand how making us forget is punishment. If we can't remember, what's the point?"

Michael rubbed the back of his neck. "Because every time you go through this, you lose more. The pain you feel increases, and yet you still make the same decision … your love for Seth over your rightful place beside the Council."

"If the result is the same every time, why make us keep doing it?" I asked.

"The Council are as stubborn as you are. And they're angry with Grace for choosing you. They believe that one day she'll find the strength to accept who she really is. To acknowledge she is an archangel and she needs to come home." Michael dropped his hand to his side. He regarded both of us for a moment and sighed.

"You're an archangel?" I raised my eyebrows. "Since when?"

"It doesn't matter. I'll never be reinstated," Grace said

Michael glanced around, as if he were checking to see if anyone was watching. "If you want to break the cycle, you have to change the moment that decided your fate. There was a time when this wasn't a cycle. When everything that's happened, actually happened."

Grace tugged my hand, and I realised I'd been squeezing it. It must have hurt, but it was exactly like her not to complain. How many times had we been repeating the same thing over and over again? When I stared at Michael,

I knew he had the answer. I also knew he would never tell me.

"How do we change the moment?" Grace asked. "How do we even know what the moment is?"

Michael stepped forward and raised his hand towards Grace. I went to stop him but he batted my arm away like he was swatting a fly. My eyebrows drew together as I watched him touch the diamond hanging from the delicate silver chain around Grace's neck. A blue spark shot across its surface, and Michael curled his fingers into a fist before dropping his arm back to his side again.

"I have a feeling you'll know," he said, smiling at Grace. When he glanced up at me he frowned. "Let's go." He turned and disappeared through the doorway.

Grace and I followed, and with every step back towards the Council's chamber, the more I thought about what was about to happen, and the more my heart ached at the possibility of not remembering Grace at all.

She squeezed my hand. *I'll remember you. My heart would never forget you. Everything will work out.*

I hoped she was right.

Michael took us back into the chamber and we stood in the middle of the room. Grace clutched my hand, and I did my best to stay calm when all I wanted to do was hit Michael to make myself feel better.

"Thoughts like that won't help you, Seth," the Council said, their voice filling the air.

"He's put me through a lot. And we like hitting each other. We do it all the time."

Michael chuckled and shook his head. The chamber fell silent and we waited. Michael watched Grace and me with an expression I could only read as smugness, like he knew something we didn't. I had another urge to wipe the smile off his face.

Michael licked his lips. "Are you ready to forget?"

"I will never be ready." Grace squeezed my hand and stared at me.

We'll always find each other, she thought.

In that moment I didn't doubt her. Her eyes were filled with the hope I needed to believe in her. To believe in *us*.

"Are we ever ready for this moment?" I asked, not taking my eyes from Grace. Something told me the answer was always no. "You've given us no other choice, so get it over with."

Michael moved so he stood directly in front of Grace. She focused her attention on him, but never let go of my hand. While we stood there, the Council explained the rules of our reinstatement. Michael would implant a mind block into our thoughts. The block would keep our memories, from as far back as the Council saw fit, hidden. Michael would be the only one with the power to reverse it. He would also remember everything, and then we'd be sent back to start the cycle again.

"Michael, please proceed," the Council said.

He stepped closer to Grace and I clenched my free fist, ready to protect her if I had to.

She is perfectly safe, Michael thought, scowling.

If only I could be one hundred per cent sure of that.

"You need to give me something." Michael stared at Grace. "It has to be a treasured possession."

"Angels don't have possessions," she said.

Michael's gaze flicked to her chest, and Grace's hand

K. A. LAST

flew to the chain around her neck. Her fingers curled around the tear-shaped diamond that hung from the end, as if it were the last thing she was prepared to give up. Michael lifted his arms to take the necklace from Grace but I stopped him.

"I'll do it." I let go of her hand and brushed her hair aside so I could undo the clasp.

Grace watched as the delicate silver chain pooled onto Michael's palm. The diamond lay against his skin, and when he looked at it, a soft blue light rippled across its surface before the stone turned clear again. Michael told Grace to close her eyes. She hesitated, but did as he'd asked. He cupped her face with his hands, running his thumbs up the bridge of her nose and across her forehead. Grace's hand fumbled for mine and clasped it tightly. I wasn't letting her go for any reason, and I gently squeezed so she knew I was with her.

I kept waiting for something to happen—sparks to fly from Michael's fingers, or light to come from somewhere—but nothing did. He simply held her face for a few moments then her knees buckled, and I caught her before she could hit the floor.

Michael removed his hands and Grace went limp in my arms.

"What have you done?"

"She's fine, Seth. You can lay her on the ground."

I gently lowered Grace until she lay on her side, stroking her hair away from her face and making sure her dress covered her modestly, before standing again.

Michael fidgeted with the chain in his hands, staring at Grace lying at our feet, waiting for ... something. I was about to ask what would happen next when she stirred. Grace slowly pushed herself to a sitting position, but before she could raise her head to look at me, the cloud dust in the floor parted and a tunnel appeared. She turned to stare into it, and I wanted to yell at her to look at me, but by the time the words touched my lips she was gone. Grace tumbled into the hole in the clouds and it closed over, leaving me feeling lost, empty, and cold.

"It's your turn." Michael motioned for me to face him.

"Where did she go?" I asked.

Michael sighed. "Somewhere safe. Now stand still."

"How can I trust you? How do I know you won't end this right here, and we'll be none the wiser? How do I know I'll see her again?"

"You don't. So you'll have to take my word for it." Michael narrowed his eyes and stared straight into mine. "Trust is a virtue, Seth. You'd do well to remember that."

I raised my eyebrows. "Says the archangel who's about to take my memories."

"I need something of yours as well." Michael held out his hand, ignoring my comment.

I fished in the pocket of my jeans for the small black pouch I carried everywhere with me. It held a diamond almost the same as Grace's but not quite. This one was smaller but in my eyes more perfect, because it had been created with her tear, not mine.

I reluctantly handed it over. When Michael opened the pouch, I went to snatch it away, but he stepped back and held it out of my reach. He pulled the drawstring open and tipped the diamond onto his palm, holding it the same way he'd held Grace's.

"Yes, this will do," he said.

The stone sparkled, and then a shimmer of blue passed over it. It happened quickly, and seconds later the diamond was back in the pouch and Michael stepped towards me. He reached up and held my face the same way he had Grace's. When I'd watched him take her memories, it had seemed as if nothing was really happening. I'd been very wrong.

My mind opened to Michael and he dove right in. I'd never felt so invaded or violated. It was different to having my thoughts read, and it was like he was actually inside my head, taking a walk around. No matter how hard I resisted I couldn't push him out.

Fighting will make it harder, Michael thought, and the sound of his voice consumed me.

The motion of his thumbs across my forehead became a background sensation, and everything I'd been through in my past came to the front of my mind all at once. Images of Heaven, and Hell, and Grace. Visions of battles won, enemies defeated, but worst of all, friends dying. My heart mourned them all over again, not realising how much losing them had affected me. I didn't have friends until Grace taught me how to love again. I didn't think I'd had anything worth losing until it had been taken away.

For a moment the thought of losing my memories scared me, and panic rose into my chest, gripping my heart and squeezing until I couldn't breathe. Not remembering didn't change the past; it only moved it out of my field of vision. My past was part of who I was. Would I lose myself? Would I be able to find Grace again? I hated the Council and Michael for what they were doing to us.

I wanted to ask Michael a million questions, but I couldn't speak with my voice or my thoughts. I stood in his grip, watching as each memory slid from my mind. All the images of Grace slid into nothingness until I was also nothing.

36

SETH
The Outer Realm

Moonlight shone off Grace's hair, rippling over its glossy surface as she stared up at me. For a brief moment I'd lost concentration, and I wondered where we were. Then I remembered we had to get back. Our mission was complete. We'd saved the twins and the Council were waiting for us.

"Fly with me first?" I asked, looking for a way to keep Grace near me for a little bit longer. The thought of my impending decision weighed me down, and I needed to be with her, just the two of us, so I could remember her the way I wanted to.

Grace hesitated, then she nodded, smiling.

I wrapped her in my arms and pulled her close. My blue orbs surrounded us and we disappeared, heading for the Outer Realm. I didn't want to let her go, but Grace pulled away and fluttered her wings.

"Race you," she said, giggling and making a line towards the re-entry star.

A million thoughts flooded my mind on how to stop her heading for home. All I wanted was to spend some time with her, because she didn't know how little time we had left. I didn't follow. Instead, I hovered in the darkness and waited for her to turn around.

At first she didn't, and my heart beat so forcefully in my chest I thought it would break free and fly after her.

How was I supposed to tell her I was leaving? How do you tell your best friend you're not going home with her?

Grace stopped, and her wings beat gently, caressing the stars. She turned and our eyes met across the void. She furrowed her brow, forming a crease between her eyes, and I wanted to smooth it out with my thumb. My fingers itched to touch her, and my arms ached to hold her, but she was already so far away.

Grace flew back to my side and slipped her hand into mine. "What's wrong? Don't you want to fly with me?"

I pressed my lips together. "Of course I want to fly with you ... but ... it's just ..."

Grace reached up and pressed a finger to my lips. Her touch made my heart ache, and I longed to tell her the truth. But the truth was forbidden.

I could never tell her how much I loved her.

Grace clutched my hand tightly and scanned the darkness of the Outer Realm. Starlight shone in her eyes, and I watched her as she watched the night sky.

"Something's wrong," she said. "Seth, tell me what's wrong." Grace stared at me, her eyes pleading.

I hated that she knew me so well, but loved it all at the same time. She was the only one who could ever make me happy, and yet she was also the one who would make my existence a living hell.

I wasn't allowed to be with her, yet I couldn't stand to be without her.

"Nothing's wrong," I said. "I don't want to go back yet."

"Then why are you crying?" she asked.

Grace reached up and held her hand beside my cheek. She pulled it away and we stared at the tear that had pooled on her palm. Its surface sparkled with its own light, and as the rays passed over it, the tear drop solidified and turned into a diamond. Grace's other hand clutched mine tightly, and she hovered with her head bent, staring at the perfect stone. It glistened again, only this time a blue light moved across the surface, as if it were coming from the inside.

Grace's brow creased, and a breath puffed from her mouth. She drew another in, and then another, as if she were finding it hard to breathe. Her wings beat faster, the breeze they created running a chill up my arms.

I grabbed her by the shoulders and forced her to raise her head and look at me.

"What is it?"

"You ... you're about to ... no! You can't do it." Grace balled her hands into fists. "You can't leave me!" She pounded my chest with both hands, her wings flapping crazily behind her. Tears streamed down her cheeks and I pulled her to me. She sobbed into my chest, and I wrapped my arms around her in an attempt to calm her down.

How was I supposed to tell her I couldn't stay?

Grace raised her head and stared up at me. "You can't leave me," she whispered. "You can't."

Wet lines ran down her face, and another solitary tear leaked from the corner of one eye. I watched as it followed the path of the others before it, and when it reached her chin, I held out my hand and caught it before it could fall away into oblivion.

We stared at my hand where the small drop of moisture sat in the crease of my palm. It shone in the same way my tear had, and it too turned into a diamond.

"This is the moment we have to change," Grace said.

"What do you mean?" I searched her face but couldn't find an answer.

"You love me, Seth. I've always known you love me, only you've never told me."

"How can I when I'm not allowed to?" I closed my hand around the diamond in my palm. "You're better off without me."

Grace shook her head. "No one is better off without the one they love the most." She took my hand and gently unfolded my fingers. "Look."

I didn't want to take my gaze away from her face, because this would be the last time I saw her. In a few moments, I would voice my decision, and she'd be lost to me forever. But I did as she asked and looked down at the diamond lying on my palm. A blue light shone across its surface, and this time *my* breath caught in my throat, and I fought to breathe properly. I blinked in an attempt to still the images racing past my mind's eye.

My eyes met Grace's, and in her pools of blue I saw everything.

My past.

Her past.

Our past.

But it was also our future.

Everything that had ever happened to us, or could happen. The pain, the loss, but also the never-ending love.

Grace cried out, and her hand flew to her chest, covering her heart, as if something had hit her hard. She stared at me and more tears rolled down her cheeks in waves. So many tears, I wondered how she hadn't dried up. We hovered in the darkness, and if Grace felt anything like I did, her head was about to explode if her heart didn't first.

"Archer," Grace said. "Emma, Ryan, Abby? Charlotte? Did any of it really happen?"

"I'm not sure. I think yes ... but I think ..." I shook my head. "I don't know."

"Why can we remember?" Grace scrunched the fabric of her dress into her fist. "It hurts."

"Michael," I said, remembering the moment he'd touched Grace's tear-drop necklace, and how he'd asked to see the tear I kept in the little black pouch. "He wanted to help us break the cycle, but he didn't want to make it easy."

I closed my fingers around the diamond in my hand, my fist stopping its glow, and I reached out to wrap Grace in my arms again. She came willingly, resting her cheek against my chest. How was I supposed to console her? I couldn't say everything would be all right, because how would it? We were right back where we'd started, at the moment that had set everything in motion, but my decision would never change. No matter what happened, or what the future held this time around, I could not live in Heaven with Grace in it. She pulled back and looked at me, her wings beating softly.

"We'll get through this," I said, because I *had* to believe that somehow we would.

37

GRACE

My eyes were hot from my tears. "*How* do we get through this?" I asked, wiping my cheeks. "We're not meant to remember anything from this point onwards. What are we supposed to do?"

I glanced at our wings, the way they moved through the air, beating in time with each other, and how they shimmered, pearly white.

"We're not fallen," Seth said, frowning. "They're expecting you to go back, and for me ..."

I waited for him to finish, but he didn't. He didn't have to tell me what he was thinking because I already knew he still intended to take the fall.

"We don't have to make the same mistakes twice," I said, slipping my hands into Seth's. "If we have to start the cycle again, maybe this can be the last time. If we change it now ... choose differently, then our future can be whatever we want it to be. My memories tell me that losing Archer broke me. But *you* are the only one who can fix me because you never gave up on us." I reached up and touched his face. "You fell for me, and fought for me, and I know you would die for me."

Seth stared into my eyes with a look I'd seen many times before. It spoke of self-hatred and anger, but most of all, sorrow.

"My decision is already made," Seth said. "It always has been. Heaven is not where I belong. But I can't ask you to come with me. If I've learnt anything, it's I can't make you do something you don't want to do."

We hovered together in the darkness, surrounded by millions of beautiful stars, and I wanted to remind Seth how much I loved him. But I wouldn't be telling him anything he didn't already know.

"With you is where I belong," I said, stroking his cheek. "And now that I remember everything we went through … everything the Council put us through, Heaven is not where I want to be either. But how our lives played out during the last cycle is not necessarily how it needs to happen again. So many factors contributed to the final outcome, but here … now, knowing what we know, we have the opportunity to decide together."

Seth leaned forward and pressed his forehead to mine, closing his eyes. "If I stay, and we go home, we can never be together. I can't bear the thought of seeing you every day, standing beside the Council, and not being able to touch you." He slipped his arms around my waist and pulled me to him, burying his face into my neck.

"Who said anything about going home? What if we

decide not to choose a side?" I said. "What if we can be fallen but not really be fallen? Maybe it's possible. Our love breaks so many rules in the eyes of the Council, and taking the fall like we did—that was our choice, but we both chose for different reasons. This time, we can choose not to defy anyone. I think Michael gave us this moment so we could make a different choice. If we make the same choices, then it would have been for nothing."

Seth pulled back and furrowed his brow. "How would not choosing Heaven be any different to what we've done before?"

"Because we wouldn't be choosing Hell either." I smiled. "We'd be choosing each other."

All the pain and suffering had tested us until breaking point, but we'd come out the other side, and we were still good. Neither of us wanted to hurt anyone, and we weren't evil like the Council had accused us of being. Despite everything Seth and I had been through, we still had room for love in our hearts.

"The Council worked so hard to get me home," I said. "But I won't stay and stand by their side if I can't have you by mine." Seth hung his head and I took his face in my hands, making him look at me. "I don't know how many times we've been through this cycle because I can only remember the last one. But if we're here, that means we've been choosing each other, over and over again. They can't force us to choose Heaven or Hell."

Seth pressed his lips into a thin line. "But they can cast us out for not making a choice."

"Then let them," I said. "I choose you, Seth. I will *always* choose you."

Seth gripped my upper arms as we hovered in the star-filled sky. His eyes shone with tears, and he dipped his head, pressing his mouth to mine. He kissed me with a passion he'd never fully shown before, as if he'd been holding back all this time, and I kissed him with equal measure. It was different, like we were kissing for the first time, and we fitted together more perfectly than we ever could have guessed.

I love you, he whispered in my mind, running his hands up my arms, into my hair, and then trailing his fingers over the edges of my wings.

I love you, too, I thought.

Light shone brightly beside us, seeping through my closed eyelids, but I ignored it, not wanting to break our connection. Seth finally parted from our kiss and pressed his forehead against mine. His breath was hot on my cheek as he turned his head. His body stiffened in my arms, and he pulled back but didn't release his hold on me.

When I looked to see what was wrong, Michael hovered near us, the darkness of the Outer Realm surrounding his glowing white wings. His arms were folded over his chest, and he wore a smile I remembered from the Michael I used to know, before I remembered what we'd been through.

"What am I going to do with the two of you?" he asked, shaking his head.

Seth pulled me closer. "Leaving us alone would be a good start."

Michael sighed and let his arms fall to his sides. He drifted a little closer.

"I had hoped you'd convince him to come home with

you." Michael stared at me.

"We don't want to come home," I said. "Why would we after everything you and the Council put us through?"

"I said ... I'd hoped." Michael smiled. "I never for a second believed that would be the decision you'd make."

Seth and I waited for Michael to continue. There was obviously more he wanted to tell us, and even though I had a million questions, I'd gotten to the point where I didn't really care for the answers. All I cared about was having a chance to be happy with Seth and if that chance would ever come.

"Every cycle has been the same," Michael said. "The pain you endure intensifies, but the same people are involved with the same ending result. Only this time, something changed, and that's why we're here."

"What changed?" Seth asked.

I stayed silent and waited.

"This time ... I let you remember," Michael said. "The cycle has been broken."

"But the Council said the cycle won't end unless I accept my wings," I said.

Michael chuckled. "You have your wings, Grace. You both do."

Seth's wings beat in time with mine, and I took a moment to admire how magnificent they were. But it didn't matter to me if his wings were white or black. I would love him even if he had no wings. I would love him no matter what.

"Surely the Council hasn't agreed to this?" I asked.

"I have convinced them that you are better off with Seth than being a broken archangel at their side," Michael said. "This is your final test. It's up to you both whether you pass."

Seth's body shook in my arms as laughter burst from his mouth. "What are the conditions of your offer this time?"

Michael beat his wings and rose a little higher. "No conditions. Provided your actions, other than your love for each other, do not defy Heaven … you will keep your wings and be free."

My lips turned up into a smile. Could it finally mean the end of all this? My smile faltered after a few seconds though, because if the events were the same every time, why would I make different choices? How would we go through the cycle again and not defy Heaven? I didn't think I'd fall in love with Josh again, but maybe I would briefly, and I would still in a heartbeat protect Charlotte. She was one of the main contributors to my reason for falling, so I would never be able to come out the other side with my wings, because what I believed was right didn't play well with the Council's black-and-white view. They may allow Seth and me to love each other, but they would never allow me to protect someone they saw as evil.

I turned to Seth and stared into his eyes, opening my mind to show him exactly what I thought and how I felt about everything. Having him inside my thoughts was a comfort I didn't know I'd missed when I had my wall up, and even though Michael could also see everything I was thinking, it didn't matter.

There was only one choice I could make … *we* could make.

"If you do this, Grace, you'll never be a Protection Angel, and you'll never see Archer again," Michael said.

In my memory I'd watched Archer die over and over. I didn't need to live through it again.

Becoming a fallen angel was never something I'd taken lightly, and my decision had always been based on what I'd believed was the right thing to do. Nothing had changed. I hadn't changed, and I was never going to. Now I knew what the Council had been putting Seth and I through, there was only one way to break the cycle, be with Seth, and stay true to myself.

I released Seth and floated over to Michael, staring into his deep brown eyes. "There is no other way. Again you've forced my hand. Over everything, I will always choose him."

"The Council will be watching—"

"Let them," Seth said.

Michael stared at him over my head, scowling. "What I was going to say … I will do my best to encourage them to leave you alone."

"What will happen to you?" I asked. "I can't imagine the Council will be too pleased."

As much as I was angry at Michael for so many reasons, we would never be where we were if he hadn't helped.

"You don't need to worry about me, Grace." He smiled.

Seth reached for me as I turned away from Michael, drawing me into his embrace. He lifted his hand and stroked the back of my head, running his fingers through my hair and pressing his lips to my temple. I pulled back and looked at the one I loved the most.

"I don't choose Heaven or Hell. I don't choose to be on any one side. I choose you, your love, and our future together." I took a deep breath. "And if that means I have to fall with you ... Then I will."

Seth leaned down and brushed my lips with his. He drew his wings around us, and I stopped beating mine, tucking them to my sides. Seth pulled his feathers closer, until we were no longer flying.

Let's do it right this time, Seth whispered in my mind.

My heart lurched with happiness, content with my decision, and I clung to him, waiting for the world to fall away.

THE END

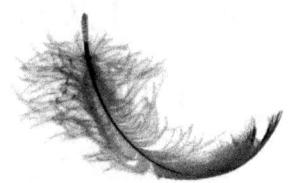

ACKNOWLEDGEMENTS

Wow! As always, I have so many people to thank, and I'm glad to be able to say that pretty much everyone who has helped get *Die For Me* to publication has been there from the start.

My parents come first. Thank you for your on-going and never-ending support, I've finally dedicated a book to you. The same goes for my brother and my wonderful sister-in-law, Kylie. You both are a fountain of encouragement.

Lauren McKellar, thank you again for being the best editor a writer could ask for. You never fail to help me make my writing shine. And you're always a text away when I have all the stupid questions.

Katrina, again thank you. You're probably so sick of this series by now because I think out of everyone you've read it the most. But you never complain, and you always push me to make my stories better. I'm so grateful to have your love and support.

Cass, what can I say? You are awesome beyond words. You're always there when I need help, and you did an amazing job as alpha for *Die For Me*. I don't think I would have gotten it written as fast if I didn't have you egging me on. Thank you. Your support is treasured.

Selina, thank you for beta reading *Die For Me*. Your feedback helped shape this final instalment, our brain-storming sessions always push me to be a better writer and story-teller.

Thank you, Katie, for your mad proof reading skills, and being there for me through my writing and publishing journey. Even though we're a world apart, I value your help and friendship.

To the girls in my writers' group, the Story Queens, thank you. Stacey, Lauren, Selina, Laura, Serene, Heather, and Rebecca, you are the most awesome support network, and I don't know what I'd do without you.

To the Aussie Owned and Read girls, thank you for all of the things. You're an amazing group of talented ladies, and I'm proud to know you all.

Any finally, to my readers, I'm sad that the series has come to a close, but thank you for sticking with me along Grace, Seth, Josh, and Archer's journey.

ABOUT THE AUTHOR

K. A. Last was born in Subiaco, Western Australia, and moved to Sydney when she was eight. Artistic and creative by nature, she studied Graphic Design and graduated with an Advanced Diploma. After marrying her high school sweetheart, she concentrated on her career before settling into family life. Blessed with a vivid imagination, K. A. Last began writing to let off creative steam, and fell in love with it. She has a Bachelor of Arts Degree from Charles Sturt University, with a major in English, and minors in Children's Literature, Art History, and Visual Culture. She now resides in the NSW countryside with her family and a menagerie of animals.

CONNECT WITH
K. A. LAST

Scan the code to subscribe to K. A. Last's newsletter.

Website www.kalastbooks.com.au
Facebook www.facebook.com/KALastBooks
Instagram www.instagram.com/kalastbooks
Pinterest www.pinterest.com/kalast
Goodreads www.goodreads.com/KALast
Twitter www.twitter.com/KALastBooks

BOOKS BY K. A. LAST

YA Fantasy Fiction

Sacrifice – A Fall For Me Prequel
Fall For Me (The Tate Chronicles, #1)
Fight For Me (The Tate Chronicles, #2)
Die For Me (The Tate Chronicles, #3)
Immagica
The Lovely Dark
Ella and Ash (Happily Ever After, #1)
Chasing Neve (Happily Ever After, #2)
False Princess (Happily Ever After, #3)
Dance of Wishes (Happily Ever After, #4)
Winter Flame (Happily Ever After, #5)

YA Contemporary Fiction

Something (All the Things: part one)
Nothing (All the Things: part two)
Everything (All the Things: part three)
The Other Side of Me (All the Things: part four)

Non-fiction

A Novel Idea! Colouring Journal for Writers
A Novel Idea Workbook for Writers

www.ingramcontent.com/pod-product-compliance
Lightning Source LLC
Chambersburg PA
CBHW060951120726
47910CB00002B/587